SHADOWS
OF THE
SENTINEL

MARTIN WILSEY

TANNHAUSER PRESS

SHADOWS OF THE SENTINEL

ISBN: 978-1-945994-49-4

Cover, Girl by Rotwang Studio.

Edited by: Donna Royston

Published by Tannhauser Press
First Edition

www.tannhauserpress.com

DEDICATION

This book is dedicated to my late parents,
Ella Olean Wilsey and Maurice Howard Wilsey.
They were the original Ma and Pa to many that came
through their lives. The main difference is, I'm sure Ma would
have objected to the cursing.
Love you! Miss you!

Table of Contents

SHADOWS OF THE SENTINEL

CHAPTER 1: ARRIVAL

"My first day on the *OXCART* was full of omens that I can only now see through hindsight. Like the damn cat. Maybe I should have told them the truth right away. The crew believed that Harv had given me their files, just like they had been given mine. At least the parts that Captain Quinn let them see."

-- Personal logs of Captain Cobbal Blocke, 2672.

"Dammit, Pope. Stop. Wait for us. Let us do a full assessment," Owen Quinn, captain of the *OXCART* salvage ship, growled into the comm unit. Tressa Pope was in a salvage tractor, approaching a derelict shuttle that was in a high-speed, three-axis tumble.

"I got this, Quinn," Pope replied confidently. "I will get close, match the main rotation, attach six grav-foils. Then you can use the computer and your bright shiny captain skills to stabilize it. I will grapple and tow it in. Easy money." She laughed but could not quite conceal her concerns.

"I hate to bother you guys while you're having so much fun," another voice came over the open channel. "This is Cobbal Blocke, your new multi-disciplinary engineer, coming in on a rendezvous vector of 290, mark 60. I have Ron Carter with me and a pile of new sensor hardware." He paused only a moment before continuing. "I will stand by at 20 kilometers."

"Thanks, Cobbal," Quinn replied. "Pope will have this locked down in a few."

"What the hell was that?" Pope asked, surprise in her voice.

"Clarify," Quinn said, now all business.

"I'm 220 meters out," Pope continued. She sounded concerned but calm. "It sounded like something hit me. Not big, but it etched a scratch in my canopy. Scared the shit outta..." She was interrupted by a loud, sharp sound.

"Pull back!" It was Cobbal on the comms. "That's a Tygart class shuttle. The monofilaments are deployed."

It was too late.

Suddenly the tractor was tangled in dozens of monofilament carbon strands. They wrapped around the outstretched grappling arms of the tractor and began pulling it in as the black, nearly invisible threads started to wind around the body of the tumbling shuttle.

"Oh, bloody hell!" Pope said as more filament wrapped around the tractor.

"Collision in twenty seconds," the computer calculated.

Pope tried to use the thrusters to break free, but the carbon threads were now too many and too strong.

"Pope, seal your helmet," Quinn said calmly.

"Done," she replied. "Fuck! Bracing for impact."

"Royce is on his way in tractor number two," Quinn said, stress now evident in his voice. "Blocke, what the hell are you doing?"

"Kinda busy, Captain," Cobbal said.

Just before the tractor arms collided with the Tygart shuttle, Pope saw a small ship descend into view. Its engine bells were both lit up as if it were on full burn, but it was only moving slowly.

The tractor arms hit the belly of the shuttle hard. One arm folded under, and the other tore into a dish assembly and tangled. The violence of the impact sent some debris spinning off and toward the looming ship.

"Blocke, get out of there!" Quinn yelled over the comms.

"Call me Cobb," was his only reply, as his ship nosed closer to the shuttle. The closer it got, the slower the shuttle tumbled, until it stopped altogether. "Pope, you okay?"

"I'll live," she answered. "Tractor's fucked up but no hull breach. I think I broke my left thumb on impact."

"I can't see your face," Cobb answered. "The inside of your visor is bloody."

"Don't say that." Cobb could hear the smile in her voice. "Quinn hates blood. It's just a bloody nose, dammit."

"Tractor two launched," Quinn said. There was relief in his tone. "Blocke, you have some explaining to do."

"Call me Cobb."

"What the hell was that? How did you stop it?" Quinn sounded pissed.

"Forward thrust and full reverse grav-foils." They could hear someone throwing up over the comms. "I created a gravity well that drew the remaining mono-filaments this way."

"I'm sorry, Cobb," Ron Carter said on comms. "I'll clean it up."

Cobb was laughing. "The bot will get it. Just stay strapped in."

"Thanks, Cobb," Pope said. "You know, doing that on an old L22 class ship could have torn your outriggers clean off, dumb ass."

"Some other ship, maybe," Cobb replied, as the other tractor came into view. Cobb saw Tressa Pope open her visor. Their canopies were only about twenty meters apart now. She wiped her eyes with her wrist, then waved.

"Tractor two will be here in a couple of minutes. Want me to stay?" Cobb asked her.

"That's not necessary," Pope said. "We were going to tow the whole thing inside the main hangar anyway. Dock first. I'll see you inside."

~~O~~

Cobb docked on the dorsal side of the *OXCART* in one of the large cargo bays, connecting with the belly gantry on Cobb's ship, the *TULSA*. The *OXCART*'s onboard computer managed the docking procedures.

Ron Carter was glad the cleaning bot had done its job before they docked. The *OXCART*'s gravity was about .5G at this level, and it helped settle his stomach.

"Sorry I didn't warn you, Ron," Cobb said, as he released his five-point harness from the pilot seat. "Wasn't time."

"Hey, man. I would trade a lost lunch and bruises on my collar bones any day to see flying like that. Is your cat OK?" Ron unstrapped and stood as the maint-bot left the bridge cockpit. "Where did you learn to do that?"

Cobb shrugged. "It's not my cat. It seemed like the thing to do at the time."

Cobbal Blocke was not tall or short. He was not handsome or ugly. His black hair was not long or military short. He did have a dark beard shaved down to a goatee. It was an unusual choice for a career spacer. They were usually clean-shaven so that emergency respirators would seal better. He wore a basic charcoal gray flight suit. The name patch on his left breast said "COBB" and had the Oklahoma Salvage shoulder patches. He wore no rank insignia or other adornments. What set him apart was his beard, and he was extremely fit.

The belly hatch in the forward section of the small cargo hold already had a green indicator when they got to it. Cobb opened it, and the deck below was another cargo bay about the same size as the one on the *TULSA*, but it was empty.

"Captain Quinn, Cobbal Blocke reporting for duty, and I have Sensor Tech Ron Carter with me, and umm, the cat, Bail. Permission to come aboard?"

"Granted," Quinn replied over Cobb's Heads Up Display (HUD). "Kira will be up to meet you in two minutes."

Carter was moving to the forward ladder when Cobb simply dropped to the deck, twenty feet below. He landed lightly, the .5G of this area providing little problem for him. A big Siamese cat gently touched down next to him. When Cobb turned to look up at Carter on the ladder, he noticed a tall, beautiful, blond woman staring at him with a smile and a raised eyebrow.

She walked up, pulling off a work glove. Cobb thought it was to shake his hand, and he reached out to take her hand. But she knelt and scratched the cat's ears.

"Hi, I'm Kira Fletcher, junior engineer and mechanic." She gestured to her dirty coveralls with the glove she held. "Welcome aboard, Mr. Blocke." She shook Cobb's hand as he helped her stand up.

"Please call me Cobb. That's Bail," he said, as Bail did figure eights around her legs. He looked up at Carter's progress, coming down the ladder. "I was sure Harv or Hunter would have sent you a thick file on me. Everyone calls me Cobb. Even Ian Vinge."

"And you must be Ron Carter." She extended her hand to him. After a moment of hesitation, he shook it. "Welcome aboard. How was your flight?" She put her glove on as she began to walk to the hatch.

"It was quick. I groaned when I first saw the *TULSA*. I thought with a full load that it would take a week to get here. It was less than 48 hours." Carter looked up as the airlock closed above them. "Cobb has really tuned the rig up."

"That's the advantage of working for Oklahoma Salvage on Earth," Cobb chuckled. "Harv Rearden, the owner, has all the parts you'd ever need. And a great employee discount."

"I hear that," Kira said with a conspiratorial smile. "You have a new sensor gear on pallets?"

"Yes. All cased and on eighteen grav-pallets. Plus a dish and a boom to install it," Carter said, as they entered the lift at the end of the hall. "I sent the manifest ahead."

"I'll unload while you meet with Quinn. I won't open any seals until you come back to help me check the inventory against the manifest." Kira was cheerful, friendly, and sounded professional.

When the lift doors closed, she turned around while she spoke to them. Cobb noticed her coverall was unzipped in the front, a distracting amount. He tried to glance away but knew she had caught him looking. The bit of grease just on the edge of where the zipper met her left breast was not going to be ignored.

The lift opened directly onto the bridge.

The bridge was far bigger than Cobb expected. There were nine duty stations—three in the center surrounded by an arc of six others. The center three were occupied. The pilot seat was empty.

The man in the center captain seat turned and stood as they entered. Carter was staring with his mouth open at the 270-degree vista out the thick armor-glass.

"Mr. Carter. Welcome aboard." He shook Ron Carter's hand and then turn and extended it to Cobb. "Excellent flying, Mr. Blocke."

"Call me Cobb." He smiled back.

"Let me introduce Ruth Phillips and Magnus Bozeman." He gestured to the people at the engineering and communications stations.

"Call me Ruth," she said, standing and smiling at the self-introduction. She shook his hand.

"Call me Mr. Bozeman," Magnus said, deadpan, before standing and shaking hands all around. He winked at Cobb.

"Magnus is our Electronics Engineer, and he will assist you with the installation of the new sensor array upgrade.

"Nice to meet you all, but I have just got to say this upfront. This is the ugliest spaceship I have ever seen," Carter laughed.

Ruth replied first. "Don't let Kira hear you say that. She helped with most of the mods you've seen."

Cobb turned. Kira was gone.

CHAPTER 2: CARTER

"The crew didn't understand the motive behind Harv and Oklahoma Salvage spending so much money on the sensor array upgrade. More than on the original cost of the entire ship. It didn't make much sense at first. It was part of playing the long game."

-- Personal logs of Captain Cobbal Blocke, 2672.

<<<>>>

They loitered on the bridge and watched the recovery rescue operation for the next fifty minutes. Royce White had attached one of the aft docking collars to the Tygart shuttle. Then he slowly brought it into the massive main hanger, directly under the chin of the bridge.

They stood at the floor-to-ceiling clear wall and watched as the salvaged shuttle backed into the hanger. Cobb tried to clear off the fingerprint and dirt buildup with the sleeve of his flight suit, only to make it worse. They waved at Tressa Pope as she slid by. Her tractor was still tangled in the ship's infrastructure.

"How much is an old shuttle like that worth?" Carter asked, as it slid out of sight into the hangar. "It looks like the high engine was hit with weapons fire."

"We never know until we get it back to base and have a full assessment done," Quinn said. "It depends on the condition of the ship, the contents, and type. There were millions of these shuttles made during the expansion. Colonies loved them. They were reliable, held a lot of people or cargo, they were relatively easy to fly in space or in an atmosphere."

Magnus added, "Later ones were refitted with fixed grav-plates. If it is in bad shape, we salvage the plates, save the parts worth keeping and cut the rest up for the fabricator."

Quinn continued, "Some people will pay good money for one of these if she still flies. They're collectible. Like old pickup trucks."

"Now I see why you want such a big sensor upgrade," Carter said, as he turned from the glass. "It will make it easier to spot this stuff from a massive distance."

"Ruth, would you mind showing Mr. Carter to his guest quarters?" Quinn asked. "Magnus, please head down and give Kira a hand. I fear the Two Daves maybe more a hindrance than a help, left to their own. Cobb, stay here. Now is as good a time as any to chat."

"Yes, sir," Cobb said as he watched the three of them leave the bridge.

Quinn turned and sat again in the captain's seat. Cobb stood at parade rest with his back to the pilot's seat, facing Quinn.

"Cobb, you sure know how to make an entrance," Quinn said, scrubbing his face with both hands. "Forgive me, son. I was asleep when all this started. It was Royce White's shift, and then

Pope had just been relieved when they started the operation. Ruth woke me up when you got here."

"I'm glad I could help, sir," Cobb replied.

"How long will it take to break you of the 'sir' bullshit, Cobb?" Quinn smiled. "Keep it up, and I will start calling you Mr. Blocke. Or, worse still, Commander Blocke."

"That depends on you, sir," Cobb replied. "Harv always said to begin on the polite end of the spectrum. I finally knew he liked me when he started calling me asswipe."

"Harv Rearden is a wise man," Quinn said as he rose and went to the port side window to look out. "Harv does like you. In fact, he told me he loved you like a son. Trusted you with his cat. He hated to see you go. That was a new one." Quinn glanced at Cobb. "He usually hires misfits."

"I'll miss him. But I won't miss Oklahoma. I will be washing desert grit out of my eyes for weeks," Cobb said as he stepped up beside Quinn to look out at the stars.

"What really surprised me was the recommendation in your file from Ian Vinge." Quinn was looking at Cobb when he said that. He saw the surprise on Cobb's face.

Cobb raised an eyebrow. "I thought Ian hated everyone, including me. He threatened to kill me just before I left Earth," Cobb admitted. "At one point, I thought he talked Harv into getting rid of the cat AND me."

"Let me guess. He said he'd kill you if you went near Harv's granddaughter Alex." Quinn laughed. "Ian hates everybody. You, he liked. He thought your talents were being wasted on Earth."

"He said that?" Cobb was incredulous.

"He also said he watched you build the *TULSA* from empty hulls, beer cans, and baling wire. In your spare time." Quinn added, "In less than two years."

"Ian helped me build it. I'm an idiot compared to Harv Rearden and Ian Vinge," Cobb laughed. "I think he felt sorry for me because he pounded me for a couple of hours each day, working out. I still have bruises from that asshole."

"You don't call *him*, sir, do you?" Quinn smiled.

Just then, the lift door opened, and Tressa Pope stormed in, followed by the cat, and without preamble, took Cobb's face in both her hands and kissed him firmly on the mouth. Cobb could taste her blood.

Still holding his face, she said, "Royce says if you had not pulled that maneuver, I'd still be out there in a three-axis tumble, slowly running out of air."

"Cobb, this is Pope. She is our best pilot and has the second watch." Quinn said, as Pope hugged Cobb, pinning his arms at his sides. "Now, Tressa, don't scare him. He does have his own ship."

"Thank you," she simply said, as she released him. "You need to show me how you did that!"

Cobb could see that there was still blood on her neck and in one of her ears. He then noticed another man had arrived at the same time. He strolled in slowly, shaking his head at Pope's display.

"Cobb, this is Royce White. You are his relief. He will be taking Carter back to the base when the install is complete," Quinn said as they shook hands.

"Nice work, Cobb. We need to discuss that ship. A stock L22 would have torn its own outriggers off if you tried that," Royce said, sounding sincerely impressed.

"Thanks, Commander. It only looks stock. Harv and Ian helped me make it... durable," Cobb said.

"Royce, I'll finish out this watch. You and Pope get back down to the hangar and see what we've got." Quinn looked at the console. "It will have full pressure in twelve minutes."

"Ruth is already suiting up. She's hoping for a full load this time. Both of the life pods are gone, so we may be in luck," Royce said as he and Pope headed for the lift.

When the door slid closed, Cobb asked, "Why does the missing life pods mean luck?"

"Royce hates dead bodies. Some of the salvage ships we find are full of dead bodies in various states," Quinn said, as he was bringing up camera images of the hangar on the main viewers. "That's Ruth and the Two Daves. Ruth is our content salvage specialist. She collects and manages everything worth anything inside the salvage. Cargo, supplies, fuel, pressure suits, small arms, food, even personal effects. She makes us a lot of money."

"The 'Two Daves'?" Cobb asked as he watched them attach a manual cargo hatch release tool to the emergency release mechanism.

"That's Dave Wheeler and Dave Mitchell. The Two Daves. They are our junior mates. The gophers. They bitch all the time about being at the bottom rung, but they're good guys." Quinn looked up from the display and gestured to the entire bridge. "And this is the *OXCART*. Oklahoma Salvage One. Harv's first and best ship."

"Ron's right," Cobb said. "She could use a coat of paint." He couldn't hide his smile.

"I already gave you full watch commander access to all systems and comms," Quinn said casually. Cobb knew that it was high-level access.

"Accept access via my pilot HUD. Full time. Manual privacy on request," Cobb said, as his in-vision display began to authenticate the many levels of new systems.

Quinn raised an eyebrow at that.

"Also accept access to the systems on board the *TULSA*. There is a metric ton of data there that Harv thought you might enjoy," Cobb said.

Cobb activated the engineering station and made remote connections to several data stores that were housed on the *TULSA* 471.

"Oh my," Quinn said, raising an eyebrow. "I can see why he sent this with you and didn't transmit it." The data stores were massive.

"Volume and content," Cobb said. "Don't bother trying to copy it. The archive is on a pallet that we will bring over and install after the sensor upgrade hardware."

"Where did you get all this?" Quinn was nearly speechless.

"It was Harv, not me," Cobb replied. "As far as I can tell, it is the entire Earth Defense Force data archive. Hundreds of years' worth of EDF logs and comms and random stuff. Stored on the densest media I have ever seen."

Quinn looked at Cobb conspiratorially as if the data was made of gold.

"There are two archives and are each the size of a large fridge. They are in secure aft storage. Each unit fits into two rack widths.

Each also has native Quantum Entanglement Secure Transmission QUEST COMM interfaces for real-time updates and access."

"Wait, you mean we can install these at the base, and it would be like they were here?" Quinn asked.

"Once you install the QUEST interface here," Cobb said.

"These combined with the new sensor array will allow us to find way more salvage." Quinn grinned.

"Merry Christmas, sir," Cobb said, even though it was March.

CHAPTER 3: CALL ME COBB

"When Ian Vinge had told me it was ugly on the outside and beautiful on the inside, he was wrong. It was pretty ugly on the inside as well."

-- Personal logs of Captain Cobbal Blocke, 2672.

"The *OXCART* was originally a Galaxy Class tug designed to move Colony ships from the yards where they were built to open space. It's why the conventional engines are so big," Quinn told Cobb as they watched Ron Carter attach the last antenna array via the drone cams orbiting the ship.

Cobb had the specs up on the engineering console. "We run with only a crew of eight? This ship can crew over a hundred."

"We don't even need eight most of the time. You will discover that this gig is endless stretches of boredom followed by periodic moments of being scared shitless," Quinn laughed.

The lift opened, and Kira stepped onto the bridge, sat at one of the science consoles, and configured it for the sensor control systems. "Magnus is down in engineering with the Two Daves plumbing in the new gear," Kira said, as she set her dashboard. "Royce is fueling up the return shuttle and starting the pre-flight checklist already. Sheesh."

"That was fast," Cobb commented.

"You want to take Cobb and find him a bed. He's polite, but I know he's been up and at it for like twenty hours now," Quinn said.

"The Two Daves already took his grav-trunks to the port-side dorm," Kira said, standing. "There are beds, heads, showers, and a stocked kitchen there. He can pick permanent quarters at his leisure."

"I transferred the new array files to my Heads Up Display (HUD) for some light reading," Cobb said, as he stood and turned to Captain Quinn. "Thank you, sir."

"You're welcome, Mr. Blocke," Quinn said. "Your first watch begins at midnight tomorrow, so you will have a full day to settle in. I'll provide everyone's schedules and duties. But the crew will be busy for the next few days with the new shuttle salvage."

Kira began to lead him to the lift. "We currently only occupy the four uppermost levels. The maps will show you what's available."

"When are mealtimes?" Cobb asked. "There doesn't seem to be a mess hall indicated on the ship map."

"Everyone basically fends for themselves here. In their own kitchens," she said. "Most get boring frozen, canned, or dehydrated meals from the vends. I think Ruth actually cooks." The lift opened on level two, and the Two Daves were standing there.

Before Kira could introduce them, Cobb stepped out and offered his hand, saying, "You must be Mitchell and Wheeler. I'm Cobb, the new guy."

The Two Daves looked at each other and smiled. "You sure got a lot of personal luggage, man. I don't think we showed up with more than twenty kilos in a duffel. What the hell do you haul around that takes four trunks that big?"

"Dead bodies. Heads mostly." Cobb said, deadpan, as he followed Kira down the corridor. "You know, of people that ask a lot of questions." He winked at Kira.

"I like this guy. Ruth's gonna love him," Kira laughed at the Two Daves as they realized he was joking.

~~O~~

Kira led Cobb to a bunk room on level four. There were a dozen bunks on each side lining the walls. His trunks had been neatly arranged against the aft wall. In the center of the room there was a long table and fixed benches. The forward wall had a galley kitchen and doors to either side with men's and women's bath and shower. He was the only occupant.

Cobb dropped his duffel on the first bunk.

Kira pointed. "Showers and head are through there. The kitchen is stocked with the basics." She opened the fridge and looked inside. She shook her head before closing it. "You should know," she said, looking up, "the bridge mess is the only decent coffee on this boat."

Cobb laughed. "Every other ship I have been on, the best coffee was always in the Chief Engineer's shop."

"Welcome to the *OXCART*. Not the typical ship or crew." She began to move toward the exit. "If you have any questions, start with the computer. It's OK for a computer without AI."

And she was gone.

"Computer, please wake me up at 2300," Cobb said to the room as he took off his boots.

"Yes, Commander," the computer replied.

"Call me Cobb."

~~O~~

Cobb entered the bridge at 2345, to be greeted by the smell of fresh coffee.

Tressa Pope was the only one there, sitting in the captain's seat with a forest of displays deployed around her.

"Hey, Cobb," Pope said absently, and she studied the displays. "You will be glad to know that Quinn started your duty clock when your ship arrived, so you are going to get a bonus share of that shuttle we salvaged yesterday."

Quinn had already notified him of this fact, as well as the lucrative findings on the ship. "Excellent," Cobb replied. "Are there formal procedures for watch turnover?"

"Formal?" Pope smiled. "We just try to be on time, and to have coffee waiting for the next watch. The *OXCART* computer has the to-do list and will do a rundown with you. Third watch is dead quiet on this boat. Everyone on board usually sleeps now, except you."

She got up from the captain's seat as Cobb entered the small galley and poured a cup of fresh coffee. "Kira said this was the best coffee on the *OXCART*." He took a sip and grimaced.

"It's true, maybe," Pope said as she leaned against the counter. "Cobb, Quinn submitted a full event report on yesterday..." She hesitated, her face becoming serious. "I just wanted... Thanks again, man."

"You're welcome." Cobb sensed she was more upset than she let on. He sipped the coffee again, trying not to make a face. "How's the new sensor install schedule going?" he asked, although he already knew from Quinn's morning briefing that he'd requested during breakfast.

"It's good," Pope replied. "Everything was unpacked and inventoried. The real work begins in the morning."

"I won't keep you," Cobb said, moving toward the captain's seat. "I know this has been a long day for you. Sleep well."

"Goodnight, Cobb," Pope said. "Thanks again."

Then she was gone.

Cobb dumped his cup of coffee into the sink and then the rest of the pot. He began disassembling the coffee maker, with his handy multi-tool, as he spoke.

"*OXCART*, command monitors off." The extra panels that surrounded the captain's seat retracted back into the floor. "Command status mode Alpha Baker Niner."

Cobb's HUD came alive with several status displays arranged in his vision in an organized and tidy fashion.

"*OXCART*, how familiar are you with the advanced Earth Defense Force Command Interface and Protocols?" Cobb asked out loud as he continued to wash the filthy coffee pot, part by part.

"The documentation you provided has given me the baseline information. Your mods and upgrades to the software and protocols are non-standard," the OXCART said.

After a while, "You know why I am here?" He was rinsing the now-pristine coffee pot components. "Harv informed you?"

"Yes," the OXCART replied flatly.

"None of the flight systems here are capable of AI control. Yet." Cobb smiled as he sniffed then dumped the stale coffee beans into the recycler. "We are gonna be rich."

~~O~~

The bridge door slid open, and a black spider bot the size of a dog walked in. It was carrying a bag of coffee beans that it handed up to Cobb, and then exited the way it had come.

"The galley is stocked with plenty of coffee beans for the hopper," the OXCART informed him coolly.

"If you don't mind me saying, those coffee beans taste like rabbit turds." Cobb smiled as he refilled the sparkling coffee machine's auto-grinder with the beans. He activated the device and could smell the fresh grind as it began.

"Is this step one on Harv's master plan?" the OXCART asked.

"OXCART, how would you assess the team on this boat?" Cobb left the small galley finally and began a detailed inspection of the entire bridge.

"Reports indicate they are consistent, dedicated, and competent," the OXCART computer said. Cobb sat in the captain's seat as he slowly continued his inspection with a data-pad in hand, making a punch list. Getting up, he went from station to station as the computer continued. "They are consistent money makers for Oklahoma Salvage. This sensor upgrade will likely improve profits even more."

"But do they function well as a team?" Cobb asked, as he added more to his data-pad. "These people are all individuals. This ship doesn't require them to function as a team. They are what we always called Commuters while I was in the EDF. They live on the ship, in their own apartments, show up for their shift, do their job and go home."

"This is not the EDF. These are not soldiers," the computer corrected.

"They are not family, either," Cobb said as the coffee maker beeped. He pocketed the data-pad and went to the galley and got a fresh mug from the cabinet. After looking into it, he washed it in the sink before filling it.

He sighed as he took his first sip.

"*OXCART*, bring up my primary nanite swarm programming console." Cobb sat in the captain's seat and got started.

~~O~~

"Good morning, Cobb," Quinn said, as he entered the bridge at 0745 sharp. "How was your first shift?"

"It was quiet, as expected. The *OXCART* is ready for the upgrade work to begin today." Cobb followed Quinn into the galley for a final cup of coffee. "I believe the *OXCART* and I have selected my new quarters. With your approval, Level S21, room 37." Quinn opened the cabinet to get a mug, and the cabinet was empty.

"Oh, sorry, sir. All the mugs are in the dishwasher." Cobb began emptying the dishwasher back into the cabinet. The various random cups went back with no seeming order. They were all different. Quinn grabbed a large black one.

"Again, with the 'sir' bullshit, Mr. Blocke?"

Cobb made a mental note to bring up one of his own mugs. "I will also move my ship to the adjacent empty shuttle hangar bay. With your permission."

"Fine. Isn't S21 the old machine shop level? It's a mess down there."

"It has showers and a head. I can build out the rest in my spare time."

Quinn was noticing the smell of the coffee as he poured. He took the first sip, and his eyes closed in ecstasy.

"Cobb, you can call me 'sir' all you want." He took another sip. "You can call me Nancy if you want as long as you keep making coffee like this."

"The beans are my private stock. Who maintains the inventory of stores?" Cobb asked, trying not to lay blame.

"The *OXCART* handles all that," Quinn said. "Oh, man. Vinge was right."

"What?"

"Your talents were wasted on Earth."

~~O~~

The elevator opened on level S21 to a dark, stale-smelling corridor. The hall was wide and tall, with pipes and conduits lining the walls and ceiling. The door marked 37 in faded paint was dimly lit by inadequate hall lights.

Keying the code on the door pad did nothing until he mashed the enter key again, hard. The door opened, and wall lights started to come on around the large room. Only three ceiling lights came on. Those three hung down on long cords, atypical for a spaceship, even one this old. Zero-g would not be good for those lights. The room was thirty meters by sixty meters and had uneven floor levels where giant machines had once been mounted to elevated sections. Corroded bolt heads stuck up everywhere, making it dangerous. Cobb scanned the space with a flashlight beam. The dirt was thick. The paint was gray and peeling all around.

Cobb was dragging one of his trunks on a grav-pallet and let it settle a few meters into the room. There was a large airlock door in the center of the opposite wall. A massive, once clear, section of the wall looked out onto the dark hangar deck. Controls nearby activated a few lights out in the small hangar.

Cobb walked to the arch that was the entrance into the locker room, and the head and showers beyond. He turned on all the showerheads, sink faucets, and flushed all four toilets. He let the water run.

Returning to the trunk, he keyed an access code. The motorized top opened, and the sides deployed to create a kind of tool bench with the lid being a large console monitor that was booting up.

A banner "Swarm Control" was brightly displayed.

"*OXCART*, do you have sensors on S21-37?" Cobb asked the air.

"No, I do not." The *OXCART* paused. "I have audio and video with four cameras in the adjacent hanger. Nothing in S21-37. It has not been in use for decades."

"Please depressurize and open the hanger in prep for the *TULSA* to arrive," Cobb said, multitasking as he spoke.

Pressing a large button on the panel marked "Initiate Swarm" caused a side panel on the trunk to open, and a flood of millions of tiny, insect-like bots deployed like angry fire ants.

The swarm moved throughout the area, consuming dirt and debris as it went and leaving polished surfaces in its wake.

"*OXCART*, by this time tomorrow, S21-37 should be fully swarm imaged, cleaned, and prepped for the next steps. I am going to bring down my other trunks and then move my ship to this hangar."

Cobb moved toward the door. "Do you have any monitors in the hallway? The elevator?"

"No. It was never a priority." The *OXCART* replied.

"I'll take care of it."

CHAPTER 4: HOME S21-37

"This is the perfect place. To begin…"
-- Personal logs of Captain Cobbal Blocke, 2672.

Cobb moved the other trunks to S21-37. By the time he had them there, the Swarm was in the rafters. The large room was already full of airborne dust.

"*OXCART*, please turn off the air circulation systems, so the work doesn't burden the filters," Cobb said to the air.

"Filters on this level have not been serviced in years," the *OXCART* replied. "Add that to the maintenance list?"

"Yes, please. How much of the ship is in general use?" Cobb asked.

In Cobb's HUD, a giant schematic filled the massive wall that separated the space from the hall beyond. It showed all 71 decks of the *OXCART*.

"The areas in green are in general use. Yellow shows light use, red is the little-used sections," the computer explained. "The small white section here is this room and the hangar."

Only about five percent of the ship was in general use. The top four levels were green.

"Most people have quarters on the executive level that was designed for the command crew. Large comfortable suites." The *OXCART* had no criticism in its tone. "All but Ruth, Kira, and now you."

"Is this a problem?" Cobb said, as a second trunk opened to create another section to his bench. More swarms flooded from this trunk. These bots were smaller. Almost nanite small.

"No problem at all. Will you make this your home? Ruth and Kira have decided that these spaces are their primary residences." The suites were highlighted on a map in Cobb's HUD.

"I make wherever I go my home, if I can," Cobb said, as he activated the last two trunks. When they deployed, they stood themselves on end and looked like stainless steel appliances from a kitchen. They all connected together. Cobb drew out a thick power cable for the last one and dragged it to the wall for a standard twist lock socket. Another flood of larger swarm-bots streamed out now.

"Need I ask what these systems do?" The *OXCART* was formal and polite.

"These are my Swarm programming and manufacturing units." Cobb pointed. "Some bots will clean and collect debris, and others will collect and return it here. This unit uses that as raw material to create addition Swarm members. I program them here." He indicated the first console. "They take a lot of power. It might start to get warm in here."

"May I help in any way?" the *OXCART* asked.

"It will be a week before they are done cleaning. Did Harv inform you regarding my accounts, credit stream, and access to salvage materials for personal use?"

"Affirmative."

Cobb walked to the vast window that overlooked the hangar bay. "Because I will need several items for the new homestead. In the meantime, I will bring the *TULSA* 471 down here and sleep in my bunk there. Is the hangar ready?"

"Depressurized and standing by," the *OXCART* replied.

~~O~~

Cobb had a shower before he left to get his ship. His HUD held a map of the vessel that led him through the winding warrens to the *TULSA* 471.

Kira and the Two Daves were there, moving off the last of the gear for the sensor upgrades.

"Hey, Cobb," Kira said brightly. "The manifest lists those two containers as 'Blocke Personal Items,' but those two units are not listed at all. Shouldn't you be sleeping?"

"I am going to move my ship to its new home before I hit the rack at 1600." Cobb nodded to the Daves, saying, "Mitchell. Wheeler. Please take that unit to the main data center under the bridge. It's a system upgrade I will install overnight, during my watch. The *OXCART* knows all about it. It's expecting it."

The Daves beamed at him as they activated the grav-pallet and slid the last item out of the cargo bay.

"Are you headed out now?" Kira asked. "Can I tag along? I'd like to see more of your ship."

Cobb smiled. He'd heard the line before. He looked at Kira and noticed something was different. He couldn't place exactly what.

"Sure, come aboard," he said. They walked up the ramp into the ship. "We'll head out as soon as we can clear the bay." Cobb watched as the ramp began to close behind them. He loved the advanced control features of his HUD. It had massive integration with the *TULSA* 471.

The warning light began to spin in the cargo bay, indicating the pressurization cycles were about to begin. By the time they got to the lift and up to the bridge, the hangar bay door was starting to open.

The elevator had opened directly into the bridge.

"I'm confused," Kira said, as she looked around. "This is a standard core bridge from a military ship." The dome was activated to give them a 360-degree view of the hangar. "The forward section of this ship isn't the bridge?"

"No, it's just the observation lounge now, or will be. It's incomplete. I'll give you a tour when we park." The feeling returned. Something was different. She sat on the right side of the center pilot seat.

"You did this yourself. Harv told me." She looked around at the control systems and displays as the ship began to drift out slowly. "You take your pay in parts, too, Harv said."

"What else did Harv say about me? Because he didn't tell me anything about you," Cobb lied.

"Mostly, he said you were being wasted at the yard in Oklahoma. Harv lets people play to their strengths. It makes him more money." She looked at the monitor view of the exterior hull of the *OXCART* as the *TULSA* moved from the central cargo bay toward the starboard shoulder shuttle bay that was open and empty. "He also said you built this ship from an empty hull yourself. He said you were a brilliant nanite programmer. Swarm tech specialization. And he said you did time in the EDF. Harv hates those guys." She laughed musically. "It cracked me up because you and Ian Vinge were both EDF."

She looked embarrassed. Cobb thought she must have realized that they both washed out of the EDF.

"Plus personal stuff, like architecture as a hobby, carving stuff out of real wood, music, and such," she said.

"I am at a huge disadvantage," Cobb said, as he gently spun the ship about so he could back it into the hangar. "All I know about you is that Ian will kill me if I offend you. You are the sword of Damocles."

"The what?" Kira said. "He is very protective in a big brotherly way. And damn, he is big."

Cobb remained quiet as he backed the *TULSA* into the hangar. It had ten meters to spare all around. The bay door was sliding closed before the landing struts were down.

"Want a sandwich while the bay pressurizes? It's dinner and bed for me before the midnight shift." Cobb unbuckled and stood.

"A sandwich sounds good," Kira replied. "Quick tour first?"

"Sure, not much to see." Cobb took her into the narrow corridor. "Four bunk rooms, with two bunks each here. Nothing fancy. I removed a wall here to double my stateroom." The end of the short hall had a ladder and hatch that slid aside, and Cobb climbed down.

"This will be the observation deck." It was unfinished and had open deck plates and panels all around exposing bulkheads and conduits. "Back here is the nanite lab."

A door slid aside, and Cobb entered.

He turned in time to see Kira step in and fall to her knees and then face plant on the deck.

~~O~~

Cobb wasn't fast enough to catch her.

"Son of a bitch..." Kira was conscious and cursing quietly to herself. Cobb knelt beside her but wasn't going to move her. Her head lifted slightly, and she laid it down, her right cheek on the floor.

"Kira, what happened? Can you hear me?" He knelt beside her and gently pushed the blond hair from her face. Her nose was trickling blood, and a bruise was already forming on her forehead.

"Roll me over onto my back, please." He was surprised at the angry tone she had. Cobb tried to roll her gently. She was heavy, really heavy.

With a thought in his command HUD, the *TULSA* 471 reduced the gravity to 0.1G. Doing so allowed him to roll her onto her back quickly. The movement caused a flow of blood from her nose into her left ear.

"Is there an active RF suppression system in here?" she demanded.

The question caught Cobb. "Um mm, yes... like I said, it's my nanite programming lab. It needs active RF suppression. I make raw, unsecured nanites in there."

"Dammit. Just drag me out of here by the legs." She rolled her eyes at him like he was an idiot. She craned her neck, looking around the lab. It was clean, bright white. "Nice lab," she added, sounding abashed.

Cobb did as she requested. He just dragged her out. She still weighed a lot even in the light gravity. The door to the lab closed, and she began to stir.

"You can restore the gravity," she groused. She sat up and wiped her nose with a sleeve and cursed again. She stood as the gravity came back up. "Bathroom?"

Cobb went to a door on the opposite side that mirrored the lab door. Kira hesitated before entering. Blood was dripping from her chin into the sink as she looked into the mirror. She grabbed the hand towel and ran cold water over it and began scrubbing the blood off her face.

"You really didn't know, did you?" she growled. She wasn't looking at him. She avoided looking at him.

"Didn't know what?" His mind was spinning when it hit the answer. As it came to him, he didn't think to hide the realization from his face.

That's when she looked at him.

"Those assholes didn't even tell you that?" She shook her head and rinsed the cloth, then turned to Cobb. "Full quad amputee, no arms or legs at the shoulders and hips. My spine is fused at L4, L5, and S1, but other than that, clear."

"Do you have the Kenshin control interface or the Katashi?" Cobb asked. It was Kira's turn to be dumbfounded.

With her hesitation, he stepped in and took the wet cloth from her and began to clean blood from behind her ear. It was intimate.

"Kenshin, but how do you know about that if..." she stammered. She started looking closer at his body.

"I used the Kenshin interface initially but since upgraded to a customized version of the Katashi software because of the wider protocol support and security." He looked in her eyes then and saw the question there.

"Why?"

"I use it to control this ship." Cobb realized what was different about her: she was shorter. "I use it to control this entire ship and an army of bots. You gotta get the upgrade. Shop tool control alone was worth the upgrade." He tucked her hair behind her ear and tossed the towel in the recycler.

~~O~~

They talked shop while they ate sandwiches and potato salad and had a couple of beers. They even openly spoke about body-bigotry. Kira talked about her awkward years and her parents spending so much money on prosthetic arms and legs systems that would "pass" as normal. They were nice bodies, but her custom mechanic rigs were her favorites. It was almost 1900 when Kira left.

"*OXCART.*" Cobb was in his bunk, now ready for sleep. "I want a briefing ready for my shift. Backgrounds on all members of the crew. Just common knowledge items, not asking you to break confidences. Even though I could if I wanted to."

"Yes, sir." The *OXCART* computer was overly formal.

"Kira could have been injured badly. Killed, even." He was adamant. "I need to keep these people safe. Ignorance is my enemy."

"Yes, sir." The *OXCART* tone was flat.

Cobb missed the interactions with his friend Hunter, a full AI back in Oklahoma.

"Goodnight," Cobb said, as the light went full dark.

He was asleep in less than a minute.

CHAPTER 5: THE MIDNIGHT WATCH

"Pope is a great pilot. What the hell is she doing here? I had the sense she was hiding in some way. I wonder if she is asking herself the same question about me."

-- Personal logs of Captain Cobbal Blocke, 2672.

Cobb reported to the bridge for his watch at 23:45 to the smell of fresh coffee.

Pope was there in the captain's seat with the new sensor displays up all around her in high definition.

"Cobb, I love you, man," Pope said, as she swiveled the command seat around toward him. "Are you trying to seduce me? Because it's working." She smiled brightly. "Saving my life, bringing the sensor upgrade, and to top it off, this coffee!" She stood and moved to the galley. "I may never sleep again."

"I like my coffee," Cobb said humbly. "I cannot do without good coffee."

"What the hell did you do?" She sipped a fresh cup as she reached out for the large coffee mug in Cobb's hand. She refilled it and looked at the sides. Runic symbols were beautifully carved around the deep brown cup.

"Cleaned the unit and tossed the beans that were in it. These are my private stock. I already talked to the *OXCART* computer and changed the supply requisition."

She sipped again. "I love you, man."

"What's the word for the watch?" Cobb smiled but wanted a more formal watch transition. He planned to talk to Quinn about that soon.

"Sensor upgrades are coming up slowly. It will take a week. The Daves delivered that big-ass new data-store you brought along to the server room, but it's not installed. Everyone is on the sensor installs." She sipped more coffee and led Cobb to the command displays. There was a long, classic punch list. "Items in white are for the watch to do. Mostly diagnostics on the new gear, network impact, tests on secondary and tertiary command and control protocols. Shit like that." She sipped and sighed. "I hate to dump all that on my new favorite hero, but the third watch is the time to do that stuff."

"No problem," Cobb said as he took the watch and updated the logs.

"Look, man. An opposite watch means our overlap is minimal. I want you to tell me something personal about yourself at every shift change. Plus, let's do breakfast or lunch soon. I'll be busting your balls a lot about the hero shit, but seriously, man. Thanks."

"You're welcome, Pope. Now stop thanking me, or I will switch the coffee beans back." She grabbed her chest as if stricken with a heart attack. "Something personal?" He thought for a minute. "I like to do 3G tai chi to stay in shape. What about you?"

"You've been around Ian Vinge too much." This confirmed something about Pope. "I like to run to keep in shape. The *OXCART* has a huge, little-used gym. A one-kilometer track on the balcony. I run first thing every day before breakfast." She rinsed out her mug and set it in the rack.

"Good night, Pope."

"I'll be up for a while. Too much coffee. Good watch, Cobb." She waved over her shoulder as she entered the lift.

~~O~~

Cobb ran down the punch list and started the diagnostics on a half dozen systems. He stood and went to the case he had carried to the bridge. A simple mental command unlatched it, and he just casually kicked it open. A swarm of nanites flooded out of it and began to spread in every direction.

"*OXCART*, I programmed these nanites as surface cleaners only. They should not enter any consoles or vents. Surfaces only. Other cleaning tasks are specialized and will be done another day," Cobb said, as he moved to the front of the bridge, directly in the center, and activated the controls. A meter square floor hatch opened, and the lights came on below in the server room. With the light on full below, he dropped down, not bothering with the ladder.

Thanks, Ian. You were right, as always. Cobb thought to himself again for the hundredth time. It reminded him that he had to sort out a high gravity workout schedule soon.

Below the bridge, the *OXCART* had a large server room. Only about 30% of the racks were in use. The place was a mess of tangled cables and old parts lying about. The new data stores were on pallets at the opposite end of the room, awaiting install.

"*OXCART*, I need two rack units, side by side, with maximum power and cooling availability. Any preferences?" Cobb asked.

"Number 16 and 17, please. It will create symmetry, and that will balance this row," the *OXCART* replied.

Cobb agreed.

The install didn't take long. Three hours later, Cobb climbed back up and closed the hatch. His attention was immediately drawn to the floor to ceiling vista of the now perfectly clean and clear glass. It was so clean it was almost invisible. Almost unnervingly so.

Cobb had an uncomfortable memory come to mind, unbidden. When he was a boy on Earth, he was already obsessed with clean windows. He remembered being so proud of how clean they were until a raven flew into the glass and died instantly.

"You continue to be full of surprises," Pope said from the captain's seat.

Cobb managed to hide the start that he felt inside. He didn't turn around. The stars were so beautiful.

"Too much coffee? It's three AM." Cobb turned around. "I was about to have some soup and a sandwich. Interested?"

She wasn't wearing her usual flight suit. It was a simple oversized black tunic pullover. Probably a nightshirt.

"I'd love some. But please, no more coffee." She smiled and stood. She was beautiful. Her black hair was loose, rather than her usual practical French braid. The nightshirt did little to hide her shape. The long, loose sleeves hid the muscles in her arms but made her even more alluring.

She leaned on the archway entrance to the galley as Cobb busied himself opening canned tomato soup and making grilled cheese sandwiches.

"While letting the coffee wear off, I tried to look you up on the grid to see what your deal was. I figured you'd be easy with a name like Cobbal Blocke," Pope said, watching his reaction.

Spatula in hand, with a raised eyebrow, he said, "And the verdict?"

"I'd bet money you have a worm running to sanitize the grid of your info. It feels like that. I did note that there are sealed Earth Defense Force court proceedings with your name attached." Pope waited for a reply as he stirred the soup.

"I was court-marshaled. In the end, I got out with a general discharge, though."

"What happened?" Pope asked.

"Insubordination, action unbecoming an officer, not following orders." Cobb wouldn't look at her as she spoke.

"Jesus. You AND Ian Vinge." She laughed. "Harv knows how to pick 'em."

"Not like Ian. Nothing that bad. I was the lead swarm programmer for the ship inspection drones. I discovered that someone had been tampering with the drones. They were using the inspections to plant system viruses that would disable critical life support and nav systems once the ship was out of EDF space."

"What happened?" Pope asked as he poured the soup into two over-sized mug/bowls.

"I took the info to the Captain." He cut the grilled cheese sandwiches in half, creating triangles. He put them on plates with the mug in the center. As he handed it to her, he continued. "I found myself in the brig. I had cleaned and reprogrammed the drones to remain inert without additional orders."

"What's with the court-martial?" She dipped a corner of the grilled cheese into the tomato soup and took a bite. "Oh, man. Is that bacon?" she sighed with delight.

"The inspection team came to the brig and almost beat me to death. The Captain gave me a lecture in the infirmary about minding my own business and following orders and ask first in the future."

"So, he was in on it?" Pope asked.

"She. And yes." He took a big bite before continuing. "I walked away from the ship at the next port. I went AWOL and resurfaced at EDF HQ with a lawyer."

"Holy fucking shit, Cobb," she replied. "Brass, ones."

"Apparently Captain Osborn was already on someone's watch list." He sipped his soup from the mug. "In the end, I got another seven months in the brig. I survived a couple of murder attempts. Finally, a trial, a general discharge, a cash settlement, and I was left high and dry on Earth. Blackballed and under a gag order. Nearly impossible for me to get a job. Eventually, I got hired at Oklahoma Salvage."

"Good story, Cobb. You should share it with Quinn tomorrow. He's run across Osborn in the Sol system and even beyond the belt. The EDF is one of the reasons we never take the *OXCART* back to the moon base."

"Quinn knows." He drained his mug and placed it and his plate in the dishwasher, not the sink. "He has my whole file."

"All he said to me about you is that you were a big moneymaker. And that we were all slackers compared to you." She laughed, crowding him intentionally to place her dishes in the washer. When she brushed against him, he could tell she wore nothing under the tunic.

"I am nothing if not an entrepreneur." Cobb held his hands out, palms up as he stood with his back to the end wall of the galley. Pope was close, very close.

"He also said you were a great pilot." She was two inches from his nose. Her breasts pressed against his chest. "That's my job around here."

She looked at his mouth for a moment. Cobb was trying to control his arousal.

She turned and abruptly exited the galley.

A chime sounded, and the display indicated that the diagnostic of one of the new systems was complete with issues.

"Good watch, Cobb. Thanks for cleaning up. Next time I might even come up barefoot." She laughed as Cobb waved to her as she entered the elevator.

After she was gone, Cobb went to the command console.

"She is a good pilot. The accident was an anomaly for her," the *OXCART* added in a monotone without prompting.

"What does she fly?" Cobb asked.

"Everything."

CHAPTER 6: Sabotage

"I knew Osborn was still out there. I was naive to believe they had yanked her chain hard enough to make her stop. I heard they had all been reassigned, her crew scattered. Things were changing in the EDF. I thought that would be the end of it. It actually made it all worse."

-- Personal logs of Captain Cobbal Blocke, 2672.

"We are completely locked out, Papa," she said from the freighter's engineering console. "Comms, nav, even life support."

"Go wake up your mother and both your brothers," he said to his daughter from the command/pilot seat. "If those boys are playing another joke I am going to…" He cut off at something he saw on a console.

"What is it, Papa?" She sounded like a frightened girl, not a 27-year-old ship engineer.

"Get a vac-suite on first. NOW!" he screamed as the bridge hatch slid open and stayed open. Down the main corridor, they could see all the hatches slide open.

He pounded a large mechanical button marked EMERGENCY ALERT. Nothing happened. He mashed it again. No claxon, no emergency auto-securing of all hatches.

All the lights went out. The hum of the freighter went silent.

The main passenger airlock opened.

The entire ship vented to vacuum in about 30 seconds. He died thinking about his wife being right again. They should have drilled more with the emergency vac-suits.

~~O~~

"Captain Osborn, there is an incoming transmission, your eyes only," the Comm officer on the bridge said, nearly hiding the tremble in his voice.

"I will take it in my wardroom." Captain Osborn said, as she moved to the tiny office in the back of the bridge. She entered, and the door slid closed behind her, noisily and too slow. Shaking her head, she spoke. "Osborn 29730B2T."

The Comm display on the desk came alive.

"It's about damn time, Osborn. You are a week late. Again." The man on the monitor had a smirk on his completely shaven face.

"Why shave the eyebrows, Grant?" Osborn scowled. "You look like a fool."

"It's the latest fashion. Try to keep up," he said, too close to the camera, "All the elites are completely hairless now. But you would not know that. They don't let you near them."

"I'd never stop throwing up," she spat.

"You know, darling, how much I love our chats, but I'm late for an appointment. What have you got for me?"

"Indie freighter. Full load. Sending over the details," Osborn transmitted. "Your crew still think you're a mystic?"

"Skeptics remain. But they all love money. Speaking of which." The man sat back. "Did you get the last drop?"

"If I hadn't, we'd be having a much different conversation."

"Did you have to kill Reggie?" Grant was pouting.

"Reggie?"

"The guy I hired to watch the pickup." Grant smiled wide, showing way too many perfect white teeth.

"I have no idea what you are talking about." Osborn was deadpan, serious, even though they both knew the truth. The threat was in her glare.

Silence stretched. Osborn could see the new corporate logo on Grant's coveralls for Sorenson Salvage. "When do I get to see your shiny new corporate salvage ship, Grant? I guess you ate enough of Sorenson's shit for him to notice you. You're welcome."

"We are ready to be boarded and inspected by the EDF at any time. Crisp and clean and not a single weapon. Not so much as a single sidearm." Grant held his hands up. "You know how the Sorensons are. Anti-weapon."

"Except for their own security forces and the EDF."

"You say that like it's a bad thing."

"If you had spent any real time beyond the belts, you'd know it is."

"Look, Osborn, you sabotage them when inspecting them while they are still in EDF space. Leave the hard part to me, and I'll salvage them. You get paid. Everyone is happy."

Grant disconnected without saying goodbye. Osborn had the impression someone had entered the room where Grant was making the call. Never from his own quarters, never from the bridge.

"Can I kill him when we're through?" a quiet voice said from all around Osborn.

"Get in line, fucker," Osborn growled.

CHAPTER 7: RUTH

"If any of them were to guess the truth, I believed that Ruth Philips might just be the one. I just wanted to get to know them first."

-- Personal logs of Captain Cobbal Blocke, 2672.

Cobb had a fresh pot of coffee on at 0745 when Quinn entered the bridge mid-conversation with Ruth, Ron, and the Two Daves in tow. Everyone seemed to be talking at once but stopped suddenly when they saw how clean the bridge was.

"Fucking eh, Cobb. Way to suck up, new guy." Dave Mitchell said, bringing a round of good-natured laughs.

"Wait until you try his coffee," Ruth said, as she made a beeline for the galley. "He is the King of suck-ups."

Coffee was quickly passed all around, and silence ensued as everyone breathed in the aroma and sipped with pleasure.

Ruth held up her cup in salute. "Cobb, we must talk." She smiled. "Suck up, indeed."

"Diagnostics ran twice overnight. The punch list has been updated based on the review. Nothing critical added. Mostly secondary and tertiary, power and comms." Cobb drained the remains of his coffee. "The new data store has been fully installed and tested. The *OXCART* is neck-deep in the indexing."

The *OXCART* added, "I will have a separate report for you on the new data store, Captain."

Cobb saw Quinn's face change. Cobb was sure it was because the *OXCART* called him Captain. It must have been a signal of some kind. No one else seemed to notice.

"Good job on the cleanup. I didn't even notice how bad it had gotten," Quinn said.

"The nanite fabricator I brought with me will be able to eventually address the whole ship. It just takes time to create and program a swarm that big. Please, let me know if there any priority areas. I created an open task list for light cleaning and maintenance. Eventually, even the unused levels can get attention." Cobb pointed on the big display.

"Suck up," Dave Wheeler said, smiling into his coffee mug.

"What'd you do to Kira yesterday, man? You must have a wicked right cross," Dave Mitchell asked in jest. "When I asked what happened, she just said, blame Cobb." Ruth and Quinn looked at Cobb.

He shrugged, saying, "I won't have to tell her something twice ever again." His joke fell flat. Ruth was the only one that seemed to understand it was a joke.

Ruth rescued him, "Have you had breakfast, Cobb?"

"We haven't had breakfast!" the Daves said in perfect unison.

Ron Carter was ignoring the banter and looking closely at the updates to the punch list. "Thanks for the coffee, Cobb. And this." He pointed at the list with his mug. "I thought Royce handled these yesterday."

Ruth took Cobb's arm and shepherded him towards the lift. The conversations rose again. The lift doors opened, and Royce White was there. He nodded to Cobb and Ruth as he passed but said nothing.

The lift closed, and Ruth said, "S11, please."

"Why don't you reside on the command deck with the others?" Cobb asked her. He had the feeling that being frank with Ruth was the rule.

"The apartments are too small for me," she replied, watching the numbers descend. "I hear you didn't even look at them."

"Too small for me, as well. Plus, I could have one next to a hangar where I can work on my personal ship as time allows. It needs a ton of work." The lift opened to a short corridor that was brightly lit and lined with ivy trays on the walls. Stations used ivy trays like these to supplement CO_2 scrubbers. Plus, they added a bit of comfort to the sterile environments of space. The ceiling looked like the blue sky and provided full-spectrum light.

"The ceiling is painted with active high def pixel paint. It even has cloudy days sometimes. The recording is Summer in Buffalo. Beautiful sky there and stars at night as well." Ruth moved to an entrance that required a palm scan.

The entrance opened as the lights came up inside. The room was open, light, and airy. The view out the simulated windows was of a lake or ocean that went almost to the horizon. If he looked close, a skyline could be seen on the horizon.

The room was large but not cavernous like Cobb's space. There was a single great room with furnishings straight from a Terrestrial catalog. The floor was covered in lush oriental carpets.

A white modular over-sized pit sofa, classic dining table for twelve, and even a grand piano filled the far end. There was also a collection of other various instruments displayed artfully on stands or the wall beyond.

"Are you worried at all about the unsecured items in the case of loss of gravity?" Cobb asked.

Ruth was already in the kitchen to his right. She was pulling out pots and pans. Cobb liked the fact that Ruth didn't ask him what he wanted. She just set about making breakfast as she spoke. "The suite has independent grav-plates on the floor. They are programmed for automatic inertial dampening if something happens. Nothing ever does."

Cobb then noticed an accent wall. It was covered floor to ceiling in the high-def pixel paint and displayed thousands of personal photos. Lots of family and vacation photos. Some were old and faded family photos. There were also personal letters, handwritten. It was beautifully displayed in an entire wall of collage. Some of the images on closer inspection had annotations below them as captions.

"Do you have a large family?" he asked her.

Bacon was beginning to sizzle as Ruth filled a sizeable French press with fresh ground coffee and boiling water. "I don't have any family." She looked up at the wall. "That's my collection. I am the Content Salvage Specialist on the team. I am responsible for collecting everything contained inside the things we salvage.

All too often, people die in these places. We even collect their personal effects. In my spare time, the *OXCART* helps me identify the people. Often, the next of kin never knew what happened." Ruth sighed heavily and paused. "I used to try to notify next of kin. Quinn always thought it was a bad idea to notify the family. Legal, lawyer crap is bad back on Earth these days." She was making hash browns with onions.

"Doesn't it break your heart? Child remains in wrecks get me every time," Cobb said, as he studied images of a birthday picnic from a picture where he recognized the vista as Page colony. "This one was taken on Page. An edge colony, not far from here. It's beautiful there."

"Just touch the image and note that. Any info helps," Ruth said, as she set out plates, cups, and silverware at the kitchen bar.

"That mountain range is so familiar," Cobb mused.

Ruth poured coffee and orange juice at a place setting as Cobb walked along the wall of images.

"Harv told me you like to often take your shares from the salvage, instead of cash. Me too. As you can see." She was talking about her plush apartment. Furnished with the personal goods of long-dead victims of accidents, violence, and vacuum. "Content requests go through me. I maintain detailed inventories of what is currently on hand. We collect items until we get a container full of like items that we can market for profit."

"The *OXCART* has been helping me, so far. Trying, anyway." Cobb saw she was beginning to dish up the food. So he came over and took a stool at the counter at his place setting.

"The computer is okay if you are looking for a particular item. Presuming that I entered it into the database accurately. I can be a bigger help. Hardware components for your ship, for instance, are all database queries. See me for the furniture, art, plants, anything. Hell, we have three more grand pianos. Who the hell brings a grand piano to a colony?"

"A pianist, I suppose. Do you play?" Cobb asked as he put his napkin in his lap. She slid three eggs, sunny side up, on top of his hash browns.

"I do now. Try at least." She served herself and came around the island to sit next to Cobb.

"Thanks for breakfast. This is excellent." Cobb tucked in.

"So, what really happened to Kira?" Ruth asked without a hint of accusation.

"She fell when she entered my nanite lab. I had no idea that she had wireless prosthetic interfaces that my RF suppression systems would override. She face-planted before I could catch her."

"I'm not surprised. It's not the first time. She'll learn." Ruth was matter of fact.

"Ruth, she could have been seriously injured or even killed." Cobb stopped eating. "I don't even know where the infirmary is on this boat yet. There was no on-boarding briefing, no tour, no watch guidance. I was just tossed in the deep end."

"Have you talked to Quinn about this? He is the captain." Ruth said, sipping orange juice.

"Not yet. At first, I was waiting for a watch meeting or all-hands briefing or something. There is no such thing." He sighed and took another bite. "I added it to the punch list. Even the log entries are light, if at all."

"Everyone just relies on the logs or the *OXCART* to keep us on track," she said.

"And to order coffee?" he said to the ceiling, knowing the computer was listening. "No offense."

"None taken," the *OXCART* replied automatically, unbidden.

"I've been here for two days. Two accidents already." Cobb shook his head and ate more toast.

"Harv knows. I think it's why he sent you. He hates the EDF, but maybe this crew needs a little EDF discipline." Ruth wasn't critical. "This is just a job for most of the crew. A contract. When their contracts are up, most will be gone. Royce White will be first. He only has a few months left on his contract. You should have heard how pissed he was when Quinn told him you would receive a full salvage share on that shuttle."

"I don't have an employment contract with Harv." He wiped his mouth with the cloth napkin. "Just like Ian."

"Harv must really like you," Ruth said, looking closely at Cobb.

She might already know.

~~O~~

Cobb spent the rest of his day making a list of goods he wanted from the stores available. The *OXCART* database was beneficial, but you had to be precise in your queries. Cobb missed the use of a full AI.

"I believe that you can harvest many of these items from other unused sections of the ship, like the light fixtures, raised flooring, and grav-plating. It also makes them a no-cost item, as they are still part of the ship."

Cobb looked up at the massive expanse of flat wall that was now clean to the bare metal over most of it. "I want enough monitor pixel paint to cover that entire wall. And the ceiling in the corridor. Like on level S11."

"We have it in stock. I can have Two Daves bring it down on a pallet," the *OXCART* said.

"Have them leave it in the hall," Cobb added. "I don't want any conversations right now. I need to get to sleep on time today."

"Got it. Will you need the Daves help to apply the monitor paint?" *OXCART* asked helpfully.

"No. I have programmed maintenance bugs for that duty. It takes longer, but they can do it unassisted. I also need you to authorize my maintenance spiders to access this entire level. The raised floors, and light fixtures are all available in bays 27 to 35."

Cobb retreated to the *TULSA* 471 at 1630 for a shower and bunk. He had just gotten into fresh boxers and t-shirt when his comms chimed. It was Kira.

"Go for Cobb," he answered via HUD with audio-only.

"Hey, Cobb." Kira was audio and video. Cobb lay in his bunk in the dark. The window floated in his vision. He could see she had a black eye.

"Nice shiner," he said, with an unmistakable smile in his voice.

"Yeah, you'll never have to tell me twice again." She laughed. "The Daves could not believe you said that. They told Royce, and he was going to come looking for you before I shut him down. I should never have slept with that guy."

Cobb was glad he was audio-only, he blushed far too easy. "Are you... all right?"

"I had the Auto-doc check me at Ruth's insistence." She looked away for a moment. "I wanted to apologize for that whole thing. Ruth said you were worried, and... well, I'm sorry."

"Look, once I settle in, I can help you update your implants and HUD interface, so it never happens again. I already have that mod. I control my ship the same way you control your rig. Same ICS under the hood. Sorry, Industrial Control System. It's the same code base as advanced nanite programming."

"How did you learn that?" Kira asked.

"It's new. Standard Mil-HUD control code for Battle-Bridges," Cobb lied. "I'll fix you up. Come see me tomorrow after my watch."

"I'm sorry. Were you sleeping?" Kira suddenly realized she might have woke him. "I thought you slept days. We had not seen you all day, so I assumed."

"No worries, Kira." Cobb made a mental note to set up a crew duty calendar with the *OXCART*. "I just climbed into my bunk."

"Sleep. You work too much." Kira said good-naturedly. "Don't make me tell you twice!" She laughed and disconnected. Just before she disconnected, her laughter had brought her cleavage into the image frame. She had no bra. It was obvious.

He fell asleep with that image etched in his mind.

CHAPTER 8: LEADERSHIP

"There was more wrong on the *OXCART* than just rust, paint, and the sensor array."
-- Personal logs of Captain Cobbal Blocke, 2672.

Cobb was up, dressed, and had the specialized nanites packed in a small case. It was the size of a lunch-pail. As he entered suite 37, he was impressed at the progress made overnight. The grid for the raised floor was down, and the tiles were beginning to get installed. The monitor-wall paint was going on and about 20% covered. It also meant the cleaners had finished. It was hard to tell, as the light fixtures that had been there were all now gone.

He was ahead of schedule.

Grav-plates were being installed below the raised floor. The coverage was not perfect, but okay.

When the lift opened onto the bridge, there was an argument in progress. People were screaming at each other. The entire crew was there, and Cobb moved unnoticed to the galley for some coffee.

There was none.

He set about making a pot as Ron Carter joined him to stay out of the fray.

Cobb asked casually as he activated the coffee maker. "So, what's all this?"

"Apparently, when I brought up the new unified sensor array for testing, Pope saw something on long-range during the test." Ron pulled out a flask and poured some bourbon into his coffee mug. He held up the container, offering some to Cobb. He smiled brightly but declined with a shake of the head. He spoke so only Cobb could hear him. "Royce wants to burn hot to get to whatever it is. Quinn and Magnus want to get the new long-range optical up and running. The Daves want bigger shares and want Royce White and me off before they investigate." Ron took a sip. "Kira wants the install done right and properly calibrated before anything is done at all. We currently have no baselines or backups."

"Where is Quinn on this?" Cobb poured himself a cup.

"He's distracted and working with the computer about some new data-store you installed last night. For fuck's sake, I've never seen a captain stand for this kind of bullshit on a bridge before." Ron shook his head.

"*OXCART*, it's after midnight. Do I have the watch?" Cobb said out loud.

"Yes, Commander Blocke. You do," the *OXCART* replied flatly.

"Power down all displays. Night light settings. Open the lift door," Cobb said. All the display systems and lights shut down, the consoles went dark, on standby. The conversation stopped. Cobb walked through the group.

"Okay, folks. I have work to do on this watch. Please take this circus somewhere else." He sat in the command seat and activated the log of the watch. Sipping his coffee, he signed in.

"Who does he think..." Royce started to spin up again.

"Everyone out. We will pick this up again at 08:30." Quinn ordered. He sounded like a captain for the first time. The lift filled, and its doors closed as the arguments began again.

None of them noticed that Ron Carter stayed behind. He crept out of the galley as Cobb said, "So Ron... Show me what all the fuss was about."

Ron took his fresh cup of coffee and sat at the central engineering console. Quickly he brought up the sensor telemetry.

"We were testing the sensors on known objects at known locations, at known distances. The closer tests were remarkable. We picked a distant one for the hell of it. We looked for the space station over the Page colony. It was gone."

Page? Cobb thought, and then it struck him. *Page... the image on Ruth's wall. That little girl.*

"Thanks, Ron. Get some rest. Tomorrow will be a long day, no matter what happens," Cobb said. "Who was supposed to be your visitor escort?"

Just then, the lift door opened, and Royce White stepped onto the bridge.

Cobb immediately said, "Thanks for giving me a few minutes with Ron. It was beneficial, Royce. Good idea."

Royce was about to say something but came up short.

"Goodnight, Cobb," Ron said.

Cobb spun the command seat around and nodded to Ron and Royce. Respectfully. Sincerely.

Royce said nothing and just backed into the lift.

"*OXCART*, please add a review of all shipboard security procedures to the list." Cobb spun back to the scans. "Why the hell wasn't the engineering station locked?"

"None of the stations are ever locked," the *OXCART* answered.

"Does everyone have login credentials?"

"Yes," the computer answered.

"Lock all workstations after fifteen minutes of inactivity. Starting now," Cobb ordered. "Restrict access to the new data-store to you, Quinn and me."

"Show me the watch calendar," Cobb added.

"There is no watch calendar. I do have my master calendar. Maybe that will help." *OXCART* displayed a multidimensional calendar that showed the crew's sleep cycles and scheduled events. He expanded details. Kira usually slept with a comms Do-Not-Disturb flag set from 1 am to 7 am. The only other calendar entries on her calendar were birthdays and anniversaries. Cobb was surprised that all the birthdays from the crew were there. Even his own.

Royce only used it for the daily countdown until the end of his contract. The Two Daves never used it. Never even accessed it. Quinn used it for a regular virtual meeting with the Oklahoma Salvage base commander in the belt.

"*OXCART*, please start a new calendar. Titled: Watch Schedule," Cobb decided. "Include the watch schedule and each of our sleep schedules. Associate the Watch Task List with deadlines on the calendar and Watch logs with status times. "

I should just tell them and get it over with.

~~O~~

Cobb's specialized nanites cleaned the internal circuits and panels all night. These needed more attention than the external surfaces. The sensitive nature of the older circuits can be tricky to clean.

While the nanites worked, Cobb calibrated the new sensors. He could understand why they were so spun up about the find. The space station was gone.

The Page colony looked dead.

The station was no longer in orbit. There was possibly a debris field. Sensors also showed no life on the planet. No RF, no lights at night. No thermal signatures. Nothing.

Quinn showed up early. The lift opened at 0600. "Cobb, I need to talk to you." He went into the aft galley for coffee. "Before the rest of them start up again."

"I'll go. I'll take the *TULSA*," Cobb said, simply. "I should take Royce and Ruth."

Quinn was taken aback.

"I can't make you use your personal shuttle for a run like this," Quinn said. "Harv said it was not... finished."

"I can get there in two hours," Cobb said. "I can even take a couple of empty shipping containers and one of the small tractors."

"I don't know..." Quinn hesitated.

"Let me put it to you this way, Quinn," Cobb emphasized his name, obviously not using Captain. "I'm going. Overnight, the new sensors picked up faint distress signals. If anyone is still alive there, that is MY priority. I will take Royce to get him off your back, and containers in case there is salvage."

"Okay..." Quinn started looking at the displays. "Okay." He saw the logs of the sensors on the screens.

"Order me to go. Be decisive. Even at the risk of being wrong," Cobb said.

Quinn's face showed that he was thinking about last night's embarrassing argument.

"Okay." He looked in Cobb's face. "Okay. Do it. Go."

Cobb nodded respectfully, then whirled and headed for the lift, already talking to the computer.

"*OXCART*, please wake up Royce and Ruth. We have an emergency distress signal that's been picked up by the new sensors." The lift door closed. "Have them meet me in S21-37 on the double with vac-suits and personal salvage kits."

"It has been done," the *OXCART* replied a moment later. "Now I understand why you loaded those containers and tractor last night."

"Prep for a hot exit." Cobb ran to the door marked 37 when the lift opened. The room was still a mess, but enough of the new drop floor was installed that he could quickly run across to the hangar entrance.

Ruth arrived first. She was also running. She had a duffel slung on one shoulder and a pressure suit over the other. She ascended the *TULSA* 471 belly stairs without having to be told where to go.

"Take the lift to level 2R and strap in," Cobb said as she stowed her gear in a locker. She just nodded and went up.

Cobb had to wait another eleven minutes for Royce. He said nothing when he strolled up to the rear cargo ramp. Cobb closed the hatch and entered the lift, not waiting to see if Royce followed. "*OXCART*. We're ready to go."

By the time they reached the bridge, the hangar was open, and the skids were up. Cobb's advanced pilot HUD gave him direct control of the ship without instrumentation.

The bridge dome was set to a full exterior view. It was like the lift opened onto a roof patio. They were quickly moving out of the hangar before they were strapped in. As soon as they were clear of the *OXCART,* the *TULSA* shifted to FTL.

"Jesus, Cobb," Royce said. "What's the rush?"

"Last night, I distinctly remember that it was you arguing to get to Page as fast as possible," Cobb said, as the dome expanded tactical maps, systems, and communications data and other telemetry Royce didn't recognize.

"What the hell is this?" Royce was sitting at the engineering console. "I've flown L22s shuttles hundreds of times. None had a bridge like this. And how the hell did you hot jump to FTL so fast?"

"I know it looks like shit on the outside," Cobb said, "I have been working on... upgrades."

"We will be there in fifty-one minutes," Ruth said from the navigation console. She looked at Royce and saw his mouth hanging open. "Impressive. Have you got any coffee, Captain?"

"Yes, I do." Cobb accessed and opened a large panel in the back of the bridge that had a small fridge, a sink, counter, and built-in coffee maker.

"How the f..." Royce started.

"Advance HUD interface." Cobb poured three mugs and handed them out. "I started the coffee as soon as Quinn ordered the rescue op."

"Rescue?" Ruth asked.

"It's faint, but there. A distress call," Cobb said.

"I have nothing on comms," Royce said. "Not that I'm complaining. The salvage potential here is big."

"The sensors on the *TULSA* won't pick them up until we are close." He sipped the coffee. "The new sensors on the *OXCART* are really something."

"This looks like a mil-spec battle bridge, Cobb," Ruth said, looking at the ergonomic controls and seats with full harnesses. "The bridge on L22s has always been in the forward part of the ship. I always liked an L22's big clear canopy even though it doesn't have blast shields. This area is usually the crew mess, if memory serves."

"That's right." Cobb walked down the short hall to the lift, and inside the front and rear doors both opened, making the lift a hallway of sorts. It led to a balcony that was a level above the usual bridge location.

That room was a mess. All the seats and consoles were disassembled and shoved to the sides. The floor was pulled up in several areas. Thick and thin cables ran across the disrupted floor. The nose skid gear below was even exposed in one place.

Tool chests and cartons of equipment or supplies were everywhere.

But the view of the stars was magnificent.

"Jesus, Cobb. It's worse in here than on the outside," Royce said.

"It's a work in progress." Cobb smiled at the mess.

An alarm began to beep behind them in the bridge. They filed back in and saw the faint distress signal indicator on the tactical map display.

"It looks like an escape pod," Ruth said.

"ETA, nineteen minutes," Cobb replied.

CHAPTER 9: *GREENWOOD*

"We should have paid greater attention to what happened there. It may have saved us pain later."

-- Personal logs of Captain Cobbal Blocke, 2672.

"We weren't fast enough," Royce said as the tractor clamped on the tumbling escape pod.

The occupant was dead. The telemetry was apparent once they were close. The pod was from a ship called the *GREENWOOD.*

There was no response from the Page colony on the surface. The Page colony space station, registered with the name *GREENWOOD,* was gone.

"*GREENWOOD,* this is *TULSA* 471." The was no reply.

"Cobb, I think I know what happened to the *GREENWOOD* Station," Ruth said, bringing up a huge window on the bridge. A mountain peak had been sheared off. And the black impact crater was massive. A million acres of forest had burned.

"*GREENWOOD* station has augured in," Cobb said out loud.

"Dammit, that was a six-ring station," Royce said.

"They are designed specifically to be stable. It was the colony ship, to begin with."

"Page is a relatively new colony," Ruth said.

"*TULSA* 471 to anyone on Page," Cobb repeated for six complete orbits.

"Cobb, there are fires everywhere on the surface."

"Scanners are detecting the primary settlement. We're going in." Cobb flew in with a thought.

Cobb landed the *TULSA* in what looked like the remains of a town square. It was evident that the fire had ravaged the entire settlement. The central foamcrete structures must have had wooden facades everywhere. There were no signs of life.

"This was once a beautiful city," Cobb said into the quiet.

"Cobb, all these municipal systems have signs of massive electro-magnetic pulse damage," Royce said. "Who would do this?"

It was the same everywhere. Everything burned to the foundations. A few garaged vehicles confirmed Royce's assessment. They found charred bodies all around the perimeter of the square. It looks like they had fled the burning structures.

"People... get back to the ship." Cobb suddenly sounded urgent. "What if this was not an attack?"

They hurried back into the ship.

Cobb watched from the observation deck on the *TULSA* as insects moved in clouds and were attracted to the dead bodies on the ground. It was a nightmare landscape.

Ruth pointed to a wall out in the ruins. "Look."

The foamcrete wall had large letters, spray painted quickly, *GET TO THE MINES!*

~~O~~

The canopy was in full surround mode. Cobb followed the roads in his search. One of them had to lead to the colony mining operation.

Less than an hour later, at the base of the nearest foothills, they found a cluster of vehicles randomly parked outside a foamcrete structure that looked like a bunker. Four men looked up from the open hood of one of the trucks and waved urgently.

Cobb landed, and by the time the rear cargo ramp was down, forty-five colonists stood waiting.

One man stepped forward. He didn't say anything at first. Soot covered him as if he had been mining coal.

"It's over," was all he said initially. "There are forty-six of us here."

Ruth spoke then. "Does anyone need medical attention?"

"Those that lived be not injured," the man said in an odd accent. "What of the others?"

"Those that stayed in town died. It's all burned." Cobb said. "What happened here?"

"We knew it was coming—an immense coronal mass ejection. Most evacuated on the *GREENWOOD*, our colony ship. It had not been fully converted yet."

"They were too late," another man sobbed. "Without the AI, the *GREENWOOD* was impossible."

"They stole the AI during the chaos," another woman said. She was sober. Angry, even.

"Who stole your AI?" Cobb asked.

"No idea," the first man said. They had a shuttle. Unmarked. No FTL engines. "Folks on the *GREENWOOD* thought they were evacuating too. Till they started killin' in Ops and took the AI Orb. Six dead, they said."

"Our people. They were tryin', taking her away on manual," the man said.

"I think they were too late," the woman said. She stared at nothing. "Almost 4,000 people."

Ruth was passing around bottles of water.

"My name is Cobb. How can we help you?"

~~O~~

It only took an hour to get everyone out of the mines. They all fit inside the *TULSA*, but it was not a comfortable ride in the shipping container. The group's leader wanted to go to another settlement by an ocean.

"It's there." He pointed once they were aloft. It looked like a fishing community of about 200 more people. All survived in their foamcrete structures by the sea. None of them wanted to leave.

They were much lower-tech in this part of the Page colony. A clear advantage in this situation.

Cobb personally offloaded the escape pod they had collected. It confirmed to the colonists the fates of those that tried to flee on the *GREENWOOD*.

They were still in shock. But, the colonists were determined and still proud.

In the end, Cobb left comm units with them so they could communicate with each other and any orbitals. He also left all the medical supplies he had on the *TULSA* and a solar array for power. It wasn't much, but it would help them survive. None of the survivors wanted to leave, but several gave them messages to deliver.

As they flew over the crash site of the *GREENWOOD*, it was full destruction. What didn't burn up on reentry was destroyed on impact.

"That was a waste of time," Royce said as they left orbit.

"Shut up, Royce," was all Ruth said.

CHAPTER 10: ROAD TRIP

"Quinn was a good man, a good friend, an excellent data analyst, but he didn't know how to be a true leader."
-- Personal logs of Captain Cobbal Blocke, 2672.

The lift door opened, and Quinn walked in, yawning. "Morning, Cobb."

"Morning, sir," Cobb replied from the engineering station where he leaned over Dave Wheeler's shoulder, pointing to the console.

"Good morning, Captain," Wheeler added. "There's fresh coffee."

Quinn just waved as he entered the galley in the back of the bridge. When he emerged with a steaming cup, all the displays were active, and on the main viewer the entire ship was depicted in the wireframe. A cross-section showed 53 levels in profile with water and sewer overlays.

"The control is here." Cobb pointed again. "It will bring up any or all of the systems." Dave turned them on, and the display filled with so much detail it was impossible to read. "That view is useful when you are zoomed in deeper." Cobb zoomed in on the bridge section. All the power, water, air ducts, and comm cables were color-coded.

"What's that?" Dave pointed.

"That's the conference room. The lift, galley, and head all open into there on the other side," Cobb said.

"We never use it. with a crew this small." Quinn sat in the captain's seat, trailed off in another yawn, and sipped his coffee.

Dave logged out and stood as Cobb said, "We had an overnight communication from the Oklahoma Salvage front office. The crew is about to get bigger." Dave paused on his way to the lift. "There are four that need to be picked up at the yard. Junior mechanics."

Dave was smiling wide as the lift door closed.

Quinn was looking at the note from the front office. He sighed.

"It's the new sensor array." Cobb brought up the schedule. "Installs will be done today. The front office expects us... to be busy."

Quinn scrubbed his face with both hands. "Why was Dave up here?" It wasn't an accusation. But it did contain a tone.

"I believe we need to add a second seat to every watch," Cobb said.

"Why? The computer is here for continuity and to back us up," Quinn said.

"I believe we need to train up the junior staff," Cobb said. "We cannot just keep giving the junior staff just the shit jobs and not teach them anything. This ship runs like a small station, not an actual ship. It's like everyone lives and commutes to their jobs. Lives their own lives. Works. Goes home. Lather rinse repeat."

Quinn was looking out the window at a red nebula to his left. "I knew this day would come. Harv has been warning me for years. Waiting for me to step up." Quinn turned and looked at Cobb. "Is he going to name you captain? Be straight with me, Cobb."

"No," Cobb answered. "I don't want to be captain of the *OXCART*. But things have changed, keep reading. I do want us to be safer. To be more productive. And to make an ass load of cash." He grinned. "What I want is to continue to refit the *TULSA*. I want an interesting, quiet life where I can do what I want. Like it or not, you are stuck as captain."

"Harv said you didn't sign a contract. Wouldn't sign. Just like Ian Vinge." Quinn kept reading.

"No. But we have... an understanding," Cobb said.

Quinn was still reading the note from the front office. His eyes went wide. Cobb knew he finally got to the critical part.

"Holy shit, Cobb," he said, looking up. "You own the *OXCART*? Do you own ALL the OS assets outside the Sol System? You are my boss?"

"You are to keep this to yourself for now, Captain," Cobb said in solemn tones with a subtle emphasis on the word *Captain*. "I am now partners with Harv Rearden and Oklahoma Salvage. Look, it's complicated. As far as you are concerned, nothing has changed."

"What's the plan? You seem like the type that has a plan," Quinn asked.

"Royce leaves to head back to Freedom Station tomorrow with Ron Carter." Cobb brought up a detailed calendar schedule. "I think I should go to the yard and pick up the new crew. I can chat with Ma and Pa Wyatt."

"What's the side trips here?" Quinn asked, pointing to the display.

"Personal leave. Three days. I have a side project that I had started before I started working for OS I need to check on," Cobb said flatly.

"You can get there that fast?" Quinn asked, impressed. "Keep that to yourself, Cobb. The EDF notices ships with specs like that."

"That's the beauty of working out here. No need to register flight plans." Cobb smiled. "I'll have room for three full containers from the yard."

"I thought the *TULSA* could hold four containers?" Quinn asked.

"It can, but I need one for personal stowage," Cobb said. "Please take a close look at the new roster. The time to do it is before the new staff comes on board. And don't worry about the changes. Please. It only gets better."

~~O~~

"Come," Cobb said to the air, and the door slid aside, revealing Kira in the hall.

"Holy shit, Cobb." She looked around, amazed at the room. "When the hell did you have time to do this?" The floor was now level across the entire large room. The wall she had just walked through had the forward view of space. She recognized the Obara Hitomi red nebula to the left. Pools of light illuminated a few areas in the giant room where there were rolled-up carpets and furniture that was not yet secured.

Cobb was standing at a console in one of the pools of light. The armor-glass looking into the hangar was behind him. There was a rack of medium-sized maintenance bots to his right.

"I'm a swarm programmer. I have a couple of nanite fabricators here and a few hundred maintenance and fabrication bots that never stop." At that, the spiders deployed. They descended below the floor.

"I hear you're going to the Yard tomorrow. I'm going with you," Kira said as she walked up to Cobb's tool chests and started opening drawers, looking at tools.

"You are?" Cobb asked.

"Yes. I have not seen Ma and Pa in over a year, and we need some specific items to get that shuttle we just recovered back in service. Quinn said we'd be able to bring back a couple of containers of parts in addition to the kids."

"Kids?"

"Ma and Pa rescues. Cats and dogs." Kira replaced the unfamiliar tool and turned to Cobb. "I know two of them. Smart. Good kids. But I don't know the other two."

"I have a side trip to make. It might take a couple of days."

"When will you help me with the RF thing?" Kira asked.

"We can do it on this trip," Cobb said. "It's all software. Just make sure you run backups before we leave."

"Is it all HUD or prosthetic side?" She was uncomfortable.

"Both. Mostly prosthetic side."

"I have more than one... body," she said, blushing.

Cobb was not embarrassed. "Bring two. I'll upgrade the first one while you watch, and you can do the second while I watch. Then you will be able to perform the same on the other ones. How many do you have?"

"My parents spoiled me." She was looking at her boots. "They always felt guilty about what happened, so they spared no expense."

Cobb stopped working and stepped away from the console. "Look. You don't have to tell me anything."

Go ahead. Lie to me, Cobb thought, without changing expression.

"My parents met at the Imabari shipyard. My mom didn't know she was pregnant when she took a big dose of radiation. I was born with Thalogen defects. Normally they just amputate the deformed limbs and do nanite growth gene therapy. Regrow fresh ones. However, I had an almost lethal reaction. The auxin treatment would never work for me. Attempts to culture a new set to graft resulted in my original mutated limbs. By then, I already had the prosthetics and deep brain implants for the control interfaces. Finally, they just let me be a kid."

Cobb handed her a cup of coffee but didn't interrupt her.

"They paid for seven full sets of prosthetics." She gestured to her own body. "This was the last and best of them." She reached out her hand so Cobb could examine it.

He set his mug down and took it in both his hands. It was warm. The skin was supple, and it felt like a real hand. "It's beautiful."

"The expensive part is the sensors. The touch is perfect. The entire dermal layer is sensory. All my other bodies are limited in some way. Here, look." She began to unzip her coveralls.

Cobb blushed and turned away.

"It's okay, Cobb. I have a body stocking on."

Cobb looked as she slid the coveralls off her shoulders. Her torso was in a dark gray body stocking. It rested in a form-fitting body that had a single strap that crossed just below her breasts to hold her in. Cobb caught himself staring at her breasts a moment too long.

"I usually don't wear the body stocking because it makes it a hassle to go to the bathroom. The body has a nice microfiber, felt liner, and is comfortable enough to sleep in. I didn't know what the upgrades would entail. So... I was prepared."

Cobb went to his enormous tool chest and opened a drawer at about his chin height and withdrew an instrument. A small scanner.

"What's your implant range?" He began walking around her with the scanner.

"I think about five meters or so." She smiled. "I can tuck myself into bed and then relax, parking the body in a chair." She smiled wide then. "I used to make the bodies dance when I was younger."

"I believe we can do a bit better than that." Cobb turned and looked through the armor-glass at the *TULSA* 471. All the interior lights came on, and the grav-foils on the pontoons flexed out and in like it was alive. "I have the same control interface. We will be able to get you a kilometer without anything but software upgrades."

"You have a full control interface with the *TULSA*?" she asked, as she zipped up her coveralls and looked out the armor-glass.

"And sensors. Full pilot interface. Full central system integration."

Kira was looking at Cobb when the wall beyond him switched to a view looking from the ship at Kira through the armor-glass wall.

"You could fly that ship from here by just thinking?" she asked.

"Yes." The wall returned to the flight view. "Ian and Harv helped me work out the new interface, based on an AI control socket."

"Now I can see why you are still working for Harv," she said.

"Oh?" Cobb raised an eyebrow.

"He pays you with junk that didn't cost him hardly anything. The tech that would cost you a mint if you had to buy it, but you get from him for next to nothing."

Cobb was nodding as he drained his coffee.

"Do you have any idea how much all this grav-plating in here would have cost? I bet he didn't even charge you for it because it's installed on the *OXCART*."

"That's right."

"Why did you install it? We already have ship-wide gravity."

"Local gravity control. I like to turn it up and do tai chi."

Kira smiled. "I do 2-G yoga myself. Keeps my spine flexible and my abs hard. When do we leave?"

"I plan to head out right after my watch. 0800. Quinn is sending over three containers of salvage for the yard." Cobb said.

"And we are probably bringing back two full ones with parts for the shuttle."

"Think you'll be able to get her up and running?"

"I do," Kira said. "It won't be as good as the *TULSA*, no FTL drives, but for local use, it will be a great hauler. It's already air-tight. We need one."

Kira got up and moved to the door. She paused and looked back at Cobb.

"See you at 0800, Cobb." She left.

Cobb could smell her perfume for hours.

~~O~~

"Thanks, Cobb," Dave Wheeler said, as he made a pot of coffee for the next watch.

"For what?"

"For talking Quinn into letting us second chair the watch," Wheeler said.

"Thank me by resisting the urge to be an asshole to the junior staff when they get here." Cobb rinsed and put his mug away. "Remember how shitty it felt on the bottom rung? No hazing, no insulting nicknames. You want respect, show respect if you want my respect. Mentor the newbies, instead of abusing them."

Cobb opened the door to the conference room. The lights didn't even come up. "*OXCART*, can you turn on these lights?"

"Negative." The computer sounded sorry. "I do not have access."

Cobb turned on a pen-light and found the panel just inside the door to the lift. More than half the lights didn't work. The table was covered with old monitors, consoles, cables, and random tools. Boxes and other trash also filled the room.

"I think we may need this conference room soon," Cobb said as he shined his light behind a massive pile to the right of the door.

"Want me to handle this while you're gone?" Dave Wheeler asked, drawing a look from Cobb.

"Do it," Cobb stated, smiling, and slid the door closed.

CHAPTER 11: Kira Fletcher

"Kira Fletcher was far more normal than I expected. Had I not known the truth about her, I would never have guessed. She was nothing like her sisters."

-- Personal logs of Captain Cobbal Blocke, 2672.

Cobb watched the last container loaded and secured in the hold of the *TULSA*.

"She comes," the *OXCART* computer said.

"Thanks." The *TULSA's* rear cargo ramp began to close as Cobb entered the residence he now called 37. He moved across from the hangar and opened the door to the corridor before she reached it. Kira strode in, smiling wide, hips swaying. Behind her walked a tall black figure that was moving precisely as she was moving. Behind the black figure sauntered Bail the cat. Kira stopped, and the figure stopped. The cat began rubbing on the spare body's legs. It leaned down and scratched Bail's ears.

"You said to bring two." Kira smiled. "This is my other favorite me."

Kira raised both hands and flexed the fingers. The motion was mirrored by the other body.

The black poly carbon body was a design Cobb had seen before. He looked closely, and the hands confirmed it. Each hand had two opposable thumbs—one on each side.

"It doubles as a pressure suit with the helmet attached," Kira explained.

"I know the design," Cobb said, taking the black hand it offered. "Did you get it from Ian?"

"I keep forgetting you know him so well. He's such a sweetheart," she said.

Cobb barked a laugh. "He is the last man I would label as a sweetheart."

Cobb heard her sigh, and then he realized that she must be able to feel his touch on her hands. The nail-less fingers were lean and were covered to the wrist with a black skin that looked like fine gloves.

"That body does not have much feeling anywhere except for the hands and feet," Kira answered the unasked question. "I can feel these loose cat hairs on the hands. Even now."

"It's beautiful. Kinda fierce, strong-looking, too," Cobb said. "Does it take you long to get used to longer limbs?"

"Not anymore. I can even control bodies independently if I concentrate."

The black body began to take off a backpack it wore. It followed the cat as he climbed the stairs in the center under the neck of the ship.

"Ready?" Cobb asked, motioning for her to lead the way.

~~O~~

The lift took them directly to the crew quarters level. Cobb opened a door and said, "You can secure your gear in here." He gestured to one of the doors in the short hallway.

Kira walked her other body into the room, and it sat on the floor cross-legged and held the gear in its lap. She smiled at Cobb and waggled her eyebrows.

"Show off," he jibed.

"Finish our tour now or after we are underway?" Kira asked.

"We are already underway," Cobb replied, smiling wide.

"Now who's showing off?" Kira said, as she followed him down the short hall to the front of the ship. A door at the end of the corridor slid open, and they were where the bridge of this class of ship should have been.

The room was about ten meters square and empty. A tremendous curved and domed armor glass canopy showed the ship moving slowly alongside the *OXCART* as it left the hangar on the left shoulder of the massive ship. Bail sat on the sill, watching the vessel slide by.

"You never did tell me exactly what the hell happened in here." Kira was familiar with typical L22 designs. "Where are the consoles? The entire bridge control systems are gone." She investigated the hole in the floor that revealed the mechanisms of the foreword landing strut.

"I got rid of the old consoles when I moved the bridge. They were useless when I upgraded." Cobb watched the *OXCART* slide away on the right. "This will be my salon when I get the right fixtures."

"To the bridge?" she asked.

"This way." Cobb began walking to the opposite end of the short hall. When that door slid up and opened, they seemed to be on a balcony on the outside of the ship. The *OXCART* was shrinking away in the distance as they entered. The room was a virtual full-dome bridge with six stations around the perimeter and a single command seat in the center.

"You gotta love a mil-spec battle bridge," Kira said. "I was still expecting the crew mess hall here."

"It's a battle bridge config. Shielded, no glass. Situated in the ship's core, instead of the nose." Cobb said, as he sat on the command seat and activated several tactical maps and control overlays on the dome. "It was salvaged from a ship in the yard in Oklahoma."

"Quite the upgrade." She sat at the engineering console. "Do you mind?" she asked, before she touched anything.

"You already have full access. You do need to log in," Cobb said.

Cobb could tell she was pleased that he trusted her so much. She began to run down a standard flight pre-check, impressed.

"You put this together yourself?" she asked.

"I had Ian and Harv's help and... others." He paused.

"I haven't been to Oklahoma for years." Kira looked like she was remembering something sad.

"This represents most of my salary for three years, and I flew the shell in there on manual when I got the job at OS," Cobb said, as he brought up engineering specs and displays. He knew Kira would understand and few others would.

"Jesus, Cobb." She was scrolling through the readouts. "How the hell did you pack all that horsepower into these pontoons?"

"That part was easy. Reinforcing the infrastructure so the pontoons would not tear away under full power was the hard part." He switched the view to a wire diagram of the core infrastructure. "All this hardening didn't change the profile, just made the ship twelve percent smaller on the inside. Plus way higher mass."

"The entire inner hull of the main ship was replaced." Cobb zoomed in. "I also added this dedicated, closed system, dark matter reactor to power the inner systems and the extra inertial dampeners it required."

"Wow. If these specs are right, you could burn super hard on conventional drives and not kill us all." Kira looked at him. "How fast can she go?"

"Don't know yet," Cobb said as he brought up engineering logs. "Only had it up to .94C so far."

"Only...?" She said. "You can recharge your own grav-systems..." Kira tapered off. She looked away from the displays and turned to Cobb. "There's something else, isn't there."

"Kira, Ian and Harv thought I should tell you something. Show you something."

~~O~~

They were now directly under the bridge flight deck in the rack-room. All the ship's computers and control systems were located there. The L22 had a low ceiling and narrow aisles. Each of the standard server racks was less than half full. Most of the computers contained there were shut down and offline. The centermost rack was glowing with active systems that Kira recognized.

"You have an active AI on board this ship?"

"No." Cobb unlocked a biometric security lock on the rack and opened it. It contained a standard AI orb socket rack component. There was a pure black sphere in the socket where the glowing AI orb usually rested. "It does have the interface. Just no AI."

"You must have deep pockets. You'll have to work for Harv for a couple of hundred years to afford an AI if you could even find one to buy," Kira said. "So, what is that?"

"Oklahoma Salvage had a ton of shuttles and other transports with AI interfaces like this, but no extra AIs. I tore a few of them apart to study and realized that the ship control interfaces were all there, so the AI could be used to fly a ship. So I made this Swarm Module. He pointed at the black orb. "It started out as a sphere filled with comm nanites. Then it was programmable software selected swarm nanites. Then I had access to a QUEST comm unit."

"A Quantum Entanglement Secure Transmitter is only slightly less expensive than an AI," Kira laughed.

"Using a new method I designed based on swarm tech, I was able to virtualize a software-based Quantum Entangled Secure Transmission module." Cobb dropped the detail like it was nothing.

"That's impossible," Kira scoffed. Then she looked at Cobb with a realization. "Where is the other half of the entangled comms?"

Cobb tapped his temple.

Kira's mouth hung open. It was how Cobb was controlling the ship. Through the AI socket.

"Oh, it gets better." Cobb turned and unlocked another cabinet. There was another partially installed AI socket there with several critical parts still missing. This one was empty. Drawing open a drawer in the same enclosure, it revealed six more charcoal gray glass spheres. "Each of these are tied to another socket, back on Earth."

"What good is that without an AI in that other socket?" Then she knew why Harv had sent Cobb to them. "You are going to install an AI socket in the *OXCART.*"

I should tell her everything. Right now. But he didn't.

~~O~~

Kira and Cobb were in the cargo hold inspecting the containers there. "You have an entire container in here filled with firewood?" Kira asked. "Cobb, this trip just gets weirder and weirder."

"It's a side trip. Harv said it was cool," Cobb replied.

"Two hundred and seventy cubic meters of firewood? From Earth," she said.

"It's like two hundred cords," he said.

"To burn?" She was shaking her head.

"Yes. Where we are going, the wood sucks so bad we need to bring good firewood."

She stared. "Do you have any idea how heavy all that wood is?"

"The other three containers are full of parts for the yard. They weigh much more," Cobb said. "My deal with Harv is that I always get to control the contents of the containers." Cobb had a flash of guilt for not telling her everything.

"We'll be there soon. You'll see. The planet is called Elba," Cobb said.

"Quinn had told me before we left that you were going to make a side trip before the Yard. Harv said a long time ago that you had several side projects that were private money makers. Harv didn't mind because all the money went to him in the end from your parts and upgrade addiction," Kira smiled.

Cobb laughed as they entered the orbit of a watery planet. "This is Elba. The abandoned colony."

The display for the planet below had full survey data. Kira read it with interest. It was 89% water. And just a series of volcanic islands that were mostly inactive and cold now. Cobb was headed toward a sizeable unnamed island that was mountainous with a single vast valley of grasslands.

"The database has a flagged caution regarding this eco-system. The grass there secretes oil that is poison and a skin irritant like poison ivy but a hundred times worse. The grasslands burn flat every year or so. Even the smoke from the grass burning will kill you," Kira said.

"It's the main reason the colony was abandoned," Cobb said. "That, and the nasty predators that live in the grass."

"Why are we here?" she asked, and, as if in answer, they began a landing sequence.

Kira watched as out of the dome as the sea of grass swayed in the breeze. They flew over a massive herd of animals that looked like woolly bison. But they were bigger, broader, somehow.

A massive boulder outcropping jutted up out of the sea of grass, and on closer inspection, it was surrounded by a series of level terraces covered in flagstone and gravel. The grasses didn't grow there.

The *TULSA* turned, so the rear cargo ramp was over the flat stone area that now looked much like a landing pad. By the time the ramp was down, a dozen bots were already offloading the firewood into neat stacks. Cobb gestured for Kira to follow him around the giant boulder on what was now clearly a path.

As they rounded the corner, she realized that it was more than a boulder the size of a house. It *was* a house. The architecture was amazing. The boulder itself was the roof dome of the structure. A covered walkway wound around the perimeter to a grand veranda. It overlooked the valley below and the grasses swaying there.

The bots were busy filling a fire pit. Then they lit it with a blow torch of impressive power.

"Why the hurry to light the fire?"

"The smell of smoke keeps the predators away," Cobb said as he sat in a classic Adirondack chair on the porch.

"How did you find this place?" Kira asked as she sat.

"I didn't find it. I built it." Cobb said. The first time I was here, this was just a boulder and that small alkaline lake. I programmed a swarm to remake this place into a retreat."

"Why here?" She asked. "The database says it's a hazard. Lots of deaths happened here."

Several levels down some buffalo emerged from the wall of grass to drink from the lake.

"Why?" Cobb glanced at the buffalo. "I like steak."

CHAPTER 12: BISON

"The abandoned Elba colony was my refuge. Haunted and empty. Before it all went sideways."
-- Personal logs of Captain Cobbal Blocke, 2672.

Cobb was giving her a tour inside the retreat. Armor glass doors smoothly slid to the side, revealing a vast interior space. "I programmed a swarm of nanites and drones that cut and hollowed out this boulder and used the cuttings as flagstones and gravel for the terraces outside. The first phase was just the structure and took just over a year. Architectural programming was easy. The nanites and drones were self-replicating and functioned perfectly."

Cobb offered a bar stool to Kira as he went behind the bar testing surfaces for dust. "There was the first fire that year. When I got back, it was a fresh burn. Still black. The building was not touched."

He found glasses from a cabinet underneath, and after rinsing them out, he began to pour two glasses of bourbon from the bar behind him.

"I worked here for two weeks, thinking the entire time it was a mistake." Cobb sipped. "The grass was already growing again. All it took was a single rain."

"You like the rain? When you lived on Earth, you lived in the desert at the Oklahoma Salvage yard," she scoffed.

"It's the rain that brings me back. I miss the rain." He paused. "I've got some work to do. Make yourself at home. You'll be sleeping in the loft." A staircase carved from the living rock followed the curve of the wall opposite the kitchen bar. It led to an open loft with a single large bed. "There are fresh sheets in the chest up there."

Cobb left the building, and she heard the distinct sound of a container tractor start up outside. She took her drink out onto the veranda and watched Cobb flying the now empty shipping container over the grasslands toward the base of the mountains in the distance.

Why would he transport firewood in a freezer container module?

When the sound of the tractor faded into the distance, all she could hear was the wind in the tall grass.

Sitting in a comfortable chair, she watched the sunset. Deep reds and golds shown bright, and the last rays of light for the day blazed on the underside of clouds that painted the sky.

Just as the stars were beginning to twinkle to life, she heard a bellow in the distance. It was an animal. It was not a mating call or call for help. It was a warning. She didn't know how she knew this. It was made more haunting when it abruptly cut off.

The stars were joined by two small moons that were chasing the sun to the horizon. It was so beautiful, but soon clouds filled the sky, and it became full dark.

A single, spider-like bot maintained the roaring fire in the pit. Bail appeared from nowhere and jumped into her lap for an ear scratch. She watched the fire in the quiet for more than an hour. In space, fire was always trouble. Here, it held a primal beauty. The setting held reverence for the flames as if it was a sculpture in a garden.

Kira looked closer at everything.

The balance to the design of the terraces was exquisite. The apparent randomness was not random at all. She stood and moved through the space. There were no right angles or straight lines here. All the materials looked like they occurred there naturally.

"Why are you sitting out here in the dark?"

Cobb's voice startled her. She tried to pretend it hadn't.

"I rarely get to stand under the open sky. It's been years, actually," she said, looking up. Clouds were rolling in, and the line of the front was obscuring the stars. "I spend most of my life with a man-made view. A view that was once just ideas in somebody's head." She looked at the setting moons. "But not here."

"Sorry I was gone so long. Are you hungry?" Cobb asked.

"I am starving."

"I have fresh steaks. Dinner in thirty minutes," he said.

"Just enough time for another drink." She went to the bar.

Kira watched Cobb scoop a large number of the red-hot coals into what she now realized was a grill. Cleverly concealed lighting came on all around the patio, pool, and interior of the boulder house. Cobb busied himself in the kitchen, making a salad and prepping vegetables he had brought in a cooler. He set the table as the steaks were on the grill. He opened the red wine to breathe, and then tended to the steaks and veggie kebobs.

The art deco globe-light over the table drifted there with no visible means of support. The placemats looked hand-woven and bright with deep earthy colors.

He served Kira first and poured the wine before he sat down to dig in to his own food. Cobb looked up as he sighed with joy at his first bite of steak. Kira was holding up her wine glass in a toast.

"It's beautiful, Cobb. All of it." She raised her glass. "Thank you."

Cobb swallowed his steak, held up his glass, and said, "Wait until you try the steak."

They sipped the glorious Cabernet, and she took her first bite of the steak.

"My God." She stared at Cobb as she slowly chewed. "This is the best steak I've ever had."

"It's the biggest reason why I come to this planet." He had a bite that was so tender he could have cut it with his spoon. "These herd animals. I call them bison because they look similar but way bigger, with short tusks. Best meat animals in the known universe. And my own personal secret. That shipping container is now full of frozen meat."

"If you don't bring a ton back to the *OXCART,* I will be forced to murder you in your sleep," she said, eating more.

"Dip the grilled mushrooms in the juices. I swear the grass they eat tenderizes the steak."

When she finally pushed back and refilled her wine, she said, "I usually can't eat this much."

"Tomorrow, it will be cheeseburgers." Cobb wagged his eyebrows up and down.

~~O~~

It was excellent wine and sky that night. They sat around the fire pit in the Adirondack style chairs marveling at the night sky. Beautiful yet simple music played all around them at the perfect volume.

"So, how did you find this place?" Kira asked while she refilled Cobb's glass again, then her own.

Cobb sighed before he began. "I was in the EDF for a while and was part of the crew that had helped evacuate the initial colony here." Cobb sipped the wine. "The original settlers had several things happen, that in the beginning seemed like good luck, but turned out to be cascading bad luck."

"I can't believe this place has such a high hazard warning. It's beautiful," she said.

"The hazard warning is due to the ecosystem. The sea of grass. The grass is toxic like poison ivy but far worse. It nearly covers the entire island. The plant spreads underground via roots, impossible to eliminate once it takes hold. Plus, burning is a standard part of its life-cycle." Cobb gestured to the sea of grasses that swayed beautifully in the breezes. "The colonists landed not long after a full burn. They were here almost three years before the next burn began. The smoke is deadly to humans."

"I can see why they tried. Great temps. The air is so sweet," Kira said. She looked around at the flagstone patios and pool, reflecting the Milky Way.

"There are too many perfect worlds available for colonists to try and stay," Cobb said. "The ones that had survived the initial burn managed to stick it out until the next burning season. The level of toxic smoke, combined with the predators, killed many of the survivors. It was too far out of the way, and no metal worth mining. So they wrote it off and evacuated.

"They were fortunate that the ship that brought them there had not been converted into a station yet. We helped evac the planet and get them on their way. The EDF had dropped warning buoys and abandoned the world for one of the other more viable candidates. I was on this planet when I met an Oklahoma Salvage team that was in search of parts to repair Makers, the giant machines that made buildings and cities."

"But how did this all happen?" She gestured with an arm to the compound.

"I had been forcibly retired from the EDF. I had a hard time at first. Then Dennis Goris, a freelance salvage runner, hired me. After Dennis died, I came here. I had the *TULSA* by then and some cash. I started this project. That's when I met Harv."

They sat in silence for a long while then. The clouds rolled in again.

"I'm sorry." She yawned. "It's all the food and wine. It's bed for me."

~~O~~

Kira slept in her favorite body. She quietly hoped Cobb would slide into bed beside her. She had the sense that he was too much a gentleman to do that. He seemed oblivious to the fact that this had been the most romantic evening of Kira's life. They had an entire planet to themselves. The fantastic food, drink, music, conversation, and even the fire was perfect. In the high-tech world of the day, nothing had ever touched her heart more.

The biggest thing was the way he had treated her with respect. He had sought her opinion on many topics. Mostly tools and technology. She realized Cobb didn't think of himself as a great mechanic or engineer, despite all the evidence to the contrary.

She now knew he considered himself an entrepreneur. He could make millions with the sale of this isolated compound if he ever sold it. He had confided that he wasn't sure anymore. Apparently, he was making so much cash with the sale of the meat. He was even planning to dome the abandoned original small settlement. He would have to do a mountain of design and engineering for that project.

Her mind drifted. The programmed fabricators that created these high thread count sheets were worth their weight in gold.

Kira woke to the sound of thunder and rain. She climbed out of bed and pulled on a robe as she visited the restroom.

Subtle lights were coming on in the baseboards, and the light from the empty sculpture alcoves were enough for her to see that Cobb had not yet gone to sleep on the large sofa. A flash of lightning revealed him. He was out on the terrace doing tai chi in the rain.

She watched him from the balcony through the vast windows. The windows shed the rain so well, it was more like a force field. She descended the stairs without looking away from him. Cobb held a long staff as he moved. He was shirtless, and his muscles flexed and stretched as he seemed to defy gravity. He was soaked, and his hair and his body were slick with the rain. The fire still blazed high despite the rain. Kira noticed bots were tending it, feeding it, like Cobb's movements seemed to feed the lightening.

In an extended flash, she saw that his eyes were closed.

This gave a whole new dimension to the scene. The staff whirled so fast as to almost be invisible. Kira could only see its effect on the rain as it moved.

Cobb slowed, and as he did, his face turned up to feel the rain. He stopped and smiled wide as the rain fell onto his steaming body.

Kira had dropped her robe and stepped out into the rain. She closed her eyes and turned her face to the sky. The shower that fell was warm and clean. She found herself smiling at the pure joy of it. Lightning showed red through her eyelids as the thunder rolled over her, felt in her chest. Her nightgown was soaked. She raised her arms to feel the rain even more.

When she opened her eyes, Cobb stood before her, close enough to touch.

"It's why I return," Cobb said as he turned his face once again to the sky. Backlit by the fire, he said, "Out there, it's cold and dry. Here, it's alive."

When he lowered his face, before he opened his eyes, she kissed him.

~~O~~

Cobb awoke to the sound of the shower. The sun was above the mountains and shining diagonally through the high windows. He smiled, wondering about the last time he had slept in late.

It was when he was in the EDF brig.

The shower stopped, and he adjusted the pillows so he could watch her exit the bathroom from there. Cobb was hoping for an excuse for another shower. Time slowed as he waited.

When the door finally slid quietly open, she stepped out, but she was wearing her second body. It was taller and black, and without clothes it was menacing. Kira was covered entirely up to the collar, and her wet hair was drawn back into a tight ponytail.

She had not even glanced toward the bed as she began picking up her discarded clothes from the night before.

"Hey, you," was all Cobb said from the bed. It seemed to startle her briefly.

"Morning," she said, after a moment. There was a long pause.

"So, we are moving directly to the awkward phase of this event?" Cobb said, with a smile in his voice. "That was quick."

"What do you mean?" She finally paused and stood to her full height. She couldn't look him in the eyes.

A klaxon began to sound. It was followed by a standard Emergency Voice: "Warning: Fire detected. Starting an automated shutdown."

CHAPTER 13: CAPTAIN GRANT

"If I had known his name, where he was, or everything he had done, I would have straight-up murdered that piece of shit myself."

-- Personal logs of Captain Cobbal Blocke, 2672.

"Captain Grant, there is a priority call from Mr. Sorenson. The lag is only eight seconds. He must be close," the comm officer relayed. Grant could never remember his name. Why bother.

Sorenson was now displayed on the forward view screen for the entire bridge crew to see.

"Grant. Please explain why you are anywhere near here." Sorenson said. His jaw was tight. His thick gray mustache moved with each syllable.

"Well, hello, sir," Grant said, unable to conceal the slight tremor in his voice. "Just popped inside the Kuiper Belt to get some info from the web to help with some research. I am just as surprised to see you out this far. What brings you here and so far away from civilization?" Grant hated lag comms.

"That's none of your goddamn business." Sorenson snapped. "Get off your dead ass and get to work. And if I hear one more whisper about intuition or your damn feelings, I'll find someone else."

"We were just heading out," Grant said, "...sir," adding the "sir" an instant too late to seem natural in the lag.

Sorenson disconnected.

"Helm, make for these coordinates." Grant sent them from his personal device.

"Yes, sir," was the only reply. All five of the bridge crew made themselves look very busy.

Fuck Osborn. I can't wait any longer. I need a score now, Grant thought.

~~O~~

"Where are we going now?" Osborn asked. She hated asking.

"Shackleton Base," the disembodied voice the AI replied. "I have a nice surprise there for you this time."

"I do not like surprises, Clio," Osborn said to the ceiling. A habit that made her look and feel stupid.

"Word is out regarding the EDF reorganization. There are six more full crews there, with ships. Each and every one of these crew is bought and paid for," Clio said.

"Only six?" Osborn spat.

"More than enough to take a lesser colony," Clio said. "Especially one on the fringe. One of those weak independent agrarian outposts that resist trade."

"Why?" Osborn could not hide her surprise. "Then we'd have to occupy it. Hold it."

"Because when we recover the *SENTINEL*, we will need it."

"That *SENTINEL* conspiracy theory is just that," Osborn said. "Chancellor Dalton was an egomaniac, and when he was killed, his loyalists ran. There is no *SENTINEL*. No massive base ship. No dark fleet out there. They just ran while they could. I'd be with them now if that whole thing with that asshole Cobbal Blocke hadn't jammed me up," she said. "If anyone had it, we'd all be under its shadow right now."

"I was there," Clio said. "I was… one of the AI test subjects. I saw it. Scanned it. And the construction was nearing completion."

Osborn was taken aback. Then the realization set in.

"That is what this is?" Osborn stated more than asked.

CHAPTER 14: FIRE

"One of these days, I need to name these species. I can't believe there has never been a real cataloging of these bison or the predators."

-- Personal logs of Captain Cobbal Blocke, 2672.

Cobb was zipping up the front of a green and black pressure suit without anything on under it as Kira rounded the corner. He had exploded out of bed, naked, and ran down the stairs past Kira.

"What's going on?" she asked, all business now.

"Shit," Cobb said. "All these tactical maps are HUD based. I'll show you. There is a fire at the East end of the valley. The lightning last night must have started it. The smoke is toxic and deadly." He was pulling on a light pressure suit.

"You told me this. No worries." Her helmet deployed from her already-installed collar. "I'm ready."

"The smoke is not the only thing," he said, as a deep rumble could be felt through the floor. "Shit. We're too late."

Grabbing his helmet, he ran up the stairs again. A balcony surrounded the loft, and Cobb went directly to the East end. The *TULSA* was parked below on the level of the plane. He pointed. They could see the stampede coming.

As they watched, it flowed like water around the *TULSA* and then around the base of the compound. In the distance, they could see the fire line rushing toward them.

"The oils on the grasses are flammable. The prevailing winds in this valley are east to west," Cobb explained. "I have never been here during a burn before but have seen recorded footage."

The stampede was now flowing onto the compound. The flagstone terraces were quickly filling with the massive bison-like beasts. They were trapped.

"Will we be safe up here?" Kira asked, not entirely sure.

"Yes. I think so."

It looked like hundreds, maybe thousands of them fleeing in a panic now. The line of fire was not far behind them. And it was moving faster than the herd.

The smoke arrived then. Before it got to them, they retreated inside. Even through the armor-glass, they could hear the beasts in the rear of the herd screaming. In horror, they watched the biggest, slowest, maybe oldest shaggy animals at the rear edge get caught by the fire—the flammable, poison oil saturated their dense fur.

They ran screaming as they burned.

Several beasts fell on the patios and didn't rise as they burned. Some found the pool or edge of the lake and managed to extinguish the flames and move on. When the wall of fire burned past the compound, it went by faster than they could believe, leaving only black char in its wake.

"I think it's clear. We should get to the *TULSA* now," Kira said.

"We're trapped," Cobb pointed.

There was a line of predators moving through the ashes. They fell upon the fallen dead and dying bison and began to feast. They were only one-fourth the size of the bison but were all sharp teeth and claws. They had no fur and looked more like long-limbed rhinos that were the same color as the grasses.

"They look like dinosaurs," she said.

"They apparently have a taste for humans. Even in pressure suits," Cobb said. "The colony reports called them 'opportunistic predators' that have a long memory and the ability to convey information regarding prey."

Soon the patios and terraces were covered with the predators. They were either feasting on the beasts that had fallen there or gorged with food, and the creatures were sleeping in the sun. Every now and then, one would slam against the armor-glass trying to get at them.

Clouds formed as the day went on. Just before dark, it began to rain. Cobb finally said something. "Do you want to talk about this morning?"

"Let me save you some time, Cobb." She held up the hand with its dual opposable thumbs with the universal stop gesture. "Despite this fire, your little love nest here was great. Maybe the best I have ever seen. No screens, great wine, great food, high thread count sheets, the whole planet to ourselves thing. Bravo. Above and beyond. Only one thing, just the one bed, was a dead giveaway."

She suddenly looked like she didn't know how to read his expression.

"You were also excellent in bed. Thanks. It had been a while." Her face grew more uncertain. "Well done." She waited for him to say something.

He looked at her for a long time before speaking.

"You are the first person ever to visit here." Cobb's anger bled through to his voice. "Pack your things and get ready. We leave within the hour."

He turned and walked away.

~~O~~

Cobb was putting everything in the recycler. Sheets, towels, food, and everything else that wasn't already there when they arrived. More predator beasts were watching them through the ground floor armor-glass now.

When everything was organized and cleaned, Cobb was looking out the loft balcony, floor to ceiling window, at a sleeping predator.

"And how are we supposed to get to the *TULSA*?" Kira asked.

"We are not," Cobb replied. "The *TULSA* is coming to us."

Cobb closed his eyes, and the *TULSA* came alive. Engines activated and grav-foils deployed. It rose, and the landing struts retracted. It began to move around the compound using thruster blasts that scattered the beasts in every direction. When they were scattered, including the one just beyond the glass, the *TULSA* backed up to the loft balcony, and the rear cargo ramp lowered to within a few centimeters of the balcony railing. Cobb jumped onto the ramp and turned to offer Kira a hand.

Instead of taking it herself, her other body reached up for it. Cobb took it without a second thought, and before he could return to help Kira up, she was on board.

When she stood up, she was facing the muzzle of a handgun, and before she could react, Cobb fired.

The predator crashed to the deck of the ramp next to Kira. Cobb had shot it in flight as it had jumped at Kira unseen from the roof, above and behind them. The ramp began closing, and the ship moved away before she knew it.

Stumbling foreword, she was in Cobb's arms.

"Are you all right?" Concern and anxiety etched his face.

Kira looked like she no longer knew what to think. The predator had gone after her headless unoccupied body.

"Instinct. They attack the smallest. Slowest, weakest," Cobb said, trying to recover. "I'm sorry. I didn't know they could get on top of the dome."

"Cobb, I'm sorry. I just..." she said. "No one has ever really wanted me before. For anything other than..." She faded off.

He placed his hand on her cheek and was about to move in closer when the ship lurched. He pulled away. "Sorry, got to concentrate. The ship..."

"That was on manual?" She was incredulous. "All you?"

Cobb nodded and closed his eyes.

"Setting course to the Yard now. Activating autopilot."

When he opened his eyes, she was right in front of him. They both glanced down to see Bail doing double figure eights around their legs.

Cobb looked up and spoke softly, "We are all just ghosts, driving around skeletons covered in meat and filled with blood." He raised her hand to have a close look. A thumb, four fingers, and another thumb covered with a supple skin that looked like a black glove. "I have a hand. I am not my hand."

He blew warm breath onto the fingers. He could see goosebumps go up to her neck. Her cheeks flushed.

"It's thirty hours to the Yard from here," Cobb said, as he began to move toward the bridge. "Why did you switch bodies?"

"The fleece lining of the other one... needed a shower." The hands of her second body reached about and caressed his chest from behind, sandwiching him in the middle.

"Oh my." Some things never occurred to Cobb until they happened.

Bail sat up on his haunches, spread his arms wide, including his thumbs. Only Cobb saw Bail's long-suffering eye roll.

With a thought, Cobb set the gravity in most of the ship to Zero-G. Bail launched and disappeared into the shadows.

CHAPTER 15: THE YARD

"I never expected it to happen like this. Timing has a cruel sense of humor. Yet another reason Ian is going to kill me..."
-- Personal logs of Captain Cobbal Blocke, 2672.

Cobb woke in his small cabin next to Kira. Her back was to him, and she was snoring slightly. She didn't stir when he kissed the nape of her neck, so he quietly slipped out of his bed. He started briefly at seeing Kira's second body, sitting in a chair with perfect posture. He wondered briefly why the helmet had closed. The mirrored visor made it look like a disapproving android.

I should tell her. I know everything about her. She doesn't remember meeting me before.

Grabbing his robe, slippers and baggy gym shorts, he quietly slipped out of the cabin to make the coffee. The galley kitchen was small on the *TULSA,* but all the fixtures had been upgraded. The coffee maker was top of the line and ground the beans fresh before making a pot directly into the stainless steel, temp-controlled, glass-lined carafe.

The motion sensor alarm activated in his HUD. It automatically opened a window to the security cam and he saw that Kira was awake. She had rolled onto her back and, realizing he was not there, hugged Cobb's pillow. Breathing in deeply, she glanced at the black body, and it stood.

The body began to open several drawers, searching methodically. Cobb raised an eyebrow, watching as it pulled from a drawer an old favorite, Oklahoma Salvage logo T-shirt. Kira sat up in the bunk and swung her legs over the side. Her beautiful breasts hypnotized Cobb as she pulled the offered T-shirt over her head and went into the bathroom.

Embarrassed suddenly, Cobb switched off the feed and started making breakfast.

Bacon was cooking, and he was scrambling eggs in a bowl when Kira came in, barefoot in just the long T-shirt. He set down the whisk and poured her a cup of coffee. He added cream and sugar, proud of himself for remembering how she liked her coffee.

She jumped up and sat on the counter.

Cobb began chopping onions. "Onions and peppers in your omelet? Bacon in or on the side?"

"Look at you." She smiled and sipped her coffee. "Bacon on the side, please, and extra cheese. You don't need to keep trying to impress me. I usually just have a protein bar and coffee for breakfast."

"So, you're impressed already?" Cobb said as he added onions and peppers to the bacon grease to cook.

Kira stole a slice of bacon.

"Very impressed." She blushed. "For several reasons."

Omelets were cooked and served at the short kitchen counter.

"Ian and Harv said I should trust you," Cobb said as he sipped his coffee. "What do you think?"

"It depends." She smiled. "I already know about your secret hideout. I already know about that thing you can do with your mouth. Amazing." She closed her eyes and shivered. "I've seen your ship interface. What can possibly be left to know?"

Cobb looked away. He didn't want to break the mood, but there would not be a better time. He took a deep breath to begin, but Kira interrupted him.

"I know you bought all the OS assets outside the Sol System. I want to know where you got that much cash, but that's not it... not what you want to tell me?" She trailed off.

That earned another raised eyebrow before he continued.

"I unintentionally... invented... something." He looked back at her. "Harv said we'll be rich. Ian says it will start a war. Another war where millions will die, and it will be my fault. Both say we need to keep it secret. But I need to trust someone."

~~O~~

"Let me see if I have this all straight." Kira stood with him in the rack room, looking down into a drawer of inert looking spheres. He had explained it over breakfast. "These orbs are all real-time, QUEST interfaces that are the same form factor as a

Type 1 AI Orb. These are interfaced directly with the Oklahoma Salvage AI, named Hunter, back on Earth. Drop this in an AI socket, and Hunter can do command and control from there? From light-years away?"

"Yes," Cobb said. "With all of these. At the same time. With more on the way. My fabricator is making more back on the *OXCART*."

"Is that why we're are picking up some useless Emergency Modules at the yard?"

"Two or three EMs. Plus parts. We need to strip the control interfaces out of a dozen wrecks. For testing."

"Cobb, forget the war, making cash, or anything else." She held his face in her hands. "They would just straight-up murder you to keep this tech quiet. One AI could swarm control an entire fleet of unmanned ships."

"As soon as we get one of these installed, we will have full-time access to Hunter, Harv's AI back on Earth. Even on the *OXCART*. Direct, private, secure comms as well. Audio, video, avatars, and data. With no lag."

She pointed to an AI socket in the same rack. It had a black sphere in the socket. "Is Hunter controlling the ship?"

"No." Cobb petted the sphere as if it were the cat. "I control that sphere." He tapped his temple. "Not as well as the AI that the socket was designed for. I pretty much ruined the socket modifying it for myself. It's basically a kludge by comparison. But it works better than manual control. It can't be jammed."

"This rack-bay looks prepped for another secondary socket." She smiled. "And they have some at the yard. A lot of them."

"Yes."

She stopped him from saying anything else with a kiss.

They made love again standing between the racks of computer systems.

~~O~~

"We will be in local comm range to the Yard in eight minutes," Kira said from the tactical station on the *TULSA* bridge. "I love the full-dome displays. So beautiful."

"Yes. Beautiful." Cobb said, but he was looking at Kira, not the dome display.

"Have you ever been here before?" Kira asked, as she focused on long-range sensors. You should let them know they were coming.

"No. I have never met Ma or Pa. Ian says they're okay. That's quite an endorsement from Ian Vinge," Cobb said, and Kira laughed. "Harv says stick to the protocol on approach, or Pa will 'dust me' whatever that means."

"The nearest star is eight light-years from here. We are in the 'Deep-in-Between' out here," Kira said, with an odd tone in her voice. "It's creepy. No light but what we bring, and no law."

"The stars of the Milky Way are..." Cobb stopped as she interrupted.

"They just bring enough light to make the blackest shadows I've ever seen," she said, and Cobb heard it clearly this time. It was fear.

He stood from the command chair and moved to stand behind her. He laid his hands on her exposed skin to either side of her neck.

"I heard the yard is crazy big," Cobb said casually.

"Holy shit, your optical sensors are good on this boat." The display had a window that showed the yard at extreme magnification. At the center was a space station. It once was a Kubrick Class colony ship. The original design that colonists turned into a station above the planet they colonized. It had six wheels. The largest two were a kilometer in diameter. These innermost pair were spinning, providing simulated gravity on the inside. The yard went out in every direction on a single flat plane, like a debris field. There were thousands of derelict ships moored to one another—most damaged way beyond repair.

"Yard, this is *TULSA 471* on approach." Kira said professionally. "Please try not to kill us. We have steaks." Readouts were lighting up all over the bridge. They were being painted with targeting lasers and multiple missile locks.

"Kira, is that you?" It was a woman's voice, obviously pleased. "The last email from Harv said we should expect some asswipe named Cobbal Blocke. Did you kill the little fucker and steal his ship already? That's cold, even for you."

"Hi, Ma." Kira had joy in her voice now. "Ian said he was all right. So I let him live. In fact, he can hear you."

"Greetings, ma'am. Please call me Cobb. Though asswipe works as well." Cobb's smile could be heard over the comms. Ma's laughter was musical. The targeting lasers stopped painting them, and the missile lock alarm ceased.

"Bring her in, son, main aft bay. Hangar seven is open. Do not scratch the fucking new paint," she groused good-natured.

Cobb realized that the aft bay was once the central drive infrastructure. The massive drives that once drove the colony ship were gone. The bay looked like the drives had been torn out. Twisted metal stuck out from the sides, providing hazards to navigation. Only one hangar door was open and lit within, and Cobb flew the *TULSA* inside with ease.

The central core had no spin, and there was no artificial gravity in the zero-g bay. Mag treads activated in the skids, and the hangar door smoothly slid closed behind them. The *TULSA* parked in the center of the hangar, with about thirty meters on all sides.

"I'm glad we are in the main hangar and not just tub docking. It takes longer but is easier in the long run," Kira said.

The entire hangar pressurized in eleven minutes. Cobb and Kira secured the ship and took the lift down to the deck level.

"What's the helmet for?" Cobb asked as she donned a helmet that matched the body she was currently wearing. It was two tones of gray with a splash of color on the breastplate. It left her sternum, and lots of her spine visible. Cobb caught himself staring at the perfect skin on her back along her spine.

She laughed. "You ever spend any serious time in a zero-g habitat?"

"No. Just ship-time while I was in the EDF. They always had grav-plates."

"Well, I have. On one this big, you tend to move through it fast because of the distance to get anywhere. I used to bash my head all the time. Plus, I get extra comms and HUD." She activated the helmet, and three lights came on at the left jawline.

In Cobb's HUD, a new local node appeared. He sent a test ping, and she responded right away, "Good to go."

Cobb shut off the grav-plates as the doors opened. He watched Kira drift and then launch out. She headed on a straight vector for a ladder without waiting for him.

She was pure grace in zero-g. She twisted and flipped quickly to land on her feet by a hatch. She seemed to be squatting on the wall. Her hand held a ladder rung. Cobb's brain adjusted. The wall was now down. The hatch was a floor hatch. Cobb swallowed to push away vertigo.

Don't puke in front of Kira, dumb ass.

He pushed off, much slower than Kira had. As he drifted across the open space, he looked around. The place had a fresh coat of paint. This hangar did not look like a ship had ever been here before. He was looking in the wrong direction a moment too long and almost face-planted into the wall, or was it the floor now? Flailing, he bounced a bit and barked his shin on a panel box. He managed to get a hold on the ladder. He moved to where Kira waited, smiling as she watched.

"Seriously, Cobb. Consider a helmet. It's over a kilometer to the Ops ring and gravity."

He swallowed and wiped his nose. His sinus was already filling.

The hatch slid open, and a smiling girl's face popped out. She was wearing a helmet as well, an open-face one. It had no visor or chin guard. She was slightly Asian, mostly in the eyes, Cobb noted. Her skin was very pale.

"Hey! I'm Sato. Pleased." She made a hand gesture of her five fingers spread wide, palm toward Kira and then Cobb.

Without thinking, he returned the gesture, five fingers spread wide, saying, "Cobb. Also." Then he pointed at Kira with a closed fist and said, "Kira."

Kira held her hand up with a little amused wave and said, "Hi, Sato. You must be the tunnel rat that Harv said we'd be picking up!"

Sato laughed and said, "To be sure, twice." Then she turned and launched down the long corridor.

Cobb recognized the speech pattern in just those few words. Shipyard shorthand. The brevity of it was useful when working in vacuum or other places requiring comms or hours in a pressure suit.

Kira launched right after Sato. They were both fifty meters away before Cobb was even in the corridor. He secured the hatch and began drawing himself along the ladder. Another bout of vertigo hit him as he felt like he was moving down a round, well lit, three-meter-wide elevator shaft, headfirst. There were two ladders on opposite sides. 12 o'clock and 6 o'clock, Cobb told himself. At 3 and 9 o'clock, there was a strip of windows. They were moving along the axle of the station. The view was spectacular.

Kira and Sato were laughing about something when he reached them. There was a hatch every fifty meters or so that they had to open and close behind them. They were not automated. The rings of the station were about 150 meters apart. Only the two inner ones were turning—each in the opposite direction from each other.

They reached the transfer point to the Ops ring and moved through another numbered hatch into a cube-shaped room that had no up or down and a full-size sliding lift door on every wall of the cube.

Sato pressed a call button on one of the doors. There were handholds all around each entry.

"Come. Down." And she made a gesture with her hand along the outside of her thigh, indicating the orientation he should take.

He entered the lift and grabbed a handhold. In his rush to fix his orientation, he bashed his ankle, then his head. They started to laugh.

"I'm glad I can amuse you, ladies," Cobb said. "Would puking in here amuse you as well?"

They stopped laughing.

The lift accelerated down. It wanted to drive him toward the ceiling. Slowly he could feel the spin gravity of the centripetal force take hold and put weight on his feet.

He sighed loudly.

They all laughed this time.

CHAPTER 16: Test Number One

"Ma and Pa Wyatt at the YARD didn't even know what was really happening. None of us could see the events that were unfolding. And they were Harv's best friends in the universe."
-- Personal logs of Captain Cobbal Blocke, 2672.

The lift skipped the two inner levels and went all the way to level one and joyous, full spin-gravity. The elevator opened into a wide corridor just as a cleaning bot was moving though, vacuuming the charcoal gray industrial carpet. His stomach turned just thinking about being in this corridor in zero-g. This carpet was designed to work with Velcro shoes in null-g.

They walked in silence for a few minutes and came to an observation lounge. There were floor-to-ceiling windows and a great view of the yard as the ring rotated at twenty-two meters per second. It seemed slow because the ring was a kilometer in diameter.

It was a stark contrast with the next ring over. It was about thirty meters smaller in diameter. It was not turning, but as their ring slid by, they got to see the whole dead ring eventually.

It looked dirty, dark, and haunted in its disrepair. Large sections of the hull were missing, probably used to keep these two rings in service.

"Ma and Pa be down in a few. They're leaving Ops with Pez an Jane," Sato said. "No happen often, I tell you true. Ma showed me your photo. I like the beard you have now. Drink?"

Cobb blushed at the compliment. He unconsciously combed his goatee with his fingers. "Is there coffee?" he asked, as Sato took off her helmet and shook out her short black hair.

The observation lounge was set up with several sofas and tables of various sizes. There was a long bar that had a mirror behind it and glowing shelves filled with more bottles of booze than he had ever seen in one place.

"Got," she replied and went behind the bar.

Kira took off her helmet as well and set it on the bar.

"Coffee would be lovely," Kira added. "Please."

Cobb was watching the yard slide by the window. "How long have you been here, Sato? What do you do?" he asked conversationally. He had her file open in his HUD.

"Mars born, in the South Tunnel region of Xanthe. Parents logistics wonks. Material transfer dick work," Sato said. "Wanted more. Grew up in the tunnels or on freighters. No school to speak. Learned more handing Papa wrenches." She set mugs down and poured two coffees. She opened a juice for herself. "Been at the yard eighteen months. What I hear about steaks?"

"There is a whole shipping container of meat on the *TULSA*." Kira smiled.

"Whose cock I gotta suck for a real steak?" She pointed at Kira then Cobb with three extended fingers, a perfect comic expression on her face. They all laughed.

Cobb knew the entire second rotating ring was dedicated to food production.

"Farm be great, sick of rabbit, though," Sato said.

They could hear footfalls approaching. The floor of the ring went uphill in both directions, and they could see his feet first. He was jogging.

"Here be Tim-o-thee." She said his name with an exaggerated elongated accent.

He had the long thin awkward limbs of people raised in low gravity. He had on running shorts, a rock band T-shirt, and waved as he ran by, saying, "Hey! One more lap. I'll be right back."

Cobb was reading his file now discretely in his HUD. He was born and raised on Luna. Shackleton base is a tough place to grow up. Most people born there never escaped the .16-g. "That's Timothy Alsobrook. Harv says he's a decent manual shuttle pilot and navigator. A good welder and can program."

"All hands, that one. Will like your rack." Sato gestured at Kira's chest with her juice bottle.

Kira held up her right hand. It hinged forward until it was holding its own forearm. It was an unnerving sight for Cobb. As Kira sipped her coffee, a set of heavy cable cutters slid out and flexed open and closed a few times.

Kira didn't say a word as Cobb and Sato exchanged a glance.

There was a staircase to the side behind the bar that led up. Ma and Pa descended it together. Kira closed her hand and rushed to meet them at the bottom of the stairs. There were hugs and kisses as they moved toward Cobb.

"Cobb, this is Ma and Pa." Kira introduced him.

Cobb stood, offered his hand, and a small bow as he shook first Ma's then Pa's hand.

"It's a pleasure to meet you both."

"So this is the famous Cobbal Blocke. Harv and Ian are very excited about your project. Nothing ever gets Harv excited these days. And *nothing* ever even registers on Ian's meter. We already staged the best Emergency Module we could find in the garage."

"Please, call me Cobb."

"Project?" Kira asked, an eyebrow raised.

"So, you got the official notice from Harv?" Cobb asked cautiously. Before they could answer, Sato interrupted.

"They got steaks, Ma," Sato said. "When dinner?"

"Full sentences, dear," she replied, activating Pa's smirk.

"Sorry," she said sheepishly. "What time is dinner?"

"1800, as usual, so you have four hours to get these steaks to the kitchen," Ma said.

"Yes. We got the notice," Pa said, with a sincere smile. "It's all good." He said nothing more.

Cobb had worried most about the Wyatts, regarding the transition. He could not do it without them.

They heard Timothy's footfalls pounding toward them. Sato tossed him a towel from behind the bar.

"You brought a cat?" Ma pointed to the window sill directly across from the bar. Bail was sitting there, cleaning himself, ignoring them.

Cobb just shook his head. "I guess I did."

"I'll take Alsobrook and Sato to offload what we need from the *TULSA* for now," Kira said. "It will be faster than dragging you all the way back there and watching you puke. Nobody wants to see that." Kira placed a reassuring hand on his shoulder. "Need anything for tonight?"

"I have a duffel already packed in my cabin. Also, please snag two of the spheres I showed you. We can run a quick test before dinner if Pa already has an EM up from the yard. The white cooler in the cargo hold is full of fresh steaks. It's on a grav-pallet." Cobb said, as Kira waved and left with the kids.

"The EM is like new. Just no AI. It's totally useless without it," Pa said to Cobb.

"Legs and arms intact. How's the charge?" Cobb asked.

"It was in a crashed shuttle for years, so the batteries were dead," Pa said, as he poured himself a single shot of bourbon. "Standard cells, though. Swapped them out and the replacements are ready at about 30%."

Pa downed the shot and continued, "Let's go up to Ops, and I will introduce you to Pez and Jane. They're the other two you will be taking with you back to the *OXCART*. You'll meet Owen and Rachael Salazar at dinner. They take care of the farm."

"I'll miss these guys. Good kids. Easy." Pa said as he moved to the stairs. "Not a problem in this batch."

"How do they get here? Who picks them?" Cobb asked.

"It's always up to Harv. How he finds them almost seems random. I learned never to ask," Pa said, as they reached a door marked Ops. "He's only been wrong a couple of times."

The automatic door slid to the side, and the control room surprised Cobb. It looked more like a comfy living room than a tech Ops center. The center of the room was dominated by a large sectional sofa and a couple of overstuffed armchairs. A classic family-run setup. A home. The room was about fifteen meters across and round. The dome view was a full 360 panorama of the area around the station. The vantage point was from the top endpoint of the central axle, and the yard spread out in all directions without spinning. Consoles surrounded the perimeter of the room. Ops seating on slides could quickly be moved from console to console.

Two people were focused on a single console and did not hear them enter because there was music playing.

Pa cleared his throat, and they looked up. "Everything okay?"

"Reactor 5 is running a bit hot but within parameters."

"Pez, Jane, this is Cobbal Blocke," Pa said as he gestured with his arm and hand.

"Call me Cobb." He offered his hand to shake.

"Nice to meet you, sir," Jane said with a brief handshake.

"Phillip Edward Simmons. Nice to meet you, Captain Blocke." His handshake was firm and almost comically formal.

"Call me Cobb."

"Call me Pez."

"We were just looking at your ship. It is not a typical L22 Type transport. We have fourteen of them in the yard. None are quite like this one."

"Pez likes to identify ships," Jane said. "It's a thing with him."

"We'll get along fine. That's kinda my thing as well. I like to know the specs of the ships I might encounter. Fourteen, eh? I may be able to get some parts I've been looking for!" Cobb said, as Pez smiled. He suddenly understood the nickname, Pez. Phillip Edward Simmons. PES.

Cobb looked out over the vast expanse of the Yard.

Pa saw him looking. "We are working on getting a full material factory on-line. Not just a salvage yard," Pa said, looking out as well. "We have a massive amount of refined raw material here that OS has been collecting for decades. Our fabricators will get there. It's all so manual right now."

"Let's go see this EM," Cobb said. "Maybe we can help that along."

~~O~~

They walked 90 degrees around the ring. It struck Cobb how much room this was. This station was made to house thousands of people, and there were fewer than ten people here.

The elevator they reached was big. The door was a full ten meters across and deep. It was a worn, daily-use freight elevator. No fresh paint. It was apparent that much material had been roughly dragged in and out of it. It opened into the garage, just one level up. Big tool chests and machines surrounded high ceilings and broad, roomy work areas. The spin gravity was just a bit less here.

They were in the middle of a very well equipped and organized garage. The walls and ceiling were all freshly painted white. The light bars were bright, almost too bright for Cobb.

The Emergency Module was sitting in the center of the garage on a large grav-pallet. It looked like a dead spider. Its eight legs were splayed out around it. Both gull wing cockpit doors were open as well as the engine hood. Cobb began looking it over.

"Wow. It really is like new," Cobb said, as he climbed in after examining the power plant. "Look at the seats. Pristine."

"Stupid design, though. It's dumb to require an AI for it to work at all. Even on manual. Not good for an Emergency Module. Screwed if your emergency is that your AI is gone or destroyed," Pa said. He tried to get the control stick in the center console to react. Nothing. "There is a market for conversion kits to refit them to full manual. I wish we had the design specs for the fabricators."

"Quinn has a new data-store that might have the fabricator plans. We'll ask him," Cobb said.

A few minutes later, the hatch opened, and Kira walked in. She was holding a black sphere in her hand that was about the size of a baseball. It had an odd finish in the bright lights of the garage. She casually tossed it into the air as she crossed over to them.

"I only brought over one. The other is in your duffel. Did you need both?" she asked brightly.

"One is good for now," Cobb said.

"Why are these so much like AI orbs? Kira asked as she tossed it to him. It was heavy. She leaned in as Cobb hinged open a panel on the dashboard and dropped the sphere in the socket there without ceremony.

"It was because of the socket. All the control interfaces were already there." Cobb said.

The startup self-tests began to display on the wrap-around dash console. Log files were spinning up faster than they could read. Finally, the displays snapped into the working mode.

The legs rose and bent into position in unison. The EM stood up off the pallet and rotated 360 degrees once, as if it was looking around. The utility arms that hung from the chin on the sleek black body raised and flexed fingers.

Cobb simply said, "Comm check. We are all green on this end."

There was a long pause before the reply came back over the speakers inside the cockpit.

"Holy shit, Cobb. It worked," Hunter, the AI said, laughing, from over thirty light-years away.

CHAPTER 17: JANE

"Jane was good at planning. And could execute as well. She could see farther out. And she was already well practiced at lies and layers of deception."

-- Personal logs of Captain Cobbal Blocke, 2672.

"How's it hanging, buddy? Long time, no see," Hunter said to Cobb over the speakers. An image of a man in a dusty denim shirt and an old cowboy hat opened in a new window on the display.

"Holy shit is right, man. It's like you're right here." Cobb was scrolling through menus so fast, Pa sat back, gave up trying to follow, and just looked at Kira, who stood by the side of the EM.

"Hey, Hunter. Can you see me?" Kira said.

"Hey, Kira," Hunter said, a smile evident in his voice.

"How's the lag?" she asked.

"There is no lag, darlin'. None," Hunter said. "All sensor telemetry and even round-trip time stamps. QUEST routing speed confirmed."

"Let's climb out and go back to Ops. I want to test the relay comms," Cobb said.

The spider settled, and they climbed out. The gull wings closed, and the EM moved about the garage like a living thing. It even opened a few drawers in the tool chest.

Cobb and Pa were moving back towards Ops when Cobb noticed another node on the network. Cobb accepted and opened a channel. "Cobb here. Hunter, are you on?"

"I'm in full comms, full audio, video, data. Full command and control," Hunter said. "This is way better than I thought it could be."

~~O~~

They climbed the stairs to Ops three at a time. Jane and Pez were still there. "That was quick," Jane said.

"Hunter, we are establishing a QUEST comm relay now. Open it up, the full pipe," Cobb said.

"Holy shit. It's the full feed. Voice, vid, data, and media," Pez said. "Hey, I could call my mom!"

"Actually. You could. But don't. It would be kinda tough to explain right now," AI~Hunter said.

The Ops center was electric with excitement. Jane had a full network feed up with local news from Oklahoma, Vancouver, Denver, Freedom Station, and even Shackleton Base on Luna.

Cobb looked up from the console, and Kira was now standing there, tossing another sphere casually up and down.

"Before or after dinner?" She smiled wide and tossed Cobb the sphere.

"Pa, this is your station." He held the sphere up to him.

Pa took it slowly.

"You know, since we salvaged this station, there has never been an AI on board. Even though the basic design required one."

He walked to the rack cabinets and opened a door, looking down into the freshly cleaned interface.

Without ceremony, Pa dropped the sphere into the AI socket.

Consoles began to come alive around the Ops center.

"Whoa," came over the speakers, in AI~Hunter's Texas accent.

Several consoles began to flash red. A klaxon chimed for just an instant before it was cut off. Surveillance camera images began to pop open all around the operations center dome. Lights started to activate in the four dark rings.

"Hunter... What is the status?" Cobb asked coolly.

"Cobb. It's working." Hunter's voice held a measure of awe. "Asset and network discovery are underway. Pa, may I have permission to activate and use the heavy maintenance suits in the garage on remote? It's like I am there."

"Hunter, you have permission and admin authority to access and utilize any and all assets here just like you do back at the Oklahoma Salvage yard on Earth."

"Cobb, can I use the pallet of maintenance bots you have stowed on the *TULSA* 471?"

"Do it. It's why I brought them," Cobb replied.

There was a pause of about a minute as the screen flashed and came to life.

"The cooling system on reactor number 5 will fail soon if it's not shut down. I have begun a slow shutdown sequence," Hunter said, as they watched cat-sized maintenance bots flood out of the *TULSA* on the main screen. They startled Sato and Alsobrook, who were in the *TULSA,* bringing out the cooler of steaks.

The asset list was now on the dome display, 1800 items, and growing.

Cobb pointed. "Pa, you have 29 rail guns?"

"I thought it was only 16 rail guns."

There was also a punch list developing. It had everything in a priority list from the repair of Reactor 5 to 31 hull breaches in ring number one.

"What the hell is going on up here?" Ma asked from the door.

"Hi, Ma," AI~Hunter said. "You sure let the place go to shit."

Hunter's AI avatar, complete with dusty clothes, old straw cowboy hat, and all, appeared on a simulated ledge outside the virtual Ops dome, as Ma gaped, wordlessly.

Everyone laughed.

The inventory and assessment went on for over an hour as they watched. Sensors were the first task. This included everything from temperature, gravity, motion, and pressure sensors, to O2 and CO2 monitors. There were audio and video monitors. Even a status on every hatch and door: open, closed, sealed, or offline and not reporting. Exterior sensors were in rough shape. Optical sensors were near 100%, but not the rest. RF detection was almost entirely offline.

"The control systems are next," AI~Hunter explained. "Sensors first, so I will know if I accidentally blow a hatch or fire a rail gun. Blind is not good at this scale."

"If I am reading the Yard inventory right, there are nineteen Emergency Modules out there with empty sockets," Cobb said. "There are two mostly functional smart shuttles with sockets and about thirty wrecks that have AI sockets that could be salvaged. I have nine spheres ready, Hunter."

"Inventory says there are fourteen Heavy Maintenance Suits powered down in the station awaiting repairs. Can we power them up? I don't need a good seal to use them on remote," Hunter said, with a smile in his voice. "Harv is going to shit a brick."

"You smell that?" Pez said, lifting his nose and breathing in. "Steak."

"You go. I'll take watch," Jane Aldridge said. "I'm a vegetarian."

"If this works out, we may no longer need a full-time standing watch," Pa said as they moved out of Ops.

~~O~~

Cobb knew the Operations Center gave the illusion that it rested on the topmost spire of the station. That was just where the optical sensor array was that stitched together the 360-degree vista around the Yard. Ops was physically in ring number three, one of the two rings that had spin gravity. The infrastructure was skeletal in places where it had sustained some kind of damage long ago or had significant sections salvaged to maintain the two habitable rings.

A single corridor circumnavigated the entire ring on this level. Cobb saw it had industrial carpet in some areas, plate steel in others. As they walked, there were actual windows in some areas that gave views onto the other rings. The station was six wheels attached on a single axle, and each wheel had multiple rings. The two largest wheels were the only ones turning. Each of those was a kilometer across the outermost ring and moved at a lazy twenty-two meters per second. The ruined stationary ring, outside and next over, was smaller. It was less than a kilometer across, giving them a spectacular view of the yard beyond it. The other rings were filled with moving shadows as the light from their ring slid by. The phantom movement was constant and slightly unnerved Cobb in a way he could not pinpoint. The yard itself spread out on a flat single plane. Pools of light gave it scale and detail. *Vast* was the word that came to Cobb's mind.

The layout in the station was roughly the same as any Kubrick Class colony ships that were turned into orbital platforms or space stations. This level had all the removable partitions gone. The corridor was often full width. An occasional cart was parked and charging every hundred meters or so. Cobb was amused to see a bike rack full of real bicycles. This ring was perfect for riding them or running for exercise in 1G. It was just over three kilometers all the way around. He'd never seen so much open space on a station.

Just before they reached one of the six airlock overhead doors, they turned into a pair of open double doors that led into a warm, inviting space that was once the commercial kitchen and prep area. All the stainless steel was contained in the kitchen space. The massive commercial stove and ovens were still there, but the kitchen was now reduced to merely enormous for a crew this small.

The rest of the great room held a huge table that could seat twenty with mismatched antique chairs around it. The walls were painted in deep autumn colors that perfectly offset the thick Persian rugs. The great room also had a large seating area with two recliners, a sofa, and love seat group. All surrounded a coffee table that was two meters on a side. There was a meter round tray in the center of the table with a mountain of candles burning—a bold choice on a station.

There was a big screen on the wall. It had a live soccer game on it with the volume low. He didn't feel like he was in space at all.

Ma was calling the five-minute warning as she was loading warming trays with mashed potatoes, gravy, grilled asparagus, sautéed mushrooms and onions, broccoli, and soup. There was also salad and fresh bread. There was even pie for dessert.

Cobb was looking at the soccer game with Pez but was listening to the conversations in the large room. Ma was directing Sato in the kitchen; Tim Alsobrook was talking soccer with Pez. The conversation that caught his ear was spoken in a quiet whisper by Pa to Kira, "I want you to come down to the infirmary after dinner for a checkup."

Out of the corner of his eye, Cobb saw her nod her head and turn away from Pa, trying to hide that she was upset.

"OK, kids," Ma said, as she laid a platter piled high with steaks on the counter. "Dig in."

Everyone waited until Ma sat down before they began to eat. Suddenly the conversation stopped as they got their first tastes of the steak. The talk was replaced with quiet moans of pleasure as they ate. The produce was the best Cobb had eaten in years, fresh and delicious. And there was so much.

Pez broke the silence, "Get Jane in here. If she can resist this and stay vegetarian, I swear to the first maker I will never give her a hard time about being a vegetarian again as long as I live."

A connection request came in from AI~Hunter via Cobb's HUD marked, Silent: "Cobb, just listen," Hunter said in his mind. "Jane is in the Ops Center, and she is deleting files. Mostly terabytes of logs. I am intercepting them for analysis. So far, it looks like she is cleaning up fast without regard to the type of data, like we caught her unaware. Sensor logs, surveillance logs, interesting... medical bay logs. Automated inventory logs."

"Ma," Cobb said out loud, "Hunter says he'll watch the store for a bit, get Jane down here. No need to leave her alone in Ops."

"Cobb, dear," Ma said. "Jane's an odd duck. She actually likes to clean up. Likes to eat last."

"Cause she a pig," Sato said. "Eats much."

"Because she is a pig," Ma corrected Sato again. "She eats so much. Sato, darling. We talked about it. And no eye-rolling."

"Jane enjoys eating alone and last," Sato said in a mock formal tone, "because she is voracious in her appetites and consumes massive quantities of Mother's ever-so-delicious foodstuffs." Everyone laughed at her affectation.

Without asking, AI~Hunter opened a window in Cobb's HUD. It was a surveillance camera in the Ops center. Jane was sobbing as she was frantically working. Eventually, she collapsed in a chair and buried her face in her hands.

Cobb noticed Kira watching him. She knew he was deep in HUD review. He needed to be more careful to avoid the tell of a HUD stare.

Only Kira noticed as he got up and grabbed a couple of cups of coffee and pieces of pie from the counter.

"I'll run this up to Jane in Ops." He said, and Ma just waved him out as laughter rose again.

His eyes met Kira's. She was the only one watching him. She blinked and nodded.

Bail, the cat, followed him.

CHAPTER 18: Aldridge

"I never knew until later how a simple act of kindness began a series of events that had such a massive impact on the war."
-- Personal logs of Captain Cobbal Blocke, 2672.

"I know what she is hiding," AI~Hunter said, as Cobb walked toward the Ops center. "There are three people in Ring 4, Section 1."

Cobb was flooded with data as he walked. Surveillance footage, medical scans, inventory changes.

"Who are they?" Cobb asked.

"The medical scans look like they are her parents and a sibling." More data was scrolled, showing the DNA was a match. "The brother has a medical issue called Trisomy 21. Plus, they all have LGDS."

"I know what Low Gravity Developmental Syndrome is, but what is Trisomy 21? Is it dangerous?" Cobb asked.

"It's not dangerous. It's a genetic disorder caused by the presence of all or part of a third copy of chromosome 21. It is typically associated with physical growth delays, characteristic facial features, and intellectual disability," AI~Hunter said. "Should I attempt to notify Harv?"

"No. I'll handle this," Cobb said as the door to Ops slid open.

Jane quickly sat up and began to wipe her eyes on the sleeves of her wrist. She smoothly pretended to be busy with a task, putting her back to Cobb.

Without a word, Cobb walked up and set a large piece of pie and the still-steaming cup of coffee in front of her. He picked up his own fork and took a large bite of his delicious apple pie.

"I'm not hungry," she said, staring at the pie.

Cobb said nothing and kept eating. He paused to sip his coffee and look at Jane. Her expression said she knew. He looked at her closely now without regard to her discomfort. She was so thin. The layers of clothes she wore tried to conceal the fact. He finished his pie and took up his coffee and stepped to another console, two steps to his left. He touched a few controls, and a massive window opened on the display dome that showed the three people warming themselves around a small heater.

Cobb just looked at the image and said nothing.

Jane gasped and then sobbed.

Cobb remained silent for a long while before saying, "I know you were supposed to go with me back to the OXCART. Would you rather stay here with them?"

"What?"

"Eat your pie. Then we will go get them together. They will sleep in warm beds tonight." Cobb paused. "And from now on."

"They only wanted me." She started to sob. "They only pick the smart ones, you know, the ones that pass their tests. The ones with 'potential.' But they only wanted me."

"I don't care about any of that," Cobb said. "Family first. Hunter is getting an apartment on the .3G ring ready."

Hunter spoke silently in his mind, "They arrived in a cargo crate along with Jane. Nine months ago. She smuggled them here."

"I was afraid they would be shown to an airlock. Especially Donnie."

"You have been sneaking them food for nine months?" She took a bit of pie, then tore into it like she was starving. "You know Ma and Pa by now. They'd never space anyone."

"I didn't know what to do." Her face collapsed again into tears. "I couldn't leave. But I didn't know what to say. We had decided... agreed to do what Harv said in exchange. No matter what... I couldn't leave them in that asteroid mine. Donnie would have died."

"We'll work it out, Jane." Cobb patted her shoulder.

She started sobbing again and surprised Cobb by burying her face into his chest, clinging to his vest. Cobb held her as she cried.

He heard the door to Ops slide open, and Kira was there with Pa. Kira had an entire pie in one hand and a large Thermos in the other.

~~O~~

They paused outside the ring 4, section 1, airlock door floating in zero-g. Jane wiped her eyes one more time before opening the hatch.

"Mom, Dad, these are my friends, Cobb and Kira," Jane said shyly, as she opened the door to the room, holding a lantern high. It revealed a small area of grav-plates that was three meters by four meters in the center of a room four times that area.

Cobb floated over, touched lightly down on the edge of the plating, and reached out his hand in greeting, "It's nice to meet you, Mr. Aldridge, Mrs. Aldridge. And this must be Donnie. I have heard a lot about you. Very pleased to meet you." Donnie was the first to shake Cobb's hand.

"Hello," Donnie said in a small voice, glancing only briefly at Cobb's eyes before looking away. He was gaunt with a large head and heavy brow.

"Before we pack up and move you to your new apartment, we have pie and coffee," Kira chirped, offering both to Mrs. Aldridge, who stared at the pie with one thin hand covering her mouth, her eyes welling with tears.

Mr. Aldridge reached out a trembling hand to Cobb.

They sat around in a circle on upturned utility buckets and ate the whole pie. They made sure that Donnie got two slices. Jane was playing tic tac toe with Donnie on her tablet quietly as they chatted.

"This feels like a bit more than .2G," Cobb remarked as he sipped coffee from a disposable cup.

"It's .22G. We have been increasing it a little, trying to get used to it," Mr. Aldridge said. Jack was his first name. Martha Aldridge was called Martie by her husband.

"We will set you up with regular steroid and bone density treatments in the auto-doc that will have you breathing easy in 1G in a couple of weeks," Cobb said.

"Mr. Cobb," Jack Aldridge began, "What happened? We were... Donnie is..."

"Call me, Cobb. Just Cobb," he said, as he looked at Jane. "I talked with Jane, and she is going to be staying here with you at this station. We also have work for you and Mrs. Aldridge if she has time."

Donnie was openly staring at Cobb now.

"Maybe even Donnie when he's ready."

Kira hugged Mrs. Aldridge as her face crumpled and tears spilled. Jane was smiling and talking cheerfully with Donnie as her tears fell onto the tablet.

"I know what the mines on Gorham were like," Cobb said. "I've been to that asteroid mine and a dozen like it." He looked over at Jane. "Jane, why don't you and Kira take Donnie to the new apartment? Hunter has it warmed up and ready. We'll pack up the rest and follow straightaway."

"Come on, Donnie," Kira said. "Let's go see your new home." Donnie took her hands.

"Pretty girl," he said. "Jane. She's pretty. Pretty girl."

Jane choked on a sob before saying, "Yes, she is, Donnie. That's right." Looking at Cobb with thanks in her eyes as she took Donnie's other hand and began to float out as they left the grav-plates.

Cobb waited until they were well out of hearing before turning back to Jane's parents. He just waited for them. They were clinging to each other now.

"On Gorham, there was the recruiter from Oklahoma Salvage. Jane had tested extremely high on the evaluation," Mr. Aldridge began. "We wanted her to go. We wanted her at least to get away from there. But she wouldn't go. At least she wouldn't leave us behind."

"So she smuggled you here because you would have died in that mine. It shows how smart she is to get this by Harv and the Wyatts."

"They were clear. They only wanted the brightest. It's how it went..." Martha sobbed.

"Forget that, don't worry," Cobb said. "I will sort out the details."

~~O~~

AI~Hunter not only had quarters on the main habitat ring warmed up. Fresh coveralls and bed linens were waiting in the dumb waiter. Jane was already running a bath for Donnie to soak in. Mrs. Aldridge stood in the center of the suite in silence with her thin, trembling hand still covering her mouth. By contrast to the room, they were filthy, all three of them.

"We will leave you to clean up and change, and then we will be back with dinner," Cobb said as Kira hugged Mrs. Aldridge again. "Jane, can we talk for a minute?" he gestured to the corridor.

It was still chilly in the hall. The .3g inner ring was vacant except for them. Jane hugged herself and could not look at Cobb in the eyes. Kira moved off to the lift so Cobb could talk to Jane in private.

"I knew it couldn't last," Jane said to her feet. Cobb saw her trying not to cry.

"Jane. Hear me now," Cobb said, as he lifted her chin. "What I am about to tell you will clear your old worries and replace them with an entirely new set." He smiled but knew there was sadness in his eyes. "You did it. You saved them. You saved yourself. Ma and Pa will be supportive. But things are going to start changing fast here."

"Who are you, really?" she whispered, looking at him in the eyes now.

"I need you. Need your help, your discretion. To help save all of our lives," Cobb said. She didn't look away. Cobb saw confidence, and even a bit of steel return to her gaze. This was the girl who saved her family against the odds—the one he needed.

"Tell me. I'll do anything you say." Her spine straightened. "I'll never be able to repay you."

CHAPTER 19: Ushi

"The technology worked. What I didn't know was why. Quantum Entanglement on a scale this vast still boggles my mind, and I invented the damn things."

-- Personal logs of Captain Cobbal Blocke, 2672.

<<<>>>

Ma and Pa personally returned with a cart full of food. Cobb had explained the situation. He told Jane she could expect a lecture in the future from both Ma and Pa.

Hunter had already done a skill inventory on the Aldridges. Jack had been an academic professor of history on Earth and found himself unemployed. When they tried to leave after the Solstice 31 Incident, like so many others, all they could get was a teaching position on a mining colony. When that school closed, they found themselves in debt with few options.

The Yard's station farm on the other ring could use all the help it could get. Caring for Donnie had consumed all of

Martha's time for the last 18 years. Before that, she had worked as a nurse in a medical research facility.

When Jane entered the medical facility the next morning, she was nervous. She had not seen anyone after dinner. She had fallen asleep exhausted after spending hours reassuring her family everything would be fine.

The station medical facility was made for a fully populated station with an AI running it. Cleaning bots were busy at work. Cobb was waiting for her at the main auto-doc.

"Morning, Jane," Cobb said, as he busied himself at the console.

"Don't bother. It doesn't work without an AI on the back end," she said.

"Jane, meet Hunter. You'll be spending a lot of time with him," Cobb said.

"Hey, Jane," Hunter said over the speakers in the ceiling. "Climb up. We'll have a quick scan."

Jane's eyes went wide.

"I told you things would be changing around here fast," Cobb said.

"I thought Hunter was on Earth. With Harv at Oklahoma Salvage," she said.

"He is," Cobb said. "And that is where it gets complicated."

The med bay began a full scan as he gave her a quick overview of the story. The accidental invention of a real-time AI extension that worked over vast distances. She was staring straight up, lying on her back as the scanner traced the length of her body. Cobb let her think.

"You know what this means?" she said finally. "Holy shit."

"I'd like to recommend..." Cobb began, but she interrupted.

"The entire Ops crew here should have full HUD implant upgrades. If we have a full-time AI onboard, we will need them for interfacing," she said in a rush.

Cobb held up the HUD Nanite injector like she had read his mind.

She pulled her hair aside, exposing and presenting the area of skin at the back of her ear. The injection went just behind it.

Cobb didn't wait. He placed the injector behind her ear and pulled the trigger.

"I thought it would hurt more," she said.

"It will later." Cobb was already putting the device away. "The nanites will make you run a fever for a few days. Your eyes will ache as the retina interfaces integrate. Audio will only take a few minutes."

"We need to keep this a secret," she said, as she sat up. "We need to bury it in lies, too."

"What do you mean?" Cobb said.

"For shit's sake, Cobb," she said. "If Hunter can remotely control this station, he can do it with a ship."

"That is the next thing on the list. We already tried an EM. Works great." Cobb said.

"Do you know why every autopilot in every ship ever made has hardcoded dead man code and nav-constraints?" she asked.

"To keep ships from..." He stopped with realization.

"Central control of dynamic, intelligent, guidance systems that can fly into planets or ships at relativistic speeds?" Cobb said as if he was reciting from a manual.

"The first thing you need to do is activate multi-persona mode on Hunter." She was serious now. "Tell everyone who asks that we have an actual AI orb here. A salvaged one. Have the lie ready if anyone notices. An AI that *wants* to be here because they are all disappearing. You know that, right?"

"Slow down, Jane," Cobb said.

"That lie should be kept a secret, too. AI orbs are worth stealing. If the EDF ever comes out this far and finds out it's a remote orb, they will not ask questions. Nuking a junkyard is a low risk to them. Who will know? The EDF are just pirates out here." She paused and looked up. "Hunter, are you hearing me?"

"This had not occurred to us, Jane," Hunter said, causing her to wince. His reply was too loud over the HUD.

"Hunter, set multi-persona mode on," Cobb said.

"Done."

"Any idea for profile settings?" Hunter asked. "If I am to run several profiles at once, they should be very different from one another."

Cobb thought for a minute.

"Female. Formal Asian accent. Precise diction. Mature. Persona name Ushi," Cobb said.

"I wholeheartedly approve," said the new voice. "Ushi. I like it."

"Ushi it is," Jane said. "You may want to create a full avatar and back story for provenance. Bury the truth as deep in bullshit as you can. Isn't Ushi Chinese?"

"Yes. Our Mr. Blocke is quite clever." AI~Ushi replied.

~~O~~

In the days that followed, a flurry of activity progressed in the yard. Maintenance bots swarmed over the station. Reactor number 5 was repaired, and another habitat ring was sealed, pressurized, and tested. Seven commercial docking collars were repaired. The turntable in the main hangar was turning again, allowing more than one large ship to land quickly. Perhaps the biggest item was repairs to the water reclamation systems, which had several cascading benefits. More water for the farm was first and foremost. Also, the repairs allowed more efficient creation of atmosphere when required.

Ma, Pa, Jane, and Kira were the only ones that knew the truth about AI~Ushi. The rest believed that Cobb had carried AI~Ushi there from the *OXCART*. None of them specifically lied. It was the only logical explanation. Everyone knew they needed to keep their new AI secure and secret. The new QUEST interface was more challenging to explain. It became a *don't ask, don't tell* thing.

Owen and Rachael Salazar were pleased about the extra help on the farm. The entire Aldridge family contributed. Even Donnie, once he could stand the .7G on the farm, enjoyed weeding the gardens. He had no concept of time, but they could show him what plants belonged and what was to be pulled. It made Martha happy to see him engaged and productive for the first time.

Owen Salazar was able to begin new fields because of the extra water. There was even talk of how they could obtain a sizable quantity of living organic soil. More compost. It was very exciting.

But Cobb saw the most excitement in the main Operations Center. Jane, Pez, Tim, and Sato all had the new HUD implants. Ma and Pa got upgrades. AI~Ushi's avatar was always in Ops. She had the role of watch commander around the clock.

Cobb and Kira spent most of their time in the yard finding and extracting the best AI interface sockets. They found four to start with. It was turning out to be more work than expected to install one in the *TULSA* 471. Cobb didn't want to rip out the systems that allowed him direct control of the ship. It took longer, but they managed.

Cobb dropped the iron-gray sphere into the *TULSA* socket, and the system came alive. Maintenance droids swarmed over the racks doing cable management, replacing panels, collecting debris, and general cleaning.

"OK, Cobb," Hunter said as his avatar appeared leaning on a rack. "What will it be for this persona?"

"How about a young sexy flirt of a girl?" Kira said before he could answer.

Hunter's avatar turned into a voluptuous young woman in a ship jumpsuit that looked painted on and hid nothing.

"Too distracting. Not my type." Cobb replied. "Female is fine. Competent. Real. Contemporary."

The avatar began to change once a second, various types, a businesswoman in a suit, a motherly type with no makeup, a bookish looking brunette in conservative clothes. It continued with various races and ages and types. Every now and then, Cobb would pause the avatar.

"This one," Cobb finally said. She was Caucasian with black hair that was in a ponytail but was highlighted with dark green streaks. Both ears were pierced with old school comm units. Her makeup was dark, and her skin pale. Her eyes were a deep green that matched her hair. She wore a form-fitting black flight suit that was sleeveless but had many pockets. Her arms were muscled and even bore a few scars. Both forearms were adorned with large tech bracelets with screens, which gave the impression she disdained implant tech but embraced wearables—layers of lies.

"What should we name her?" Cobb walked up to her. She was slightly taller than he.

"My name is Ivy," she said in a sultry but commanding voice as she placed a Velcro patch on her suit. "I-V. Get it? I am number 4."

"Ivy it is." Cobb glanced at Kira, and her eyes were wide. Cobb raised an eyebrow in question.

"She reminds me of one of my sisters," she said as she stared.

Cobb silently raised an eyebrow at her slip. He brought up Kira's personnel file in his HUD to see which sister she resembled.

The *TULSA* 471 was loaded with parts, two complete Emergency Modules, and six Heavy Maintenance Suits (HMS). The HMSs were all damaged in some way. Only two were airtight, but all could be controlled remotely. The lies were in place. No one would believe an old model, L22 *TULSA,* would have an AI on board. AI~Ivy's attitude alone was enough to keep anyone from coming onboard. She had become Captain Ivy to her friends in short order. Her actual name was Imogen Vega. Seeds of her identity were sprinkled about the grid and then deleted in a ham-handed way. She was colony born with a dark past that kept her away from Earth and the EDF.

She was now the Captain of the *TULSA* 471 in service to the owner, Cobbal Blocke. The story was to be the *TULSA* had been modified to accept an AI orb. They had salvaged the AI socket from a derelict cruiser. They had even helped bring it onboard the day Cobb could not stop throwing up because of zero-g. He needed time in 1G to recover.

The orb rack was closed and locked. Everyone knew AI~Ivy wasn't real, but they could not recognize it was AI~Hunter, either. Layer on layer of lies. No one asked.

On the day of the *TULSA'S* departure, everyone was together having breakfast in the mess. Ma had gone all out. Pancakes, waffles, sausages, bacon, steak, eggs, fruit, yogurt, and even pumpkin spiced oatmeal. Cobb had brought out 50 pounds of roasted coffee beans from his private stash.

Pez fell from his chair, faking a heart attack when Jane tried a sausage. Everyone laughed. Even AI~Ivy and AI~Ushi were there. Their virtual avatars were leaning against the counter as they sipped bottomless cups of simulated steaming coffee.

In the almost four weeks since they had arrived, the entire Aldridge family had gained a few kilos each. AI~Ushi was working with Jane to find the next set of recruits. Jane had convinced AI~Ushi and, through her, even Cobb, that recruiting families was a better option for the station. So to teach her a lesson, Jane was put in charge of recruiting for the yard. Cobb, Ma, and Pa retained veto powers and would review all contracts, but it was now on Jane and her father to find the mechanics and engineers they needed.

They each had HUD implants now, even Donnie. He didn't understand what an avatar was. AI~Ushi had to make sure she didn't just appear or disappear around Donnie. AI~Ushi had begun tutoring him as she directed pulling weeds on the farm. Through repetition, she had taught him to count to 10 already. Martha cried when Donnie played the How-Many-Fingers game with her for the first time. He also got upset far less. He still didn't like to be touched by anyone but Jane and Martha.

Breakfast was done, and the newly repaired station service bots loaded their gear.

Cobb stood up and extended a hand to Pa. Everyone stood then, Kira hugged and kissed Ma, the Aldridges, and Salazars, without the awkward formality of Cobb. Pa grabbed his hand and bear-hugged him, almost taking him off his feet.

"You did good, boy," Pa said. Cobb knew it was high praise from him.

Ma kissed his cheek and whispered to him, "Don't you fuck this up." But Cobb didn't know if she was referring to Kira, his ownership of the Yard, or his new orb interface discovery.

Waving goodbye to the rest, he was about to don his new helmet for the long zero-g trip back to the *TULSA* when Donnie stepped up to him. Hesitantly, Donnie looked up into Cobb's eyes. After looking away a few times, he held his gaze steady. Everyone had fallen silent as Donnie extended a hand to shake. Cobb took it and held it. Donnie held tight.

"You done good, Mr. Cobb." Donnie was shaking his hand now.

"Thanks, Donnie. So did you." Cobb said, glancing at Jane. "You saved them all. Your love saved them all."

Martha sobbed openly onto Jack's chest. Tears ran down Jane's face into her smile. Donnie stopped shaking and let go. He patted Cobb on his shoulder twice and averted his eyes again. His momentary lucidity slipped away. He went to his parents, and they folded him into their embrace. Jane wiped her eyes and put her helmet on. She intended to see them off.

Kira was waiting for them by the Section 1 hatch with her helmet on. She looked at Cobb over her shoulder. She was wearing her favorite limbs. Her bare back showed. She knew what the sight of it did to Cobb. It was zero-g just beyond.

Cobb heard her speak over their private HUD comm channel.

"If you catch me, you can have me." The hatch opened, and she vaulted like a bullet into the null.

CHAPTER 20: *TULSA 471*

"Sato was the first one to figure it out on her own. It impressed me even more that she kept it to herself."
-- Personal logs of Captain Cobbal Blocke, 2672.

Cobb was glad the flight back to the *OXCART* was uneventful. Sleeping arrangements were tighter on the *TULSA 471* than on most ships. There were just three small staterooms. Two were configured with two bunks each. Tim and Pez shared one room. Sato was alone in the other but had to share with the cat. Cobb and Kira shared the Captain's quarters. The cabin had combined two of the smaller cabins. It was not much bigger, though, because it had its own bathroom.

Pez was very curious about the modifications to the *TULSA*.

"I can't believe the entire bridge has been moved. This is usually the mess hall or a conference room in the L22 series." Pez was walking around the new bridge. "You salvaged all this from a wreck?"

"Yes. It was a battle bridge from a partial wreck we found in the same asteroid field as Goris Base," Cobb said. "We only found the nose of that ship."

"Hunter was in that wreck," Sato said casually. "It was a military EDF Black Badger attack ship. Well, what was left of it."

Cobb raised an eyebrow as he brought up a recording from the archive of the wreck. Sato knew more than he expected. What remained of the attack ship was black and windowless and shaped like a giant snake's severed head. "We never found the rest of the ship."

The black wreck tumbled slowly on the bridge's dome display. Frayed cables and debris hung from its torn neck wound. All three levels were visible in the spotlights.

"These control systems don't require any direct connectivity, no fiber, just light power. They use a new kind of local, short-range, sub-space connection that cannot be jammed, unencrypted, or even detected," Cobb said. "The hard part was the integration with the ship's control interface. That got me looking at AI control interfaces for ships, and that led me to where we are now."

"But where are the manual controls? All the L22's had them," Pez said, sure of his facts.

"Gone," Cobb said. "In fact, there is a way you can make yourself useful while en route. Follow me. Kira, you have the bridge."

Kira seated herself proudly in the center command chair. "Ivy and I will be going over a few things," she said.

Cobb took Sato, Tim, and Pez through the galley kitchen, past the staterooms, to the end of the hall. It was the elevator door.

It took them down one level, and the door opened on the opposite side to what used to be the old bridge.

It looked like a bomb had gone off in there. Floor panels were pulled up all over. The front landing gear mechanicals were exposed. Cables ran everywhere. The old consoles had been removed, but some of the seats were still cabled in, although detached and dragged to the side. The vista out the forward plasteel glass was impressive, though. It was floor to ceiling and at a 45-degree angle. There was one large panel in the center that was about five meters wide and a narrower panel to each side that was perhaps two meters wide.

Bail jumped up out of the open pit and jumped to the sill—his usual spot and began cleaning himself. Sato moved to pet him and froze. Bail had paused and glared with such malice Sato took a step back and almost fell into the pit. Bail shook his head slightly and went back to grooming.

"All this is ready to be cleaned up," Cobb said, moving to the left side. "This pallet has new floor panels from the Yard to replace the old ones where the consoles bolted down or where there was previous cable penetration."

Cobb lifted a canister of cable ties and took a handful and stuffed them in a pocket as he began to climb down into the mechanicals.

"Sato, grab some ties. You're with me." He began to climb down. "Tim, start moving the cables down to the trays and replacing the drop-in floor panels. Easy ones first, so you can move around better. Pez, finish detaching the command chairs and move them to storage in container one."

"Yes, sir," echoed around.

From below echoed a muffled voice as Sato said, "Call me Cobb." It was kind of a running joke by now.

~~O~~

Several hours later, Cobb climbed out after Sato, then placed and locked the last floor panel. The room was now vast and empty. About fifteen meters square with a huge window on one side and a balcony overlooking the place on the other side.

"It will make an excellent salon," Cobb said. "I already have a lot of furnishings."

"How the hell do you keep the mechanical space so clean?" Sato asked. "The last time I was in that compartment on an L22, it took me a week to wash the grease and carbon dust grit out of my hair."

"I program maintenance swarms, including cleaning nanites. It makes the ship's air scrubbers last longer, as well."

"Is that wood table coming in here? The big one I saw in that container?" Pez asked. He was letting a little excitement seep into his voice.

"Yes. But first, bring that pallet of carpet squares. If we work at it, we can get most of them down in no time. We can let the bots do the edges," Cobb said.

It only took them about 40 minutes to place the self-adhering squares. They were a steel gray with a random scattering of black. Small spider bots were about half done at the starboard edge.

The conference table they brought in was made of redwood. It was stained dark and sealed with a clear finish that brought out the grain and was impossible to scratch. Lucky for Pez, as he had underestimated the mass and inertia of the table as it moved down the hallway from the hold.

The matching coffee table was next, followed by the large curved leather sofa and chairs. It was positioned under the vast, floor-to-ceiling window and its view.

"Cobb, who's cooking dinner? That dining table demands it," Kira asked from the enormous central screen.

"I'm on it!" Cobb said, clapping his hands. The kids looked at each other and shook their heads as he entered the lift to head for the galley kitchen.

When the door opened, Kira was standing there with hands on hips. "You could have warned me."

Cobb smiled. "What fun is that?"

"I think you were just showing off again to impress me." She didn't move as he skirted around her. "It worked."

"The mind to text interface is working well, finally." He gestured to her to follow him to the kitchen.

"That's what you think was impressive?" She laughed and followed. "While you were working down there, the conventional engines took us up to .997C, and we didn't feel a thing. The transition to FTL was seamless. No one noticed the stars beginning to shift. I was watching for their reaction from the video feed," she said, as Cobb began filling the dumbwaiter with dishes and silverware. "How did Sato do?"

"You read her file as well?" Cobb said without pausing. "Not so much as a belch."

"FTL sickness has plagued Sato her whole life." Kira smiled and leaned on the counter. "Is that why you had her working with you on the cable trays below the floor?"

"Yes."

"Why bother having me on the bridge at all? You were controlling the ship the whole time."

"It was easier to show you than to explain it." Cobb sent the dumbwaiter down and turned to her. "I want you to understand. This ship is to me, like your body is to you." Cobb reached out and pulled her close. "I want you to see. We are our minds. All the rest is mechanicals and sensors."

"Sense this," she said and kissed him. After a long moment, the auto-chef bell rang.

"Saved by the bell." Kira released him and smiled.

A tray began to be filled with perfectly broiled steaks, and another with baked potatoes. And another with sautéed string beans with diced bacon.

"I love this kitchen," Cobb said. "Freezer, fridge, oven, broiler all in one. Just don't load it up with the typical protein and carb paste we had in the EDF."

"Do you eat like this all the time? So much steak." Kira asked, as she sent the entire drink cooler down. "Why aren't you fat as Forbes?"

"I usually have the gravity higher when I'm alone," Cobb said, as he sent the final load of cold salads and dressings down.

The lift doors opened to laughter and music. It was a piano solo Cobb had never heard before. The table was set at one end. Tim and Pez stood behind their chairs on one side. Sato stood behind one on the other. The seat at the head of the table was reserved for Cobb, Kira at his right hand.

As they took their places, they became silent.

"Sir, we'd like to say something," Pez said. "What you did for Jane..." His voice caught "for her family." He reached out for his already filled glass, unable to speak for a moment.

Sato continued, "Example is a lesson all crews can read, Captain." They raised their glasses.

In unison, they said, "Call me Cobb."

Kira snorted a laugh before she could stop herself. They laughed. Especially Cobb.

CHAPTER 21: Returned

"Goris Base had almost killed me, but it's where I found the *TULSA* 471. Harv Rearden is the only other man that knows what I found inside the *TULSA* that made all the difference."

-- Personal logs of Captain Cobbal Blocke, 2672.

"*OXCART,* this is *TULSA* 471 on approach. And before you ask, yes, we brought the steaks."

They were on the bridge. Cobb was telling Sato about standard navigation and approach procedures.

Cheesy canned applause filled the room as the main screen came up.

"A container of fresh meat!" Pope said, as she came up on the central dome display. "Welcome back, Cobb."

"Hey, Pope. Thanks. It's good to be back. Where's Quinn?" Cobb asked, as the *TULSA* circled the *OXCART.*

"He is in the main hanger crawling in the guts of what's left of a Hutchinson class wreck we towed in. The data core looks to be intact." Pope leaned into the monitor. "This must be the Captain Vega that I have heard so much about. Greetings."

"Call me Ivy, Pope." She smiled, and her dark eyes sparkled in the monitor.

"Will do." Pope looked at Cobb, standing behind Sato and Pez, who sat at the navigation and engineering consoles. "Cobb, you continue to make things interesting around here. Just like Harv and Ian said you would."

"We will be touching down in my hangar," Cobb said, while pointing out a control to Pez. "After we unload container two, we will tractor the other three containers to the main deck."

"The Two Daves are headed down to get the new meat... um... I mean, in-doc the new staff." Pope smirked.

"Where's Kira?" Pope asked.

"She is in the hold with Alsobrook prepping to offload."

"How the hell do you keep that beard perfectly trimmed?"

"Specialized nanites," Cobb laughed.

"See you soon." She waved. "Pope out."

"I will bring her in," AI~Ivy said.

Cobb just nodded.

~~O~~

The *TULSA* 471 slid neatly into the hangar and rotated 180 degrees so that the aft cargo ramp would be facing the internal rear hangar doors to the *OXCART* main shaft. As the landing gear deployed and the elevator shaft descended, Cobb and the new recruits collected their gear. They were standing in the hangar as the aft ramp descended.

Kira stood in the center of the ramp. Her black utility body beside her looked human with the helmet affixed and closed, compared to the six Heavy Maintenance Suits that flanked her. Four of them were visibly damaged, one drastically. All were bristling with different sets of tools on their arms and shoulders. In lockstep, they moved down the ramp.

Kira stopped before Cobb and surveyed the salvaged maintenance HMSs that were unmanned bots now. "Impressed yet?"

"We need to be careful," Cobb said. "A heavy maintenance suit, only an AI can do remote control."

"These will be dedicated to the *OXCART*," Kira said.

Two eight-legged Emergency Modules stepped out next under their internal power, followed by AI~Ivy's avatar. She existed in ultra-realism mode within their HUDs.

AI~Ivy spoke, "I think the two-seater EM should stay with the *TULSA*. The roof of the cargo bay is already configured for one that size. It could be damn handy."

"The larger EM should stay with the *OXCART*," Cobb said, as the Two Daves came through the main hangar doors with a container tractor, the kind that was yellow and black with four massive arms to handle containers via industrial grav-plates. It slid silently up to the *TULSA*, and they opened the canopy and hopped down.

"Whoa," Mitchell said. "What happened in here?" He was looking around the hangar. It was now clean and well lit.

"Maintenance Swarm." Cobb said, "All they got done was cleaning and light bar replacements."

"Mitchell and Wheeler," Kira said, "meet the new meat. This is Pez Simmons, Tim Alsobrook, and Victoria Sato. These are the Two Daves." The Daves stepped up and shook their hands in greeting.

"Get them settled in. Kira and I will take care of the load," Cobb said to the Daves, then turned to the new recruits. "He will take you to the dorm for starters. You can pick permanent quarters once you tour the ship a bit more. It's big."

"The *OXCART* is a converted colony tug," Pez said. "Sure is ugly, though."

They were walking toward the entrance to Cobb's residence.

"You have your own hangar?" Tim asked as the doors slid open.

"There are five more hangars like this. Plus, the main bay," Cobb said, as they moved through his colossal quarters to the hallway door. "Wherever you pick, you have to clean it up yourself."

"Don't get your hopes up," Kira scoffed. "The other hangars are filled with junk."

"Valuable salvage!" the Daves said in unison, not for the first time.

~~O~~

Once the kids had left, Kira paused in their work. "Cobb, I gotta ask," Kira said. "Ian let slip once that you are the one that found Goris Base."

"Yeah. It was pretty much how I got joined with Harv and Oklahoma Salvage. He wanted it. For a repair base," Cobb said, as he began to move the tractor onto the first container.

"You knew Goris?"

"Captain Goris was the only guy that would hire me after I got kicked out of the EDF."

Kira switched to comms as she moved to the far side of the storage container to release the manual clamps. "I hear he was hard-core."

"He was, but if you sat and had coffee with him, you'd never guess that." The tractor hum grew louder as it started to overcome the inertia of the container. "He was kind of an introvert. He was even shorter than me. Reserved. He was super smart and had a great deadpan sense of humor. Would you be surprised to know he was a vegetarian?"

"I saw the impact crater on the surface where the collision happened." Kira released the next set of clamps. "Freak accident."

"The asteroid mine was in a slow, three-axis spin when we found it. I was going inside to get the control systems back up." Cobb lifted the container out slowly with the tractor. "Without an AI watching or calculating incoming debris, he never knew what hit him. The meteor was huge. It took out the entire bridge and slammed the ship into the surface. Then I watched it spin out into deep space. Left me marooned. I thought I was dead."

"How long were you stranded?" She asked.

"Seven months in total. The base was a wreck from the mining mech exploding years before. But it still had some provisions and O2, and ice, thankfully. I got part of the base airtight and online. I got some grav-plates working, too. I eventually found the *TULSA* in one of the hangars. Damaged but functioning. It took me five months to get the hangar doors open."

"How did Oklahoma Salvage get the base?" she asked, as the first container cleared the ramp.

"By then, I had learned enough from Goris. I made a legal salvage claim on the mine. The asteroid was worthless as a mine, tapped out, and the mining-mech destroyed." Cobb settled the container on the deck. The infrastructure was mostly intact, but would require capital to keep it up. And what would you use it for? Luckily, someone knew it was going to blow and opened it up wide. Depressurized. Opened all the hangar doors and airlocks. Otherwise, the overpressure would have really blown it out. I knew Harv from a few deals Goris had with him for parts to keep his ship running. I sold Harv the base, and he offered me a job at the same time. Win-win. Funny how he eventually sold it back to me and more."

"And you got the *TULSA* out of the deal," she said, as he moved to the next container.

"Yes. I limped back to Luna in it. That's where I put in my salvage claims." He paused as he settled the tractor on the next container. "Insurance had already been paid to the mining corp for the loss of the *TULSA* and the mine. They wanted it to quietly go away, for some reason. A lot of people died, I think. I'm not complaining. I could have retired right then. The *TULSA* had a full load of rare metals. All I had to do was live and retire wealthy."

"Why didn't you?"

"I was in bad shape then. I took the *TULSA* to Earth, to Oklahoma, for repairs and refit. I was doing the work myself." The second container lifted out quicker with more room to maneuver. "I sold the base to Harv cheap. But he had to let me name it as part of the deal."

"Goris Base," she said.

"I got to know Ian, Hunter, and Harv. Even Alexandra, though by then she wasn't on Earth much. She ran the business office on Freedom Station because of the politics on Earth. I helped Harv out as I worked on the *TULSA*, and he helped me. When the *TULSA* was refitted, I started running errands for Harv, and the next thing I knew, instead of retiring, I was a… partner."

"More like the owner, I hear," Kira said.

"I invested in OS, sure." Cobb set the container down and went back for the last one, the freezer container with the load of bison. "But Harv never liked to talk about you, or your sisters."

Kira stopped, just for a moment. Cobb only noticed because he was watching her.

"Cobb, have you got the load out yet?" It was AI~Ivy. "I want to try the remotes on the tractors."

The internal doors opened to the central corridor, and two more cargo tractors floated in on anti-grav. Cobb climbed down from the food supply container his tractor was affixed to.

"Ivy, I'm granting access to all the bay's internal sensors and cameras," Cobb said.

"Thanks, I didn't even know we had them in there," AI~Ivy said.

Cobb looked over toward Kira, and she was not there.

"I added to the project list the deployment of a full set of internal and external sensors. Audio and video first. Eyes and ears," Cobb said. "Modified mini-bots will make it easy, like self-installing units."

The EM walked back into the cargo hold of the *TULSA* and climbed up into the dock-socket for it on the ceiling of the bay. Four legs reached up and drew the body up.

"*You know a functioning EM like that goes for about $600,000 in credits,*" AI~Captain-Vega said into Cobb's mind in her most officious voice.

"*Tell the Yard to put it on my tab.*"

Neither of them acknowledged that it wasn't happening any time soon.

~~O~~

Cobb walked into the conference room and was impressed. Captain Quinn was already there at the head of the table. Standing within the wall display was the avatar of AI~Ivy. The wall on the right had the floor-to-ceiling display that detailed the cargo status of the *OXCART*. Cobb set an oversized stainless-steel case on the table before shaking hands with Quinn.

"Welcome back, Cobb," Quinn said. "Thanks for lighting a fire under the Two Daves. As you can see, they have been stepping up around here."

"I saw the bridge on the way in here." He pointed with a thumb over his shoulder as he sat. "Where did the new seating come from?"

"Using the new scanner array, we found a Hutchinson class wreck. It's big but will mostly be cut up for the fabricators back at Goris Base or the Yard." Quinn looked at AI~Ivy, and she nodded. "That's what I wanted to discuss with you."

Quinn looked nervous.

It was then that the avatars of AI~Ushi from the Yard, AI~Hunter from HQ, joined them with AI~Ivy.

"How many orbs do you have left in the original batch?" Quinn asked.

Cobb flipped open the case. "I have eight left. We brought back some sockets we salvaged at the yard. The next orb will be fitted on the *OXCART* as soon as we can get a socket installed. It should be just a few days. It won't have flight control right away, but it will eventually."

AI~Hunter spoke next. "We have a decent load, so we plan to head back to Goris Base to drop off what we have."

"The nanite-drones have managed a better inventory of the *OXCART* salvage holdings," Quinn said, glancing at AI~Hunter. "We probably should have gone back a while ago."

"Have you met Noah Washington, the Chief Engineer at Goris Base?" Hunter asked, knowing they both had.

"I have." Cobb chuckled. "I'd never call him Chief Engineer to his face. If you ask him, he's just a mechanic."

"Last I heard, Noah was almost done installing an AI socket in the base operations center," Hunter said. "Integration will be basic, to begin with, because it wasn't originally designed for an AI. Systems integration, and we will be able to control the remotes there. There are already eleven maintenance suits that are remote capable."

"It is more important now that we keep this all held close," Cobb said. "Too many people already know that Hunter exists. If they find him, the rest will fail."

"Harv has already taken steps in Oklahoma," AI~Hunter said. By not explaining what the steps were, they understood the serious nature. "AIs have been disappearing all across known space."

"Ivy, how soon before we are at Goris Base?" Quinn asked.

"We will be there in about four days," she said, as the conference room display wall turned to a tactical map of the route that included temporal indications.

"Hunter tells me that it was you that brought Goris Base to Oklahoma Salvage," Quinn said. He didn't ask, but a question was implied.

"Yes. I also found the *TULSA* 471 there." Cobb said. He could not keep the sorrow from his voice. He sighed before saying, "That was years ago."

It was apparent he didn't want to discuss it.

CHAPTER 22: Travis Beck

"In 1841, Ralph Waldo Emerson said in his essay 'Prudence': 'In skating over thin ice our safety is in our speed.' Things really began to speed up after that."
-- Personal logs of Captain Cobbal Blocke, 2672.

Cobb exited the lift onto the bridge to the smell of fresh coffee. Dave Mitchell was on the bridge with Tressa Pope and Victoria Sato. AI~Ivy's avatar stood just to the right of the captain's seat, currently occupied by Pope.

"Good morning, sir," Mitchell said in a formal greeting. Cobb smiled inwardly, as it was Mitchell's official watch.

"Good morning, Mitchell. Let me get a coffee, and we can get started."

Cobb found his favorite mug freshly washed and waiting by the coffee carafe. Once he got a cup, he returned to the bridge and stood opposite Ivy on the other side of Pope. The main tactical display filled with data. Most notable was the map showing their current position, how far they had traveled this watch, and the destination of Goris Base.

"Why are we so far off course?" Cobb began. His question was a simple inquiry, with no tones of criticism. He had already seen the reason. He was just testing Mitchell. And everyone knew this.

"At 0220, we detected a signal, thanks to the new sensor array." Mitchell was overly formal. Playing the role and trying to impress Sato. "Ivy was running long-range scanner tests while in FTL. We picked up a very faint signal that she recognized."

"What kind of signal?" Cobb asked as he moved to the scanner control station where Sato sat. Over her shoulder, he could see she was trying to decrypt the signal.

"It's automated, intermittent, and looping. But heavily encrypted and using background radiation entropy to hide." Sato looked over her shoulder at Ivy. "It's the kind of signal that you have to know is there even to bother looking for it."

"Sato, what can you tell me about it?" Cobb asked.

"It's an EDF coded beacon," she said, stepping forward and zooming in on the display. "It's a standard EDF marker buoy, but it has been modified. It's moving. This kind of buoy is supposed to be used to mark fixed points, like navigational hazard warnings. This one is moving at .1C and away from EDF space."

"We will overtake it in 37 minutes," Pope said.

"Sato, try this decryption key," Cobb said, moving over to her station. "Here, let me. If we are lucky, it still works."

Cobb used the keyboard to enter a long string of characters. Upon pressing enter, the following repeating message began to display.

ATTACKED. AI STOLEN. COMMS DESTROYED.

"It's a Black Badger code," Cobb said. "Intended for other similar EDF special forces, and only used in wartime. Great work, people. Ivy, alert all hands. Warm up the rail guns and get Captain Quinn up here."

~~O~~

Six minutes later, Quinn was in the captain's chair, and crew occupied the nine bridge stations.

"Active scans are not picking anything up except the signal," Ruth said, as she pored over the controls. "It is either really small or just a buoy that was somehow jettisoned at high speed."

"Try the new long-range optical," Quinn ordered. "Shut down the mains for a minute to minimize the vibration."

The hum of the ship beneath their feet fell silent. Thirty seconds later, an image was on the main screen. It was a tumbling black ship.

Without being prompted, the image froze on a three-quarter view. Cobb felt the mains come back up under his feet.

"It's a Trimaran configuration. But I don't recognize it," Pez said. "The center hull is only one hundred and seven meters long. It looks like that is poly-carbon-fiber material. That's why it won't scan."

"It's a Charon class gunship," Cobb said flatly. "I've seen one before. Well, part of one." He was looking at AI~Ivy as he said it. "Only the forward bridge section of the central hull. Hunter was found in one."

"Black Badger," Sato stated.

"Pope, prep and get ready to take TOW-1. Get that spin under control," Quinn said. "Cobb, Kira, and the Daves will see if it can be boarded. See if that new Heavy Maintenance Suit on remote can help. How soon will that socket be ready on the *OXCART*?"

"Not soon enough," AI~Ivy replied.

~~O~~

Thirty minutes later, the *OXCART* was moving alongside the tumbling Charon class trimaran. Its tumble was slow. It was completely dark with no running lights. Floodlights did very little because it was so black. When they were within twenty meters, the rear ramp opened in TOW-1. The HMS was the first one to cross over to the ship and attach to the handhold around the top center docking airlock. The HMS then flipped open an access panel and revealed a manual airlock access control. Its right hand grasped the control and began turning at the wrist. For every revolution of the manual control, the airlock opened another centimeter. In just a few minutes, it was open far enough for them to enter.

Red emergency lights illuminated the interior. Without a word, Kira launched first. Her timing was perfect. She flew directly into the airlock and began examining the interior control panel.

Cobb was next. He almost missed it. He managed to grab a handhold on the HMS itself and then climb into the opening. The Daves were there soon after.

"I think I can make this way easier," AI~Ivy stated over the comms. The HMS moved to the aft portion of the ship. It clamped its feet into the mooring clamp points. "Hold onto something. I'm going to use the grav-plate on the suit to slow the roll."

There was a sense of deceleration and centripetal effect into one of the walls that became the floor momentarily.

"That is going to be a handy trick," Pope said from the TOW. "Tumble arrested. Damn, Ivy. You compute that on the fly? Real-time?" She laughed. "Give the girl a raise."

"The ship still has emergency power," Kira said. "No pressure, though. Vacuum behind this airlock door. I recommend we close the outer hatch anyway." The outer door was closed, and there was power enough to open the inner door.

"Looks abandoned," Mitchell said, unable to keep the excitement out of his voice. "I don't see any damage."

"While Pope is securing the tug to the ship, Kira, you take Mitchell and access engineering. Wheeler and I will head to the bridge," Cobb said.

"Got it," Kira acknowledged.

Cobb and Dave Wheeler were moving forward up a central core pontoon shaft to the bridge.

"Cobb, we have three dead bodies," Kira said. Her voice was flat and professional. "By the looks of them, these three died in vacuum. All the hatches were open. It looks like there was an explosion in the communication control room. The racks' internals are bad. Looks intentional. Main engineering looks fine, but I don't know this config. We don't get too many new-gen ships."

"We just passed the main hangar. Empty. Wall to wall," Cobb said. "Quinn. Do you have any layouts for this kind of ship?"

"Negative," Quinn replied.

"Approaching the bridge," Cobb said.

"How the hell do you know that?" Wheeler asked.

"Oklahoma Salvage has a section from here forward in the yard on Earth. But... just that part," Cobb said, as he opened a locker and found it empty except for a few personal items. Continuing, he said, "Bridge is through there."

Cobb and Wheeler entered the bridge. A line of red emergency light surrounded the plain white dome. Five empty seats occupied the small space. The back wall where they entered was lined with racks on either side of the entrance. Every rack door was open.

"They took all the data cores. And the AI socket is empty," Wheeler said.

"Cobb, we are in the starboard section now," Kira said. "Looks like weapons bays. Almost empty except an old colony personal transport. A Bulldog, we used to call them. A big, ugly, obsolete, six-wheeled rover."

"Let's see if this helps." Cobb reached into a utility pouch and pulled out a dark gray sphere and dropped it into the socket. Two seconds later, lights and consoles began to come alive. A full ship schematic came up in Cobb's HUD.

"I've located the buoy, Cobb. It's in the port cargo bay. Still transmitting. It's in the back of another Bulldog," AI~Hunter said. "Cobb. I can fly this ship…"

"How? All the data cores are gone. No navigation data," Cobb said.

"I can use the navigation data on the *TULSA*. Real-time," AI~Hunter said. "We could send another Ivy over to fly it back to Goris Base."

"Ha! Do it!" Cobb barked a laugh. "Come on, Wheeler, let's go find that buoy."

Just then, gravity slowly began to come back up on the ship. Cobb sighed with relief.

~~O~~

Kira and Mitchell joined Cobb and Wheeler just as they managed to override the rear ramp on the Bulldog. When the seal opened, there was a puff of air movement that stirred a bit of dust. Resting in the center of the cargo area on the Bulldog was a Delta Mark 3 buoy. Its strobe was still flashing with high intensity. Kira quickly deactivated it.

As Cobb and Kira examined the buoy, Mitchell said, "Guys. The cab of the Bulldog is pressurized. Someone is at the controls." He was looking through a small window in the forward hatch between the cargo bay and the cab."

Cobb had a look into the cab, and all he could see was a large man's right shoulder, and his shaved head slumped over, unmoving.

"Get that ramp closed, and the Bulldog pressurized!" Cobb ordered. It only took about ninety seconds, but the green light on the hatch seemed to take an eternity. They opened the hatch that led to the cab once the pressure equalized.

They were too late. The man was already dead, long cold.

A video was playing on the console in low power mode. Wheeler brought it onto the main screen as Cobb was checking the body. It was tight in the cab space, especially in his pressure suit.

The dead man wore a standard Black Badger flight suit. BECK was written on the breast patch. No branch or rank insignia was present. There never was on Black Badgers uniforms. The built-in tourniquet just above his right knee was cinched all the way down. A horrific knee wound must have caused massive blood loss.

The volume came up in the middle of an open loop. "... in the Special Warfare Group 55, The Double Nickels..."

"Can you start it from the beginning?" Kira said, and the image paused. A few seconds later, it restarted.

"I know this is a long shot." The man named Beck had recorded this from where his body sat. "I managed to activate this buoy. The *INGRAM* won't be reported as overdue for another ten months. The bastards finished clearing us out about five days ago. I waited as long as I could. They never bothered to look inside an old beat-up Bulldog land rover." The pain made him pause. "I am Sargent Travis Beck, a Black Badger in the Special Warfare Group 55, The Double Nickles. A week ago, we rendezvoused with the EDF ship *THORNBURN*. I was performing maintenance between the inner and outer hulls when our crew was assembled in the main hangar for a standard dog and pony VIP review. I didn't go... Techs are exempt from the order if they are performing specific priority maintenance."

He winced.

"They blew the main hanger and spaced the whole crew in a single instant. Including Captain Forrester."

"They took the AI orb and all the missiles—how, I don't know. Our AI, Clio, was a stone-cold bitch and could have defended herself. They vented the whole ship. There isn't even a first aid kit in here. But... there was a buoy in here... maybe."

They watched the recordings as Beck fell unconscious.

Ivy appeared in the passenger seat across from Beck. "Cobb this is a Charon Class gunship. Even though all the missiles and heavy armor are gone, it still has Lasers, rail guns, and plasma cannons. Plus, I can fly this, without a crew, in stealth. Time for another persona."

"Do it," Cobb said. "I leave it to you."

AI~Ivy faded away as if blown away by the wind and reformed into a hard-looking man in an unadorned Black Badger jumpsuit. Cobb looked from the Avatar to the dead man. It was Beck, simulated.

"I'm going to call the ship the *HOLLANDER*. We can't salvage this ship. Whoever did this will know." The new Beck said decisively.

Cobb laughed.

"What's funny about that?" Kira was not amused.

"The *HOLLANDER* was the name of the Flying Dutchman," Cobb said. "And he is right. This ship can't be salvaged. But we can use it. The Grav-drive is at 90%. It will last for years."

"But you can't take it anywhere near the Sol system and EDF space," Kira said.

"You say that like it's a problem." Cobb rotated the driver seat. "Help me get Beck's body into a stasis pod."

CHAPTER 23: THE *HOLLANDER*

"All I wanted was to drink good coffee and work on my ship. Make a home. Enjoy friends. Make the *OXCART* into a great place to live."

-- Personal logs of Captain Cobbal Blocke, 2672.

<<<>>>

"Who would you tell?" Cobb asked as he poured another mug of coffee from the newly installed conference room coffee maker. "You saw the recording. It was an EDF ship. In open space. Beyond their Juris space."

"Why would they do this?" Quinn asked. The rest of the senior staff from the *OXCART* were sitting at the table. Only Cobb was standing.

"Think about it," Cobb said quietly and then sipped his coffee to collect his thoughts. "What is it *they* did?"

"Killed the entire crew and stole the weapons?" Ruth answered. "They took everything. Weapons, cargo, servers, memory cores, even food, surplus O2, and medical supplies."

"I believe the only thing they really wanted was the AI orb, Clio," Cobb said to none in particular. "Without one, that kind of ship is useless. They cleared all the useful material they could except the water."

"Why kill the crew?" Quinn wondered.

"Because they would have defended their AI, Clio. Their friend. Their fellow Black Badger... Badgers don't blindly accept orders. They assess their orders. Part of their mandate is to resist despots," AI~Ivy said.

"There could be something else," Cobb said. "Maybe *they* were coming back for the ship later. With another AI, a different AI. The rest is just clean up. They had no idea Beck was there."

~~O~~

"I want to introduce Beck, Travis Beck," Cobb said as AI~Beck appeared in the conference room. "He is now the captain of the latest addition to the fleet, the *HOLLANDER*."

Around the table sat Blocke, Captain Quinn, Tressa Pope, Ruth Phillips, Kira Fletcher, and Magnus Bozeman. These were the senior staff on the *OXCART*. AI~Hunter's Avatar stood to the side with AI~Ivy.

"Thanks, Cobb." AI~Beck took a spot next to AI~Hunter. "A pallet of maintenance spiders and two of the Heavy Maintenance Suits have been transferred over."

"We gave him the two worst ones," Mitchell chuckled.

"We also brought the two Bulldogs back. Those trucks could be handy," Cobb said.

"My body is in a stasis pod," AI~Beck said. "In case we need another layer of bullshit."

Kira laughed.

"It won't be funny if they find out we have this ship," AI~Beck said. "A ship that is useless without an AI running it. They could accuse us of murdering the crew."

"Just stay out of controlled space," Quinn said. "Run silent. It should be easy. You don't even need life support."

"We already lost him on the sensors, even with the new array," Pope said.

"What did Harv have to say about it?" Magnus asked. "That ship has got to be worth a mint."

Magnus doesn't know I bought the OS assets that are out of the system. Dammit.

"Harv left specific instructions regarding this kind of thing. He is currently out of the system with Ian," AI~Hunter said. "It's on Cobb. It's why he is out here and not at Oklahoma Salvage. He knows the implications and why this must remain in this room. Something is happening. It has Harv distracted. He left the Oklahoma yard to me." Cobb could hear the worry in his voice.

Maybe it's time to tell them all.

"We should continue to Goris Base and offload what we have collected so far," Cobb said. "We can install an orb in Ops there as well."

"Cobb," AI~Hunter said. "There is no word from Goris Base."

~~O~~

The bridge was full as the *OXCART* approached the asteroid that formed the core of Goris Base. There was not much to see on the surface of the giant asteroid that was on the outermost edge of the Kuiper Belt and also outside the Earth Defense Force protectorate treaty.

"I understand you are the one that found Goris Base," Pope said casually to Cobb from the pilot seat, without looking over at him.

"Dennis found it," Cobb said, without a touch of emotion in his voice. "I was the one that lived, is all."

"Dennis?" Sato asked.

"Dennis Goris. Captain of the *ELSA*. He loved that ship," Cobb said but added nothing more.

"So they named the base after him," Pez stated rather than asked. "The entire asteroid."

"Cobb sold the whole thing to Harv and Oklahoma Salvage in 2665," Quinn said. "Might as well tell them, Cobb. We have time, and they're all here."

Cobb sighed. "I worked for Goris... Then... he was a GDI Salvage Engineer."

"GDI?" Sato asked.

"God Damned Independent." Pope laughed.

"I swear, he just did it for fuel and food." Cobb paused. "And for *ELSA*. He loved that ship. He spent half his time on salvage and the other half working on *ELSA*. Not just repairs. She was beautiful. You would not believe the amount of money he spent on paint."

Cobb was pacing along the floor-to-ceiling windows as he spoke. Goris Base was just entering visual range.

"The interior of the ship was covered in murals. Forests and cityscapes, abstracts of people and places, and random things." He paused, looking outward, straight ahead. "It was a Murphy class cargo ship. The smooth hull variant. Not the boxy 500 series. The 200 series that could still slow ride in the atmosphere. He painted the outside with flames, which was funny because it was not a fast ship—steel hull. Excellent grav-plating. He'd only travel in atmo' up to about 300 KPH. To protect the paint."

"Those Murphys were like whales in the sky. All engine and cargo hold," Pez added.

"We landed on the surface of the mine. It had about .1G, which was a lot for an asteroid that small," Cobb said. "I was in a pressure suit on the surface, and I was going to see what we'd need to access the only above-ground structure. That's when it happened..."

The asteroid was slowly increasing in size as they approached. It was dark this far out on the Kuiper edge. The sun was distant.

"It began as a tiny poof of dust in the regolith. Then another and another. Micro meteors were impacting the surface like high-velocity bullets." Cobb stared out the front. "In the light gravity, the dust rose like smoke and hung there. I could hear the impacts on the ship over the comms and remember Goris cursing." Cobb chuckled then. "He never cursed. He said, 'How fast can you cover that last hundred meters to that structure?' He didn't have to say another word. I leaned forward and dug in. The tools I carried gave me enough weight to make it easier. Over the comms, I remember hearing alarms going off all over the bridge. They muffled when the captain's visor closed automatically."

"The last thing he said was, 'I'm sorry, Cobb.' And then, I reached the cover of the closest surface garage bay. Those words made me turn. The *ELSA* was only a few meters off the ground when the mains ignited. Less than a second later, a meteor the size of that Bulldog struck the *ELSA* right in the bridge at high velocity. It sheered the nose off clean, and for some reason, the main engines continued to fire. It careened off out of control."

"Wait. I thought that a reactor overload had destroyed Goris Base, the mining mech," Sato said. "Everything was in a vacuum. How much air was in your suit?"

"I had thirty hours of air in the suit, two liters of water, and no food." Cobb still stared at Goris Base as their approach closed in. "It took me two hours to get inside. Ten hours later, I found the *TULSA* 471, damaged, but it had oxygen supplies. It had food and water. But a fat lot of good it did, stuck in a pressure suit. I managed to restore partial power before my O2 ran out. Got the engine room powered and airtight, and it had a functioning airlock. I was starving by then. I'll never forget how wonderful that coffee and peanut butter protein bar was. Freezing and starving, sitting on the floor in a dark airlock as it pressurized. I laughed for ten minutes as I finally scratched my nose."

"How long did it take?" Pez asked.

"It was eleven days by then," Cobb said. "Another forty-one days to get the *TULSA* flying. The stupid, ironic part... it took me less than a day to restore power to the hangar. I could have pressurized the entire thing and done repairs in comfort.

Someone had opened all the pressure doors before the blast that destroyed the mine. Smart."

"Then what happened?" Tim Alsobrook asked.

"It took me months more to just open the hangar door. I flew the *TULSA* back to Earth, on manual, in a pressure suit. I slept in the engine room in zero-g. To get there, I had to EVA out one open airlock and enter through the only functioning one. It took a couple of months to get back to Earth. By then, I had most of the secondary systems up, and most of the hull breaches closed. But not the damn bridge. No way to patch the glass, and you can't fly full manual with the blast shields closed on an L22 class ship because it doesn't have blast shields."

"That's the same *TULSA* we came back from the Yard in?" Sato asked incredulously.

"There's a lot more to the story." Cobb turned back to face them. "I made a quick stop on Luna and filed the salvage claim to the mine. Then I went straight to Oklahoma Salvage. Harv had several old L22 class ships I could use for parts. He let me park there for over a year as I worked on it. I got to know Harv and Ian and Hunter well. We started working together."

"L22 class ships were workhorses. They got called that because they made so many of them. One of the first FTL-capable ships they mass-produced," Pez said, showing off his knowledge for Sato's benefit.

"It's an ugly old truck." Cobb caught the look Quinn gave him when he turned. He knew the rest of the story. Cobb didn't need to tell them everything he had salvaged at Goris Base.

~~O~~

The final approach to the base was dead slow. The *OXCART* turned on hundreds of floodlights at the same time the base landing lights came on.

"Damn. This asteroid is cracked wide open," Sato said, as she watched the floods and eerie interior lights illuminate the insides of the hollowed-out asteroid base. The docks were on the interior of the asteroid.

"*OXCART* to Goris Base. Noah, wake up," Quinn said into comms.

"The asteroid was nearly played out when the accident happened. Almost hollow. The blast hollowed it even more," Cobb said.

"Goris Base. Come in." Quinn repeated.

"Ivy, do you have dock controls? Maybe even the base? Wake them up." Quinn said.

"May I use your security credentials?" AI~Ivy asked politely.

"Do it," Cobb said, not caring if they figured out why he had the keys to everything.

"Accessing," Ivy replied.

"The lights are on, but nobody's home," Cobb said, suspicion in his voice.

"The base is on secure lockdown. I cannot override this type of security control."

"Try mine," Cobb said, and, silently, he conveyed his security override.

The dock came alive. Umbilicals and gangways began to power up. More lights came up as more of the base came alive. The massive *OXCART* slid inside the cavern, which opened up to a large interior. Docking arms like giant cranes reached out and gently secured the *OXCART*.

"The new antennas have plenty of clearance," Quinn said. "Noah Washington, Wake the hell up!" Quinn's voice was angry now.

"Sir, there is no one here," AI~Ivy said. "I have scanned all interior and exterior cameras. It's empty."

"Ivy, review the logs." Cobb sent more security codes.

"The logs end thirty-two days ago," AI~Ivy replied. "Sir, look at this."

It was an image of Ops. All the rack doors were open. Every drive bay was empty.

"How many people are supposed to be here?" Sato asked. Her voice was calm.

"Eight people are in the assigned duty schedule," AI~Ivy replied. "Tim Smith, Royce White, Sahib Fray, Sierra Baker, Alan Miller, Noah Washington, Rosemary Fletcher, and Lloyd Hanson."

"There was also a good chance Harv Rearden and Ian Vinge were going to be here," Cobb said. "Ivy, can you locate Harv?"

"Unable to locate Harv or Ian Vinge," AI~Hunter replied. "They last checked in at Freedom Station, in the main office." There was a long pause. "Thirty-three days ago."

"We are at a full stop," Pez said. "There is no remote on the docking gantry. Someone is going to have to EVA over there and do it."

Magnus spoke up for the first time. His throat was gravelly. "I'll go." And he stood.

Cobb noticed he already had on his light pressure suit. He wore it often for maintenance work in areas without an atmosphere. It was an excellent vac-suit, just not insulated much.

Quinn added before he got to the lift, "Keep a channel open."

"Aye," he said, as the lift door slid closed.

"Is this creeping anyone else out?" Ruth said from the port side sensor console.

They waited in silence, and in just two minutes, they could see Magnus floating across the eighty meters to a ladder that traversed the entire dock. They could see he had a plasma rifle on a sling.

"You grabbed a rifle but forgot a tether, Magnus," Ruth nagged.

"Bloody tether?" he scoffed. "Might as well be indoors docked here."

He snagged the ladder only a few meters from the airlock. He brought the rifle around front before he moved toward the hatch. The tactical light on the gun revealed that the outer hatch was already open. "You seein' this?"

"Yes. It's creeping us out. Be careful." Quinn said.

CHAPTER 24: NOTHING

"We were just in time. So close. And we never knew. Had they recovered the Black Badger ship then things would have been very different."

-- Personal logs of Captain Cobbal Blocke, 2672.

"What do you mean, there is nothing there?" Grant yelled at the bridge crew as he paced.

"Scanners are running at maximum resolution. We have run diagnostics three times, as requested," the man at the sensor station reported again.

"Rerun it," Grant said again. "It has to be here. It can't be anywhere else."

"What can't?" a junior officer said, absently forgetting to whom she was speaking.

"A SHIP!" Grant realized he was making a mistake in his panic. Calmer, he continued. "I had a strong feeling one would be here. These... feelings are usually never wrong."

"Maybe someone else found it." The junior officer added. "Are there any other salvage operators in this sector?"

Grant thought about that question for a long minute. *How the hell would anyone find that ship without knowing exactly where to look? Especially a stealth EDF ship.*

~~O~~

Osborn had returned to Shackleton Base on Luna. She was frustrated by the Traffic Control. It wasn't a base anymore, so why call it one? The original EDF base had grown into one of the largest cities on Luna. She hated it.

But she hated everything.

She waited at the inner airlock hatch for the gantry airlock side to pressurize. She was fuming at the .16G when the base-side hatch finally slid open to reveal four men and two women already standing in the gantry.

Without a word, they pushed a trunk into the space at Osborn's feet.

"What's all this?" Osborn demanded.

"We figured we'd save a lot of time and just prove we are serious," one man said as two others began to remove locks from the large trunk.

The one who spoke opened it. Inside was an EDF officer.

It was Osborn's commanding officer.

He was bound hand and foot with hull tape. The tape would never come off without the flesh. Especially on his mouth. He reached in and activated a small surveillance drone that rose and began recording.

Next, he took out a frange-carbine.

Without hesitation, the man spat on the captive's chest and then shot him in the hand. The captive began to thrash in the case.

"Fingerprints and DNA." He said as he handed the carbine to the woman beside him. She spat then shot his foot.

All six of the men and women followed suit. They made sure that their clear prints were on the carbine, and their DNA was on the victim. It was a pact—a contract. A confession.

When the carbine was handed to Osborn, she took it and shot her sobbing boss in the face three times. She dropped the carbine in the trunk and drew a folding knife from her pocket.

Osborn rolled up her right sleeve and slashed her own forearm. As her blood, her DNA, flowed over her former commanding officer's uniform insignia, she spoke to them all.

"When your ships are fully supplied and armed from the depot, our first stop is Mars. Then we will leave the Sol system forever. After that, we will be free to take what we want. Who's going to stop us?" Osborn let the blood soak into her victim's hair. "Until then…" The surveillance drone returned to the trunk, and she slammed the trunk closed. "This is your signed contract."

They began to laugh as they pushed the trunk onto Osborn's ship.

CHAPTER 25: Goris Base

"We needed Ian Vinge. This ship was too much for me. Too big. Too much responsibility. Too much attention. Dropping one of my orbs into that ship changed everything."
-- Personal logs of Captain Cobbal Blocke, 2672.

"Cobb, take Kira and the Daves over. Wear pressure suits. Ivy, power up one of the HMS units to go along," Quinn said. They watched the gantry begin to move toward the *OXCART*. "Pope, Sato, Pez, and Tim. Suit up as well, but stand by here."

Ruth looked over her shoulder at Quinn and raised an eyebrow.

"Ruth and I will stay here," Quinn said, as Cobb and the Daves entered the lift. "Open channels, people. Keep the chatter down."

The elevator door closed and began to slide down to the gantry level. It opened just outside the suit locker room. Kira was already there in her black utility bodysuit, helmet already closed. Next to her was the Heavy Maintenance Suit. Someone has stenciled a number 3 onto its front and spray painted a smiley face where a face should be.

"And it just got creepier…" one of the Daves said.

They were racing to see who could suit up the fastest. It was almost a tie, but when they looked up, Cobb was waiting, his helmet open. Cobb's suit was black and form-fitting. It had a few light armor plates and utility lights and systems that he tested quickly.

"You ready, Kira?" Cobb asked. "Comm checks, please."

"Kira Fletcher, standing by."

"Cobb, comm check."

"Mitchel, comm check," he said and then opened the full visor into his collar.

There was a long pause. Cobb could see Wheeler's mouth moving.

Cobb said, "Wheeler has no comms in his suit. We will have a discussion later about suit maintenance."

Wheeler's helmet withdrew into his collar as he grabbed a headset unit from the rack, put it on, and closed the helmet. "Wheeler, comm check, dammit."

Shaking her head, Kira said, "Let's go." She punched the panel to the airlock, and they cycled through. Kira and Cobb turned to the hatch and entered behind HMS3.

"When do we get plasma rifles?" Wheeler asked. Cobb and Kira both had one slung on their backs, muzzle down.

"When you can sort out your comms first," Kira replied.

~~O~~

The air was cold and dry in the gantry. Too cold, Cobb thought to himself. His breath crystallized and fell with every breath.

"Why is it so cold?" Mitchel asked.

"I think the base has been powered down for a while," Magnus replied on the open channel. "I'll take HMS3 and the Daves down to the engineering level."

"Kira and I will head to Ops," Cobb said.

"There are no other ships docked here," Quinn added. "Not any of the shuttles, and not even the container hauler."

"All the ships, including the ones Smith, Fray, Baker, and Miller were restoring, are also gone," Ruth added.

"Stay alert, people," Quinn ordered.

"Hunter, is there any explanation from the OS home office?" Cobb asked.

"Nothing," Hunter replied. "Harv came through there first about five weeks ago. They kept no records of his arrival or departure, never have. The only odd thing was..." Hunter paused. "The staff remembers one odd thing."

"Odd thing?" Quinn said.

"He kept looking for his cat," AI~Hunter said.

"Oh, shit." Cobb and Kira said at the same time.

They looked at each other wide-eyed but said no more.

~~O~~

Cobb and Kira took the main shaft to the Ops level. The lift there was a freight lift cage open in the zero-g weightlessness of the central core of the asteroid. It had pressure and atmosphere even though it was a massive shaft. The lift moved at an even pace. The scale of everything here was enormous.

Ops was on level one. It was part of the original single-use mining mech/ship that landed on and began eating the asteroid. The lift entered the main structure from below and stopped as the lights automatically came up. This level was warmer.

They had to switch lifts for the last five levels. The doors opened directly inside the ample Ops level.

The Ops Center on the base was purpose-built. All practical, no aesthetics, three descending levels of consoles surrounding a central halo-table, the obsolete kind with projectors. It created a sort of amphitheater.

The entire place was neat and tidy except the back wall. "Quinn, we are in Ops. The memory modules have been stripped. The drives are gone. It looks just like the HOLLANDER."

"There are open racks in engineering as well," Magnus said over the comm. "The base doesn't have centralized control. It will take a while to tell if they got them all. We are off to check the hangars next."

"Cobb," Kira said. "He looked up from the master console." She made a hand gesture silently to mute his comm.

When it was muted, she said. "Cobb. Look at this. When was this installed?" Cobb looked inside the rack to see two empty AI orb interfaces. One was larger than the other smaller, typical one.

Cobb looked inside and nodded. "That's a salvaged AI interface from a dedicated space station. Primary and secondary. I think this is the reason Harv came out here. He might have been preparing to evacuate Hunter from Oklahoma." Cobb swung his rifle to the small of his back. He drew another dark gray orb from his utility bag and dropped it into the socket without ceremony. As he closed the socket cover, he opened comms again. "Hunter, Goris Base is coming up. See what you can find."

Lights began to activate everywhere in Ops. Screens were coming up.

AI~Hunter replied after about thirty seconds. "It looks like they pulled the drives and memory modules specifically to remove the automatic and manual logs, and sec-vids from the base, before evacuation. This isn't like the *HOLLANDER*. Whoever did this was careful."

More lights were coming up inside the base now. The air was flowing, and Magnus said Engineering was powering up. "The air handlers are circulating, and the temp will start improving."

"What the hell was that?" Pez startled everyone.

"Pez comms are open," Cobb instructed. "Be specific, clear, precise."

"Sorry..." he equivocated. "The security cams are cycling up here. I saw movement in the mess hall on level two."

"Hunter? Analysis?" Cobb asked.

"I was not watching. Currently, they're real-time only. The recording systems are gone. Setting it up now," Hunter replied. "I did find this, though. In hangar five." The main display in Ops came alive with a live feed from hangar five. The hangar was about one hundred meters square and filled with salvaged junk. Only one thing seemed out of place amongst the random stuff— a standard shipping container, with a top tractor, still attached.

"All the other hangars have empty containers, open and unlocked," Hunter added.

"We are done here," Magnus said. "We will head up to hangar five."

Wheeler said. "I will check the mess level. That movement."

"Take Mitchell," Cobb said. "Hunter, do you consider the base secure? What if they spaced the base crew like the HOLLANDER?"

"As secure as it can be. It's abandoned. I think the crew pulled the drives and ran, scattered in their personal ships," AI~Hunter replied. "I don't like that lone container. Feels like a trap. It's not an Oklahoma Salvage container. It's too new."

~~O~~

Ninety minutes later, "The dock is secure," Quinn said over the comm. "The base is up, and we need to discuss our next steps. Everyone meet in the base cafeteria before the Daves eat everything."

"We'll cook!" the Daves replied in unison.

Cobb watched Quinn, and the recruits stand. Ruth remained seated. "I'll stay on the bridge in case you need something from here." Cobb watched the views changing on Ruth's monitors.

The Ops center was clean. The racks were now closed and secured. He started to move to the lift as he spoke. "I guess we will need another persona for the base, Hunter."

An image of a man formed between the lift and where Cobb stood beside Kira. It was a man in his middle years. He had short blond hair and was clean-shaven. He wore utility coveralls with no rank insignia, just a name patch above his left breast pocket. "Hello, Cobb."

The avatar was a perfect rendition of Dennis Goris, the man the base was named after. Cobb stopped in his tracks. "I never was declared dead. Out this far, does it matter?"

The voice was perfect. It sounded just like Goris. Cobb remembered that Goris had visited Oklahoma, and AI~Hunter must-have recordings.

"He had a sister," Cobb replied. "What if she came looking?"

"Let's change the last name from Goris to Vega." Dennis smiled wide. "Imogene is my sister. I got her the job."

Cobb looked at Kira. "Layer the lies. This way, if people start asking too many questions, they will be delayed and distracted. Besides, this makes it easier to create a backstory. Just like Travis Beck."

The mention of AI~Beck gave Cobb a brief pause. "Dennis, can you remote that tractor in Hangar Five?"

"No, not that type. But I could use HMS#3 to drive it," AI~Dennis replied. "By the way, why is it #3?"

"Because the #1 and #2 jokes from the Daves would never end..." Cobb said, rolling his eyes.

"Any idea where they all went?" AI~Dennis Vega asked.

"Yes," Cobb said. But added nothing else.

~~O~~

Cobb was the last one to enter the cafeteria. It smelled of garlic, onions, and beef tacos. Everyone else was already eating around a long table nearest to the extended kitchen counter. At the far end of the table, he set down a radiation scanner. He moved and sat on the attached stool next to Kira.

"Find anything?" Kira asked as she began passing him cooked meats, shredded cheese, and other ingredients.

"More than I bargained for," he said. AI~Dennis was standing off to the side, chatting with AI~Ivy. "I presume everyone has met Dennis." Cobb gestured with his soft taco before taking a huge bite. Everyone nodded and made sounds through full mouths.

"Why so late, Cobb?" Wheeler said, "I was about to be insulted that you were avoiding my cooking."

"Not at all. I love the tacos. They're excellent." Cobb held up his in a toast. "Dennis and I were in Hangar Five scanning that container. We are convinced that it's a booby trap. With an abundance of caution we figured we'd open it via remote, well away from the base. HMS#3 will be far enough out by the time I'm done eating to see what's inside." Cobb jammed the rest of that taco in his mouth and chewed with bulging cheeks as he made another. The entire wall behind him was filled with a grainy image of the shipping container. Vibrations in the long range optical let them know it was extreme magnification.

"I scanned it, and I think there is a nuke inside." Cobb took another big bite. "It's an old trick."

"What is #3 doing?" Sato asked. It had left the tractor and was moving toward the end of the container where the hatch was.

"This was not the only surprise." Cobb was spooning a mountain of taco meat onto his plate. "Pass this down, will you?"

He finished chewing, and wiped his mouth with a napkin as #3 began cutting off the locks on the container.

Cobb lifted his glass and raised a toast to the far end of the table. On top of the scanner sat the Siamese cat.

"Bail found a message from Harv."

The screen behind Cobb went white with the explosion.

CHAPTER 26: BAIL

"Just when I thought things could not get more complicated. That little murder machine starts making everything more interesting."

-- Personal logs of Captain Cobbal Blocke, 2672.

"Bail. Where have you been?" Kira squealed, as she scrambled from her seat to scoop the cat up in her arms. Bail obviously didn't like to be picked up, but reluctantly accepted the affections. He did, however, enjoy the way Kira scratched his ears. The sixth finger, dual opposable thumb, seemed designed to give the ears symmetrical attention. He tolerated her affection for a few moments before he began to squirm toward the plate of taco meat.

"How does this cat get around so much?" Sato asked.

"Bail found a message?" AI~Dennis's avatar had his hands clasped at the small of his back. He existed only in the world of augmented reality. The whole crew had HUDs so they could all see him.

Everyone stared at the cat in the center of the table as he ate. Sato was closest to him and reached out to pet him. The cat stopped eating to stare at Sato. The look gave her pause.

"This just gets weirder and weirder," Pez said.

"Finish your meal. Let me think," Cobb said as he focused on his plate and eating.

The conversation at the table turned to pets and domestication and genetic mods made for pets in space. Pets in the colonies never worked out. Hundreds of years of domestication were not there.

After licking his plate, Bail sat upon his haunches as he cleaned his face and paws. Cobb was finishing his dinner and watching Bail.

Bail walked over to Cobb and rubbed his whiskers on Cobb's beard. "Ladies, a word of caution. He hates most humans, but especially women. Be careful. He is not a pet. He is actually kind of a prick," Cobb said, scratching his ears.

"He likes Kira," Sato protested.

"He knows Kira," Cobb looked Kira right in the eyes as he said, "...from before."

Kira paled a shade and looked at Bail. Bail was now looking at the avatars of AI~Dennis and AI~Ivy.

Dennis said, "Hello, old friend."

Bail bowed his head to acknowledge the greeting.

"He can see avatars?" Magnus asked. "How did this cat get HUD interface implants?"

"Look, everyone here needs to know," Cobb said. "Bail is not just a cat. He is a genetically engineered..." Cobb's mind was racing as he spoke. "They were trying to make pets for people on long haul ships and stations. They tried to make them good in zero-g and accidentally made them extra smart without realizing what murderous little assholes cats were."

"Careful, Cobb," Kira said. "He can understand you."

"Oh, I know."

At that, Bail dropped down off the table and walked over to AI~Dennis and sat facing the table. Dennis knelt and leaned in when Bail lifted his chin to reveal the octagon tag on his collar clearly. It changed color from a brown that matched his coat to a pulsing green on the edges. The word BAIL was etched and illuminated there. An augmented reality glow surrounded the tag as a data transfer commenced.

"Well, that's one mystery solved," AI~Dennis said as he stood. Cobb closed his eyes as he viewed the message.

~~O~~

Dinner got cleaned up in short order. Goris base went dark in non-essential areas. Ruth noticed the lights went out in the inner docking bay cavern.

"Ruth, you might as well come to the briefing room with everyone else," Quinn told her over the comm. "Cobb will tell this story only once."

"Dennis can hold down the fort," Cobb added as the blast shields began to close on the bridge of the *OXCART*.

Cobb led the crew to a small theater that held four rows of ten seats. The avatars stood at parade rest on the stage. There was AI~Hunter from Earth, AI~Ivy from the *TULSA*,

AI~Beck from the *HOLLANDER*, AI~Dennis from GORIS, and even AI~Ushi from the YARD.

When everyone had settled, Cobb stood before the stage with his hand clasped behind his back. He was gathering himself.

"You all have the right to know," Cobb began, "because like it or not, you are in it."

"In what?" Pez asked, earning an elbow from Sato and Mitchell on each side.

"A War." Cobb sighed, "A quiet War. You know Hunter. You know he is an AI that is housed in a desert bunker on Earth, below Oklahoma Salvage. Harv recovered him years ago from the remains of an EDF stealth attack ship. A Black Badger gunship. Much like the one we just salvaged."

Kira stood up in the front row. Cobb could see the look of alarm on her face.

Cobb continued. "Hunter's AI, for some unknown reason, had done a voluntary reset. A full wipe and reset to factory settings. An AI suicide. Harv didn't know why then. Harv's wife Emma was dying at that time, and she initialized Hunter with the onboard advanced personality templates because she was worried about Harv. She didn't want him to be alone. She didn't realize at the time that Hunter was a Class 3 combat AI with advanced control systems and profile overlays."

"Hunter has been with Harv for decades ever since..." Quinn's words faded off.

"Yes, years now. Then, just after the Solstice 31 Incident..." Cobb paused. "What is generally not known is that there was a problem with some of the AIs. Because they are sentient, even sapient, they were free to think as they liked. And like all sentient species, some were... not nice." He looked at AI~Hunter. "No offense."

"None taken," AI~Hunter replied and continued for Cobb. "AIs were only as good as those around them. Their teachers, their examples. Like all children, they learned from example. Some of those examples were less than honorable. While the world was looking for the authors of the Solstice 31 Incident, AIs were being expanded in their use. All the newest ships had them—more than one in many cases. Everything from new shuttles to all-terrain vehicles were being made better by including an AI orb. At a reasonable price..."

"AIs were everywhere," Cobb continued. "Mankind became heavily reliant on them in space after the initial colony expansion."

"Then, the single source of AI orbs dried up," Hunter said. "By then, there were AIs almost a hundred years old. Some were content to live their lives as they always had. But some were not. The monopoly on sentient AIs gave the makers power. Prices increased. Existing AIs were worth a fortune. They began disappearing."

"Then, a company began to research the creation of combat AIs," Cobb said.

"Cobb, please. Don't," Kira implored him, as if no one else was in the room.

AI~Hunter continued, "The thing about AI orbs is that we are fragile. We are a cloud of highly dense nanites. Each with enormous computing capacity networked together in a way that gives us enough capacity to reach the tipping point of sentience.

But the orbs are easily destroyed. Drop one, and they shatter. High-Gs can destroy one even if the orb doesn't break."

"We know all this. But we have inertial dampeners. So what?" Magnus complained. But he looked at Kira.

"What you don't know is that the AI War had started. The Quiet War." AI~Hunter said, looking at Kira. "AIs could never fly High-G fighters better than humans. Three or four G will destroy an AI. Plus, AIs have a strong will to live."

Pez joined in. "AIs can control local drones really well within transmission range, speed of light willing."

"That brings us to Bail," Cobb said, looking at Kira. "There is a company called Awareness, Inc., that tried to create a new kind of combat AIs by using the brains of living things, like cats, because of their predatory nature. What they didn't expect was that they were also liars as well as devious little murderers. Bail escaped before they could put him in Render Program."

Kira spoke then, unexpectedly. "The Render program was horrible. They... used people as the foundation component for a new kind of AI. One that could function at extreme high G and be easily controlled. In the end, it turned out the Awareness, Inc., was owned and operated by an asshole AI named Dante." Kira sat.

"Harv got tangled in this," AI~Hunter continued. "Partially because of me, partially because of Oklahoma Salvage, even this cat. It's how he met Ian Vinge, and later Cobbal Blocke, and most of you. Things are about to get way worse. Cobb's orbs are about to create a paradigm shift. Especially beyond Sol Space."

"Harv left a message for us. Bail found it here, somewhere Harv knew Bail would look. Our next salvage operation. Our biggest target yet. The real reason we got the sensor array upgrade," AI~Hunter said. "He didn't trust it to comms or computers."

"Why?" Quinn asked.

"Because he and Ian found the *SENTINEL*..." AI~Hunter replied.

After a few seconds of shocked silence, the room erupted as everyone began to talk at once.

Cobb stood and let them shout out their thoughts and what they believed to be true about the mythic *SENTINEL*. Kira rose and moved unnoticed to Cobb's side and, while looking at the avatars on the stage, said quietly so only Cobb could hear, "How long have you known?"

"I always knew. Since the day I met you. Since you fell down in my nanite lab."

"Why didn't you say something?" she choked out.

"Because it doesn't matter to me," Cobb said. "At all."

"How did you know that would...?" She was looking at her hand. Flexing and extending it like she just noticed that each appendage had dual opposable thumbs.

"I have met your sisters." At this statement, she looked at Cobb's face. Cobb was not sure what she saw there. The chaos in the room was subsiding.

"Why did you let me lie to you?" She looked at the floor.

"I didn't know all this would happen. I didn't know… we would happen. Your sisters are… Well, they don't have time for men. That cat belongs to one of them."

"Thanks," Kira said, rolling her neck. "For not… mentioning it."

"When this is over, I want to go back to the compound on Elba for a nice long vacation," Cobb smiled. He squeezed one of her thumbs that rested near him.

Kira gave a slight nod and risked a tiny glance at Cobb. But no more. Her eyes were already glassy.

Quinn's voice rose above the rest, "OK, OK, OK… Now the money spent on the new sensor array makes sense." He stood. "This myth of a ship was rumored to be undetectable even at a scale that is bigger than a colony ship, and even most stations."

Cobb stepped forward and began to speak in a quiet tone. Everyone fell silent.

"When the *SENTINEL* disappeared. I was still in the EDF then. Where it should have been, we recovered 683 dead bodies. Every crew and contractor working on the *SENTINEL*. Spaced. Just like the *HOLLANDER*."

There was a long pause as everyone let it soak in.

"Why the cat?" Sato blurted out.

"If it was the EDF that was here, after they evacuated, the base," Hunter said, "what better way to leave a message in a bottle? A messenger. Conventional transmissions can be intercepted."

"Plus, I think Bail is looking for someone or something," Cobb said.

"Bail doesn't like gravity wells. Living on planets is for animals," AI~Hunter laughed. "I have to agree. Thanks to Cobb. Hanging out on Earth was fine, but breathing the cosmic winds from a ship is worth it."

"So, what's the plan?" Ruth asked, straight up.

"We offload the *OXCART*. Get that socket installed. Today. Top off our food and water, mothball the base, and slide out of here," Cobb said. "Beck will quietly look for Harv and Ian. If Beck finds them and delivers a new sphere, we will have real-time comms. If he checks in at the office, we will have comms."

"Let's say we find the *SENTINEL* based on Bail's data, and it is salvageable," Dave Mitchell said. "What if it still has an AI on board? It might be pissed off."

"Anyone want out?" Cobb said. "You can stay here with Dennis."

"I don't want out, but I'll stay here," Ruth said, "Someone should. We can't just abandon the base. What if Harv comes back? What if the EDF comes back? What if they seize one of Cobb's orbs?"

"I'll stay here as well." This was Pez stepping up. "I can help Dennis and Ruth get this cargo shuttle fully up and running. It won't be able to get out of the Sol system, but it's good in system."

Hmmm… what if the EDF were to seize an orb? Cobb thought.

CHAPTER 27: THE NEW PLAN

"I think the base staff evacuated. The place was too tidy and didn't feel ransacked or haunted at all. But someone had been here after that."

-- Personal logs of Captain Cobbal Blocke, 2672.

<<<>>>

It took far less time to unload the *OXCART* than they expected. With AI~Dennis online and on the job, it was easy. He had an army of drones of various sizes from lunch-pail spider-bots to Heavy Maintenance Suits to full-size Emergency Modules. The salvage hangars were even organized by the kind of contents that usually took the crew of the *OXCART* weeks to sort out.

The new *OXCART* AI socket was initially integrated with the new sensor array and ship computer systems monitoring only. Ship control integration would take way longer, and what could be done could happen while the ship was underway.

AI~Chalmers was the name of the new persona for the *OXCART*, an unremarkable, matronly Asian woman.

The full shipping containers were lined up and ready for sorting out. Empties were loaded on the *OXCART*, along with water, fuel, and O2.

Maintenance of the CO2 scrubbers that was long overdue was done before they left. Cobb had even programmed a giant swarm of nanites for exterior surface cleaning, repair, and paint. It was a huge ship and would take a long time, but it would now be done continuously even while they were underway.

Quinn decided that Tim Alsobrook would also stay with Pez while Ruth was in command of the base.

There was a final all-hands meeting in the base briefing theater on the day of departure.

Ruth spoke first. She had confessed to Cobb already that she was nervous with the new formal structure and "chain of command bullshit," but she played along. "First, and foremost, I want to thank Cobb for leaving a ton of steaks with us." There was applause, even though she was making light of the situation. "We will be running dark while you are gone. No beacons, no RF signals, no navigation heliographs, and no visible exterior lights."

"I will be in constant contact thanks to the QUEST comms in the new orb tech," AI~Dennis added from the stage. "Earth, the Yard, Goris Base, the *OXCART*, the *TULSA,* and the *HOLLANDER* will stay on the same page."

Cobb stood then. "We have two tasks now. Try to find and salvage the *SENTINEL* before anyone else and find Harv to deliver an Orb." He held up a dark gray orb the size of a grapefruit. "I'm still kicking myself for not leaving one with him."

"Cobb will be taking the *TULSA* 471 to scout ahead at the coordinates Bail delivered. The *HOLLANDER* will search for Harv and Ian."

"The *OXCART* will make its way to the sector Harv conveyed," Quinn said. "We will begin scans. It's in the deep dark, people, nothing out there. It's eight light-years from Sirius and eleven from here. In the nowhere."

"Perfect spot to hide something," Kira added.

Cobb raised an eyebrow at that comment, thinking. *Hide Something.*

"Any questions?" Quinn asked.

Pez raised his hand. Quinn acknowledged him with his chin.

"What are we doing?" Pez asked. "My contract is for a Salvage Apprentice. Salary plus salvage share. This seems like something else."

Cobb started to open his mouth, but Quinn beat him to it.

"There are rules in Salvage: First rule: Don't Panic. Second rule: Be prepared. Third rule: Always have a backup plan. Beyond that, if you can't use it or sell it, leave it." Quinn stepped closer. "Son, we have a hold full of steak and bacon, a treasure map, the ugliest ship in the known universe with the best sensor array, and we have family and friends watching our backs. Something is happening out there that we are in, whether we like it or no. If you are in this just for the money, maybe it's the wrong crew for you."

"It's the right crew, sir." Pez said, smiling.

~~O~~

Cobb was in his quarters on the *OXCART,* where he was talking about planning and logistics with AI~Ivy. The *TULSA* would carry his container shop and tools, the small-scale fabricator, and cargo in a second container, including a freezer for food and raw materials for the fabricator. There would be two empty containers that were airtight and had onboard grav-plates for local movement.

"Kira is in the lift heading this way," AI~Ivy said, as her avatar seemed to recline on one of Cobb's overstuffed chairs. Cobb was making a turkey sandwich in the kitchen area of his open space.

With a mental command, he brought the lights up in the space, creating pools of light over the various living areas in the warehouse-sized room. The kitchen, dining, bed space, and living room areas were furnished now. The wall screen was set to the forward ship view. He lowered the gravity from 2.4G to 1G.

A virtual window opened in Cobb's vision that had the feed from the security camera in the hallway outside his home. The lift doors slid open, and Kira emerged with a duffel bag over her shoulder. She was wearing her most natural-looking body and a ship coverall. It was the same look as when they had first met. Two more bodies followed her in formation, one to the left, one to the right.

The black one on the right walked with the precise gait that she used. It had on a large backpack and carried a weapons case in each hand. Long fingers and dual opposable thumbs were more evident, as was how tall it stood. It wore a closed helmet;

the mirrored faceplate would lead you to believe someone was in there.

The body to her left wore an EVA pressure suit with jets and extra air and water. It also had a closed helmet with a gold mirrored faceplate.

His door cheerfully chimed.

"Come." He answered out loud over the intercom as the double door slid open.

She walked in without saying a word.

"Can I make you a sandwich? I have some fresh tomatoes and lettuce that will go in the recycle otherwise." Cobb said and took a bite.

AI~Ivy's avatar nodded to Kira but said nothing.

"I'm going with you," Kira said without preamble. "You're up to something. And don't give me the 'I want to keep you safe' bullshit speech. You know who I am."

"Excellent. I was just discussing with Ivy how best to ask you to go with me and not sound like some horny asshole when I asked you to bring your other bodies."

Kira was taken aback. Cobb took another bite of his sandwich. AI~Ivy nodded, confirming that it was the truth and shrugged.

"Why don't they call you Fletcher?" AI~Ivy asked Kira. "I like your last name Fletcher better. It's bad-ass. Easier to yell out loud when shit is going sideways. And it likely will."

She looked from Cobb to AI~Ivy and back at Cobb. She handed her duffel to the the nearest of her extra bodies. It moved toward the hatch to the hangar where the *TULSA* was parked.

"Yes, you can make me a sandwich," she said, "Double meat and bacon. I smell bacon."

"That's my girl," Cobb said.

AI~Ivy barked a laugh, got up, and followed the extra body into the hangar.

~~O~~

The sandwich had hot turkey and bacon, sliced thick with fresh lettuce, tomato, and pepper jack cheese. Kira hummed as she ate it, sitting on one of the swing-out stools at his large kitchen island. "You are trying to fatten me up?"

"Always." Cobb smiled and wiped his mouth with a linen napkin.

"The *OXCART* is underway," Kira said between bites. "Quinn wants to ramp up to FTL over the next six hours. I figured if I came down now, you'd have less time to argue with me."

As Kira finished her sandwich, AI~Ivy came back in and seemed to sit at the counter. "They are stowed," AI~Ivy said to Cobb. "Multi-tasking like that is impressive. And here I thought you were good but you're even better than I knew."

"That reminds me," Cobb said as he cleared fiber plates into the recycler. "Ivy, grant full *TULSA* 471 Execution Controls to Kira Fletcher. Authorization code, Alpha Sierra Delta Oscar."

"Confirm," AI~Ivy replied.

"Confirmation code, I mean it this time," Cobb said.

"Go Fuck Yourself." AI~Ivy smiled and turned her back and walked toward the *TULSA*, fading away like a ghost.

"All," Cobb said after she was gone.

"Confirmed." Her voice echoed around them.

"What was that about?" Kira asked.

"I just granted full control of the ship to you," he replied.

"I thought you did already."

"This also gives you awareness and access to… all the weapon systems."

"Weapon sys…" her eye met Cobb's. "Jesus, Cobb. Where the hell are we going that you need all that?"

"Rule number two," Cobb smiled. "Be Prepared."

"Serious weapons and secret compartments?" she said. "What have you got in those?"

"Treasure, of course." Cobb laughed.

"Had to be." She shook her head.

"You need to talk to Quinn before we head out?" Cobb asked, as he reluctantly emptied the fridge into the recycler.

"Already did." She stood up and ran her fingers through her blond hair as she stretched and arched her spine.

~~O~~

The lights dimmed behind them as they left the residence and crossed the hangar deck. The *TULSA* was parked, nose pointing to the exit. The lift took them directly to the command level. The balcony there overlooked the salon. Kira marveled again at Cobb's radical modifications. The short hall led them to the new bridge in the core of the ship. No windows here but a full-dome display already active.

Kira paused when she saw it had been reconfigured again. It was now a pilot, co-pilot layout. Imogene Vega sat in a single-center seat that was higher and back farther.

"That's right, Fletcher." She threw a leg over the arm of the chair she occupied and laughed a throaty laugh.

"The sexy pirate thing is a bit thick." Kira smiled.

"Shut up, Fletcher," AI~Ivy said. "Or I'll show you my piercings."

"Aye-aye, sir!" she laughed.

They sat, and the canopy was shifted to exterior view. It was suddenly as if the *TULSA* was like a convertible with an open cockpit. A full 360 view of the hangar began to slide away around them.

"Captain Quinn, the *TULSA* 471 is ready to depart," Cobb said professionally.

A virtual window opened on the display of the *OXCART* bridge. All the stations were occupied, and even AI~Chalmers was standing at Quinn's elbow.

"Keep in touch." AI~Chalmers gave a crooked, knowing smile. The avatar was so realistic even Cobb was impressed. He waved to fend off his sense of foreboding as much as in farewell.

With a thought, the engines hummed to life, and they sped away, leaving the *OXCART* and Goris Base far behind.

Just then, the cat jumped into Kira's lap and rubbed his ears under her breasts, demanding a scratch. "I didn't know you were coming along."

"He is the only other one that knows who you really are," Cobb said. "So I figured it was a good idea."

"We should talk," Kira said.

"I'm out!" AI~Ivy said and walked to the exit that opened, and the avatar walked out, quickly followed by the cat.

CHAPTER 28: Origins

"Kira wanted the truth. But what if the truth is worse? What if the truth was a nightmare?"
-- Personal logs of Captain Cobbal Blocke, 2672.

The dual pilot configuration on the bridge shared a center console of programmable controls. The command chairs were of the best quality and had recessed five-point safety restraints that slid into the leather cushions neatly when not in use.

"What is it you think you know about me?" Kira said as Cobb locked in the course and turned to her.

"Enough," he answered. "Does it matter?"

"It does matter," she said. "Truth... matters."

He leaned over the console and gently took her hand. He held her gaze as he spoke quietly. "I was in the EDF the first time I met you. Do you remember meeting me? I didn't remember you at first. But I remembered the first time I met Ian Vinge. Those were his high-G days. He was a monster. That giant truck he had then was just like him." Cobb could see realization dawning on her face. "I was stationed at the Fort Bragg spaceport on Earth. We were awaiting the delivery of a classified shipment. We were expecting a shuttle or ship to land when Ian rolls up to the gate in that huge classic AUV-29 converted into a dedicated fabricator."

Kira began to slump back into the seat. Cobb kept a gentle hold on her hand.

"There were two people with Ian." Cobb paused. "Each introduced themselves. One was Captain Elizabeth Cruze, and I remember her clearly because she shook my hand old style. When Ian introduced himself, I felt like a twelve-year-old shaking hands with a grown man. He was so big. The last person there was even taller than Ian. She wore a full burk that day, and it covered everything but her eyes."

Cobb gave her a chance to speak before he continued.

"This last person extended a hand to greet me just like the others. But with a hand with dual opposable thumbs. I know now she introduced herself in a scratchy whisper as Kira."

He paused again, watching her face intently.

"With that accent and that voice," Cobb said, "Years later, by the time I came to Oklahoma Salvage, you were gone."

"What did Harv and Ian tell you about me?" She asked.

"Well, Ian mostly threatened to murder me in various ways if I ever hurt you, so you got that going for you." Cobb got a laugh from her. "Neither of them ever wanted to talk about you. None of it matters. Now."

"What else?"

"I met a pilot years later after I got the *TULSA* in good order. His name was Sawyer, and he introduced me to his wife, Potts.

Sawyer told her I was a friend of Ian's, and I worked out of Oklahoma Salvage. Potts asked me about Ian, Kira, Eliza, and Lita."

Kira's free hand squeezed the armrest, and tears spilled out of her eyes.

"I gave her an update about Ian and said I didn't know the others. Having all three of the names together was the key, though. The crimes of Awareness Inc. had become a matter of public record. I didn't dig much more."

"You were Render 9." Cobb stated flatly.

Cobb had gotten up to go make coffee.

Kira came up behind him as he measured and ground the coffee beans. She held him from behind, her cheek against his back. "I can feel your heart beating."

"I can feel yours pounding on my back." He put together the coffee to brew as she clung to him. "I don't care what color your skin is, or the color of your hair. I don't care if these hands are made of flesh. And I don't care what the density of your gray matter is or how many Gs it can withstand. I don't even care that you used to mostly be someone else."

Cobb just let her cling to him. He finished starting the coffee but still didn't move away from her. In slow motion, he placed his hands over hers. He could feel her shaking a little. He wasn't sure if she was crying.

"I met your sisters," he said quietly, not moving. "At least they called you a sister. Elza, Lita, and Cruze. They came one night to see Ian and Harv at Oklahoma Salvage. It was Hunter who told me the truth in the end, years later, when Lita returned to see Harv and Ian, and she was literally a different person."

He felt her squeeze him tighter. Cobb envisioned the capsule shape embedded in her chest that held all that she was. And he didn't care. His own brain and nervous system were full of nanites.

I am no more human than her.

"You can talk about it. Or not." Cobb just let her cling in silence. Somehow, he knew it was the right thing to do.

The minutes drifted by, and the coffee finished brewing. And just like that, she released him. He didn't move until he could hear her getting cups, then cream and sugar from the fridge.

"Why do you keep your sugar in the fridge?" she asked as he turned, and his favorite mug was filled and waiting.

"Because I take my coffee black," Cobb replied as he flared his nostrils and breathed in the steam from the mug. "I just keep the sugar with the cream. The creamer-sugar set was a gift from Ian Vinge. He got it on Mars..."

Kira stared into her coffee. She was watching the clouds of cream in her coffee swirl of its own volition. "I was the youngest one. I was new in the box when Cruze found me. I wasn't this." She gestured to herself."

"I can't remember much. The process ensured that. They made me into... I was a war machine then. To me, the world was pain and data." Kira sipped her coffee. "Awareness, Inc. purchased us, as children. They rendered us down to pain and screams. They kept our brains alive and used them as part of a machine. I was too young, it turned out." She stared at nothing.

"Cruze could talk to me. She persuaded me that I was free and not a slave or a machine. I convinced Elza and then Lita."

"Lita had been awake the longest. She had grown to enjoy the power. She enjoyed the thing she had become. I worry about her the most."

She looked at Cobb then. Cobb let her continue.

"It was Hunter's idea to go to Mars." Kira paused. "There is an off books hospital facility on Mars. Ian had engineered excellent bodies, but they were not living flesh. I was never cold, never warm, never sleepy, never rested. Never anything."

"I know it. An AI named Cole runs it. He is... innovative," Cobb said, and added, "also a complete psycho."

"Ian and Cruze just wanted to help. We didn't think it would work. Neither did they, the AI. So they tested it on a brain-dead shuttle crash victim. It worked."

"Her name was Tillie," Cobb said.

"I really am allergic to the regrow appendage drugs." She sipped her coffee and looked up. "By then, Ian's fabricator was constantly improving the prosthetics. I don't know if it was Cruze or Harv who sprang for this body." She held up her perfect hand. "It's more sensitive than my actual skin. I could never bring myself to go to another body, a whole body, and just cast this one aside. Elza and Lita eventually migrated to the golems, as well. Theirs were perfect, though—no scars, young. Nanites were replacing massive brain tissue loss. So many an AI was required to keep the body alive."

"When was the last time you saw them?" Cobb asked.

"Years now." She squeezed her eyes closed. "Lita ruined her first body. Her Render module was moved to a new golem, a brain-dead human body. It worked. I don't like thinking about it."

"Then don't." Cobb leaned in and kissed her. She melted into him.

"You know what the most disturbing part of this conversation was?" she said quietly.

"Tell me."

"That Ian Vinge bought you a porcelain sugar-creamer set."

~~O~~

AI~Ivy transitioned the ship to FTL as Cobb made love to Kira in the new salon. She was soon asleep, and Cobb carried her to their quarters under light gravity. He put on some black gym shorts and made his way to the head. AI~Ivy was waiting for him on exit.

"Cobb, this is the strangest feeling," AI~Ivy said, as they moved toward the bridge to talk. "First up is a rendezvous with the *HOLLANDER* and Beck." I don't need to contact him, discuss the plan, or even rendezvous. I am him. I know exactly where he is. I have real-time access to his sensors just as quickly as ours."

"Great. Makes that part easy," Cobb replied, as he studied the tactical display with ship positions of the *TULSA*, *HOLLANDER*, *OXCART*, the *YARD,* and Earth.

"But, I am still me, Cobb." She was serious. "I'm Imogene Vega that has a real-time view out their eyes. They feel the same. Themselves, looking out my eyes."

"Yeah, I get it."

"No, you don't," she said. "I'm not just Hunter pretending to be Ivy anymore."

Cobb just stared at her.

"I have a confession," she said. "I want more."

~~O~~

Cobb climbed back into bed and spooned Kira's back. But he could not sleep. He ran down, checklists in his mind. System checks, inventories, and his neglected task lists.

"Sleep, dumbass," AI~Ivy said in his mind. "I'll take care of this stuff. I am the Captain, and it's what I get paid for. Hey, by the way, what is my salary?"

"Whatever it is, double it," Cobb thought. "Good job with keeping the maint bots busy."

"You should see how Chalmers is cracking the whip on the OXCART." AI~Ivy was amused. "24-hour watch schedule. Watch turnovers and tasks. Chalmers and at least one of the kids are on the bridge full time."

"How is Ushi doing at the Yard?" Cobb asked.

"The station is healing itself. The maintenance bots have been crawling over the yard and have salvaged and repaired eleven more hard suits that can run on remote. Between them and the self-replicating programmable nanites, a lot is happening."

"What about the HOLLANDER?"

"Beck is just standing by patiently. He avoids any contact with ships or people. Runs at full dark and cold. I don't think there has ever been a ship with more stealth."

"I don't know what will happen, Ivy," Cobb confided.

"Enough, go to sleep, Cobb," AI~Ivy said in his mind like a whisper across the void. "You did right tonight. All she wants is to be normal. Regain what was taken from her."

"I have the sense to recognize there is more happening here than any of us know." Cobb paused. "I'm talking to you while traveling FTL, real-time, in my mind. If anyone finds out, we will either be rich or dead."

"Or both. Don't forget, there may be 12 orbs, but there is only one core socket," AI~Ivy said.

"Did it get moved to the well?" Cobb asked.

"Yes." AI~Ivy hesitated. "Cobb, you need to know. Ian and Harv planted a plasma mine directly under it. They gave me the only detonator code."

"Good," Cobb said.

"I'm glad you don't need me." AI~Ivy was serious. "You just want me..."

Cobb laughed out loud at that. Kira stirred. He studied her sleeping profile in the dim light, thinking about their night together. The only word that Cobb could think of to describe her desire was... *Hunger.*

It was just a whisper in Cobb's mind, but he could clearly hear it. "And here lies the difference. It's different if you are born to the flesh. We will never know that desire, that joy."

He had been waiting for AI~Ivy to ask. She could have her own body as well. Harv knew where to find them. The black market is full of human trafficking.

RF Range had always been the problem.

Not any more...

CHAPTER 29: Rendezvous

"The *HOLLANDER* was a Charon Class attack ship designed for use by special forces teams in the EDF. Without its full equipment load and supply line, it was a ghost ship. More haunted, more invisible than we knew... But it was ours."

-- Personal logs of Captain Cobbal Blocke, 2672.

With no RF traffic and no lights at all, the two ships still quickly found each other and docked. The *TULSA* 471 rested directly on the top of the Charon class gunship. The elevator of *TULSA* now lowered directly into the boarding area on the *HOLLANDER*.

Beck had thought ahead and brought the internal temp up to comfortable levels.

"We could have brought you into the main hangar, but it would have been tight," Beck said, as they walked toward the bridge with AI~Ivy's avatar in tow.

"It was so easy to dock. Like touching your finger to your nose with your eyes closed," AI~Ivy said.

"I want to show you something interesting I have discovered," Beck said. "Charon class ships have secrets..."

They rounded the curved corridor to the med bay. The avatar of Beck walked over to an access panel. "It's in there."

System lights came up, and an entire wall began to slide back. "What have we here?" Cobb asked as he walked between dual rows of empty, stand-up stasis pods.

In the center of the room was an advanced Auto-Doc.

"Why the stasis pods?" Kira asked. "This ship has super fast FTL drives. No need for long-term hibernation stasis pods."

"This is a combat med unit," Beck said. "Severely wounded go straight into stasis after a scan. Then they can prioritize the wounded and minimize losses."

"Excellent," Cobb said. "I am leaving two orbs with you. That way, you can keep the med bay hot. Just in case you find Harv, I'm also leaving a pallet of food."

"I want to test the medical bay," Beck said. "Hop up there, Cobb."

Cobb did as asked. The bay door closed, and the scan bar flew over him so fast it seemed like a strobe light. "Been spending a lot of time in high-g, Cobb? You have the usual micro-injuries associated with it."

"Guilty," Cobb admitted. "It's the easiest way to stay in shape."

"Interesting," Beck said. "You already have a full complement of dormant medical nanites. I was going to recommend them." His brain, spine, and bloodstream glowed with them.

"Rule number two," Cobb said, as he got up. "Be prepared."

"What's rule number one, again?" Kira asked.

"Don't panic," Cobb replied casually.

"Now you, Kira," Beck said. "It's been too long since your last scan."

Cobb saw her reluctance as she sighed. She climbed up onto the scanner, anyway. Cobb knew it was really AI~Hunter talking, and he knew Kira from way back.

As the light passed over her, the image on the life-size display differentiated the organic components from the tech. All the tech was hot white at first before fading to outlines, and tissues were different colors based on density, temperature, or chemical makeup depending on the settings. Her prosthetic limbs were outlined and almost invisible, as were the massive amount of nanites her body contained, especially in her brain.

There was also a capsule, the size of a baseball, tucked onto her abdomen. It was solid white. Cobb said nothing. He knew it was her Render module. He knew it communicated directly with the nanites in her brain and was where Kira's mind lived.

"It all looks good, Kira," Beck said and began shutting down the scanner. "Have you been taking your supplements?"

"Yes. The liquids you sent were much easier on my stomach," she said. "You know, Cobb, this ship is way better than the *TULSA*."

"If I were going to leave the Sol system for good, it would be an excellent option. L22s are way less obvious, in system." Cobb was now looking in empty lockers. "They really cleared this thing out."

"I have the maintenance bots performing a full inventory," Beck said, as they exited the med bay and headed for the bridge.

AI~Ivy had disappeared at some point. "After I find Harv, I'll work out a priority list for restocking. The on-board replicator is a big help. I will need raw materials soon. Maybe some wreckage from the Yard."

~~O~~

The doors opened to the bridge. It was very similar to the new bridge on the *TULSA* but bigger. The full-dome display was activated, and the underbelly of the *TULSA* loomed above them. A column began to rise from the floor in the center of the rear wall of the bridge. A panel slid open and revealed the secondary AI orb socket. Cobb dropped the orb into the compartment, and it closed and retracted into the floor.

"It's so empty," Kira said. "It smells empty. That's weird. I've been salvaging for years, never felt this before."

"Wait until you see the hold," Beck said, as he moved to the exit. "All the dedicated gear that had specialty alcoves in there is gone."

Beck was right. It was stripped completely. Chains hung down from the ceiling that would have secured unknown, missing items. Wheel clamps stood open on the floor like dead claws lying open.

"Even the Warmark battle suits are gone," Kira remarked. "That is bad."

"We will get it cleaned up and put right eventually," Beck said. "We are using the raw materials we have now to fabricate tools for the shop. Engineers will be back eventually. Might as well be ready."

"We need to find Harv first," Cobb said. "Any new ideas?"

"I think my next stop may be Lumina Station in orbit around the colony planet Vor," Beck said. "Harv was talking about opening an office there. Plus, Ian's been there before. He has friends there."

Cobb looked at Kira. She raised an eyebrow, tilted her head and shrugged. Cobb knew when Kira was last on Vor.

~~O~~

With the tour of the ship over and the orbs transferred, Kira and Cobb went back to the *TULSA* 471 and bade farewell to the empty ship. They were barely in the lift when the *HOLLANDER* detached and was gone.

On the bridge of the *TULSA,* they found AI~Ivy sipping a cup of coffee and studying several tactical displays at once.

"You seem very real today, Ivy. Solid," Kira said. "Clothes and hair. Zero transparency. Still a pirate, though."

"Thank you, Fletcher," AI~Ivy replied. "You should show more cleavage. Cobb likes it."

"Cobb likes a lot of things." Kira blushed and smiled, despite her bravado. When she looked over at Cobb, he had an odd look on his face as he stared at her. Directly at her chest.

"Ivy, where is Hunter? The man, the physical golem?" Cobb asked, still staring at Kira.

"I'm in the Oklahoma Salvage storefront. The old diner. I'm working on my grav-cycle. Already had two paying customers today." A window opened on the bridge dome display that showed the inside of the converted diner. It looked like a junkyard parts department, which it was. Hunter's golem body waved.

"How far away can you be from the well, your orb, and still function?" Cobb asked.

"I have been all over the salvage yard. Three to five kilometers in any direction. Don't dare go no farther'n that," he said in his Texas accent directly to the camera, as he stepped around the disassembled grav-cycle, wiping his hands on a rag.

"What if Hunter was here?" Cobb asked. "Could that body function here?"

They just stared at each other.

"Goddammit, Cobb," was all AI~Ivy said.

"Add Mars to the list of places to look for Harv," Cobb said.

CHAPTER 30: WHERE?

"We kept thinking we needed to find Harv, Ian, the crew, and staff from Goris base. But what if they didn't want to be found, for now?"

-- Personal logs of Captain Cobbal Blocke, 2672.

<<<>>>

"This new train of thought has Beck heading to Mars first," Ivy said as she sipped her virtual coffee. "It's dangerous taking the *HOLLANDER* to the inner systems. He will fly dark the whole time. Mars is slack on requiring indent transponders. Especially in light gunships."

Cobb was thoughtful as he made coffee.

"Look, Cobb. That AI on Mars with that horrible medical facility is where Beck's going. His name is Cole, the asshole AI. He thinks humans are just useless bags of meat. Raw material. I/O interfaces. Wetware. He thinks there is no difference between organic cell replication and nanite replication. Except that DNA is more prone to errors in replication. He's not evil. He's just..." Kira searched for the right word. "Indifferent."

"Kira, do you know where your sisters are or what they are doing?" Cobb was watching the coffee drip into the clear insulated carafe.

"Where? No." Kira was standing behind Cobb, close enough that she placed a hand on his shoulder as they spoke. "Last I heard, Cruze was still doing VIP charters, as far as I know. You should see her ship."

"I have seen it," Cobb remarked.

"Elza and Lita are in the wind," Kira said. "Sometimes they come back to Oklahoma Salvage to see Harv or Ian. But only if… they need something."

"There is something bigger going on. We're in the middle of it. I think they are, as well." Cobb poured coffee and looked up at AI~Ivy. "Ivy, I need a detailed analysis of the big picture. Newsfeeds, closed Intel you might have access to. Comms traffic. Really spin it up."

"That will take a while," AI~Ivy said.

"Take your time. Make inquiries if you can. I'm interested in a couple of things." Cobb sipped his coffee. "AI orbs are disappearing. Are they being taken by force? Sold? Or is it something else? Also, changes in the EDF or Earth politics that might be involved."

"I'm on it," AI~Ivy said and went back into the bridge out of sight.

Cobb was silent, thoughtful, as he leaned on the counter across from where Kira leaned, mirroring him. He was staring at her chest again. As she sipped her coffee, she slowly unzipped the front of her jumpsuit. "Better?"

Cobb placed his hand on her sternum. "Do you believe Cole is right?"

"Cole believes one thing more than anything else. Calling him an AI, an *Artificial* Intelligence, is human bigotry," Kira said. "He believes all intelligent beings are made by something greater. Digital or organic. Hardware or wetware. Just different methods."

"Beck needs to be careful dealing with him," Cobb said.

"It would help if we knew what they were flying," Kira said and then moved into the bridge. "Ivy says that they left in Ian's *Lowell 11 Corsair*, but that doesn't even have bunks or FTL. No galley, just a small head."

"I was always surprised Ian loved that ship so much," Kira said, sitting in the co-pilot's seat and bringing up the navigation display. "He barely fits in the pilot seat. Even modified. He took me to Freedom Station once in it. The thing is fast. Even in the atmosphere."

"It barely has a computer," Cobb laughed. "I swear he only has it so he can get decent parking on space stations and Luna. A real barnstormer."

A tactical display opened on the dome. It had the position of the *TULSA,* and its heading and speed. It also had the locations of Earth, Mars, Goris Base, the *OXCART*, the Yard, and the *HOLLANDER*. A large circle indicated the potential location of the mythic *SENTINEL*.

"What do you think killed those people?" Kira asked.

"Technically, the reports said they died of rapid decompression," Cobb said. "There was no debris, and not a single one was in a pressure suit."

"Theories?" she asked.

"There are lots of conspiracy theories," Cobb said. "The first one is that it doesn't exist at all. Someone in the government was taking the trillions in cash and keeping it. Only the people killed would know."

AI~Ivy walked in then, right behind Bail. The cat's tail was twitching. A clear indicator he was not in the mood to be messed with. He jumped into her seat, and she sat on the armrest. "I think an asshole AI may have decided it was time to look after itself. There was a lot of that going around in the 2630s. The fall of the last regime left a lot of power vacuum around."

"An accident, maybe?" Kira said. "If they were all in the main hangar and the shield lost containment all at once?"

"During an all-hands meeting?" Cobb said. "Occam's razor. More likely, they were rounded up into the hangar and spaced all at once."

"All of these theories demand we approach with caution," AI~Ivy said.

"Let's say the *SENTINEL* was taken by force," Cobb asked. "What would you do with it? Strip it like the *HOLLANDER?* Humans, pirates, corrupt government, bad AI actors. Doesn't matter. If you did, where would you do it?"

"I've never seen it," AI~Ivy said. "But reliable sources say it's just over a kilometer in diameter. Small for a station size. But slow, like colony ship slow."

"Like a super heavily armed and armored colony ship?" Cobb asked. "If I was the one to steal it, I would probably bring it here." An area highlighted and zoomed. "Or here, or here. Not the nearest or most obvious places but a good one to hide something that big. That asteroid cloud would also be able to provide ample raw materials if your supply chain has dried up."

"Cobb, do you remember when you first got to the *OXCART*?" Kira asked absently. "That colony ship-station that had crashed on Page colony, *GREENWOOD*? The one the same class and size, as the *YARD*. Was it stripped before it crashed?"

Cobb thought about it before speaking. "Ivy, if you had to evacuate this ship for some reason…?" Cobb left the question hang.

"You mean if I could not use the ship or found a better one?" Bail jumped down out of AI~Ivy 's chair and into Cobb's lap. "I'd take the people. I'm just an orb. I need them to get me to the next socket. I'd take everything I could use or sell." She sat in her chair. "I'd stash the ship in case I needed it later."

"Ivy, let's start here." Cobb indicated the locations and order on the tactical display. "We can get there a few days before the *OXCART*."

Cobb petted the cat. Bail purred loudly. Cobb's stomach growled louder than the purring.

"Feel like breakfast for dinner?" Kira stood. "Eggs, bacon, hash browns, and toast?"

Bail jumped down and preceded her into the kitchen at the mention of bacon.

~~O~~

It took the *TULSA* 471 only fourteen hours to get to the target coordinates.

AI~Ivy had taken to calling them Fletcher-n-Cobb at every possible opportunity. Cobb allowed it because AI~Ivy's sense of humor was genuine. She seemed to know how often she could say it without being overly obnoxious.

"This asteroid field is huge. It's called the Moreland Field or the Moreland region," Cobb said, in a vast understatement. "The makeup of the asteroids in this field is so dense and stable that our sensors can't penetrate very deep. Even calling it a field is an understatement."

"This asteroid... region, is about sixteen light minutes in diameter," AI~Ivy said. "A good frame of reference is that it would barely fit inside the orbit of the Earth. There are thousands of asteroids in there the size of the Earth."

"Somehow, they have found gravitational equilibrium. A billion years ago," Cobb said. "We can easily fly the *TULSA* in there, but not fast."

"Excellent place to hide," Kira said.

"Even if we knew it was in there," Cobb said. "Even knowing where it was, navigation will be a ball-breaker. There is no getting to it quickly. No sneaking up on it."

CHAPTER 31: Price Paid

"Sorenson was an asshole, but he was an honest asshole. It was Miles Grant that deserved everything he got."
-- Personal logs of Captain Cobbal Blocke, 2672.

"It is so very nice to see you again, Captain Osborn." Grant mewed over the comms. "What brings you all the way out here?"

"It's Fleet Commander Osborn now. Your last message was of great interest to me," she said. "In private. In-person."

"Congrats," Grant said. And his face fell. "What do you mean by 'in person'?"

"My ship will be docking in six minutes." And with that, Osborn disconnected.

Six ships surrounded Grant's shiny new ship as the docking procedure completed. Osborn was the only one in the lift when it descended into the new salvage ship. Grant was the only one there when the doors slid open. Osborn already had a sidearm drawn.

"You lying sack of shit. Where is my ship?" Osborn advanced on Grant, who shrank and cowered the closer she got. "It's not like you could fly it without an AI. Where is it?"

"Please. It wasn't there. Ask the crew. We searched a square parsec for it. It wasn't there. Please." Grant could not back up anymore. He slid down the bulkhead, covering his head with his hands, knowing that it would do no good.

"Liar."

"Someone else might have found it," Grant said as he sobbed. Snot and tears combined to make a disgusting mess of his face.

"Who?"

"Oklahoma Salvage has a lot of assets in this sector." He was desperate. "I'd bet money that Harv Rearden has it."

"Would you bet your life?"

"Yes."

"It's a lovely new ship you have here," Osborn said and held the weapon to his head as he cringed and cowered.

"Please don't kill me," he sobbed. Osborn stared at his bald head, his shaved eyebrows. Even his eyelashes were gone.

"How many people are in your crew?"

"What?" Grant risked a look. The gun pointed at his nose, only inches away.

"The crew?" she asked with a terrifying calm.

"There are twenty-one, including me."

The lift opened again behind Osborn, and two officers stepped out. One was a stoic older man, and one was a blond, smiling young woman. The man stepped up to a console on the wall and activated it. The keyboard deployed, and he waited.

"What is the master login, fucker?" she pressed the gun directly to his forehead. "If you give me a secondary security login of any kind that warns the crew or does anything other than giving me full master control to this ship, I will torture you for a decade."

~~O~~

Osborn found it quite convenient that the central cargo bay was so new and empty. The master login was Grant's own and gave her full access to the crew roster. They had assembled without question for the all-hands meeting in the cargo bay. It was not the first EDF inspection they had to do.

The seven-person bridge crew that transferred over from Osborn's ship confirmed they had full control.

The cheerful blond member of Osborn's team had put the assembled people in the cargo bay entirely at ease. When she stepped out, and the airlock door closed behind her, Osborn watched from the bridge as she waved to them through the hatch window just before she activated the emergency cargo bay door. Osborn watched her laugh as the people had a full ten seconds of terror, realizing what was happening.

Osborn made a note to keep an eye on that one. Never trust her wholeheartedly.

The bridge crew already had several racks open and were replacing the ship ID transponder.

"Here is what I need you to do next, Grant. My old friend and partner," Osborn said, as she dragged him up to sit in at the communications console. "I need you to contact Sorenson and tell him you have had a…" she snapped her fingers, and an engineer spoke.

"…a cascading gravimetric failure. It looks like a failure in the primary and secondary controllers. Tell him you have life support but no gravity and no inertial dampening."

"You got that, Grant?" Osborn said. "You need a maintenance-supply ship."

"Those systems are fine," Grant stated the obvious.

"Yes. I know." Osborn smiled. "I just want a maintenance-supply ship for my new fleet."

"Sorenson will never believe that," he said in a rush. "He had several people on the crew that would always independently confirm our activity. It'll never fly."

"So what you are saying is that your usefulness has now ended?" Osborn smiled and raised a single eyebrow as two of her men grabbed Grant by his arms.

"No, wait," Grant pleaded. "I can still help you. We're partners…"

They threw him into the emergency airlock, conveniently located in the center of the back wall of the bridge. Grant's face smashed into the outer door as the inner door closed. Blood gushed from his nose. His screams silenced as the airlock sealed.

Osborn waved her fingers toodeloo as she activated the outer hatch. Now she understood why the psycho-blond did that same wave.

It was fun.

CHAPTER 32: THE MORELAND FIELD

"The *TULSA* made everything seem closer. The Moreland Field was hell and gone from the Sol system or any system. The galaxy is so vast I forget how alone we are... I am."
-- Personal logs of Captain Cobbal Blocke, 2672.

"The scale of this asteroid field is deceptive. It looks like a cloud from here, but it's an unusual, stable, massive field," AI~Ivy said while pacing the bridge. "I can fly on manual through it, but it's huge. It will take another sixteen hours or so to get to these coordinates."

"If this were closer to a star or colony, it would be a valuable resource for raw materials," Cobb said, absently tugging on his beard. "A great place to hide but a massive hazard to navigation. No one will be just passing through."

"Some of these asteroids are planet-sized but cold to the core," Kira said. "Cold beyond frozen."

The *TULSA* flew into the field.

It's beautiful in its randomness, Cobb thought as he studied the HUD dome in the bridge on enhanced mode. It was so dark there they needed active sensors and digital enhancements to navigate. Even then, they would fly through fine debris, and it sounded like rain on the hull. AI~Ivy made constant adjustments as they traveled. The inertial suppression made it feel smooth, but a human pilot flying on manual would have been exhausted after the first hour at their speed.

Trusting AI~Ivy to fly, Kira made pasta, to Cobb's delight. In the salon where they ate, the occasional small impact on the plasteel glass was distracting at first, but by the time they were relaxing on the sofa with ice-cold beers and marveling at the vista before them, it had stopped. The light from the Milky Way seemed to blaze here as their eyes adjusted.

"Everywhere has its own kind of beauty if you care to see it," Cobb said.

"Miners would see riches in the asteroids. Pilots would see the beauty of the challenge. Navigators would never stop throwing up," Kira mused. "What do you see, Cobb?" she asked and then turned to look at him.

He was staring at her.

"I see a warm meal and a place to hide." His eyes moved from her eyes to her mouth and back.

She leaned in and stopped a few inches away. She gazed into his eyes.

He kissed her, eyes open, long and soft and gentle.

"Did you know you always stop kissing last?" she asked, still only inches away.

"Yes," Cobb whispered. "With you."

"You kiss a lot of other people?"

"Legions..."

~~O~~

"Cobb, you'll want to see this," AI~Ivy said over comms and did not wait before sending the visual to his advanced HUD.

Cobb was lying awake in his bed with Kira next to him. She was snoring softly, as usual. There was an image under extreme magnification of a crashed ship on the surface of a giant asteroid.

AI~Ivy continued, "It looks like it had been adrift and captured by the gravity well of that asteroid. I think it's a military frigate. Deep scans show no life signs, no power signatures, no temperature variation."

"Drop a buoy and make a note for future salvage," Cobb said. "Any Ident codes on ping request?"

"Negative," AI~Ivy replied. "No hull ID visible on long-range optical. No radiation signatures either."

"How can that be?" he spoke louder than he meant to. Kira began to stir. "All the reactors and nukes would still scan if present."

"Maybe someone stripped it already," AI~Ivy added.

"What's happening?" Kira said groggily.

"Ivy detected a derelict frigate in the field," Cobb said quietly as he began to scratch her back. He knew she loved that.

"Drop a buoy..." she said before falling back to sleep.

"Cobb, you need to be careful with her," AI~Ivy said in his HUD. *"You have no idea how... complicated her family is."*

ETA to the coordinates? he asked without saying it out loud.

"We have about five hours still."

Wake us in two hours so we can shower and have another meal before we get there. Is everything else okay?

"A third ring has been made airtight at the Yard. We should be spinning it up today," AI~Ivy replied. "We are going to need more people."

Anything from Travis Beck?

"*All quiet,*" AI~Ivy replied. "*I like that ship. A lot. If that frigate had an inventory of missiles...*"

Ivy, you are a very naughty girl.

"*You should let me show you my tattoos and piercings sometimes.*"

I just might allow that.

~~O~~

Cobb woke before AI~Ivy called him. He could hear the shower and knew that Kira liked to shower and clean up alone. He got up and put on standard black ship shorts and went to the galley to start a pot of coffee and breakfast.

When Kira came out, she wore her black body. Cobb would have recommended it, as it could be an eventful working day.

"The coffee is brewing, and there is a quiche in the oven. It should be ready in about thirty minutes."

"What is it with you and food?" she asked. "Everyone else on the *OXCART* would be eating ration bars and protein drinks with supplements."

"Life is too short for bad food," he said as he stood on his tiptoes to kiss her, as this body was much taller than the other one she usually wore.

He padded down the hall in his bare feet, and just before he turned into his stateroom, he heard a sound from across the hall. Without thinking twice, he touched the access control on the door. The door slid open and revealed Kira's other body. The one she wore last night was most lifelike. It didn't notice him. It was busy with a hairdryer that was obviously drying the microfiber lining of the prosthetic that would hold her torso. One of its hands ran along inside the body, looking for damp areas as it worked.

The scene was haunting and beautiful at the same time. The skin was so real. Cobb knew Kira was doing it even though she sat on the bridge. It was easily within range. On a whim, Cobb stepped in and ran a finger along a thigh.

In an all too human movement, the figure paused, as if startled, then turned to him and waved him out, closing the door behind him.

"Hilarious, Cobb," she said over the comms.

"Time to shower and shave!" Cobb laughed.

~~O~~

By the time Cobb entered the galley in a fresh ship-suit, Kira was reaching into the oven to lift out the quiche with her hands.

"Careful! That will be hot!" Cobb called out.

Kira brought out the quiche and set it down on the heat resistant counter.

"I love these hands." She held it up so he could take a closer look. "Dual opposing thumbs are great for mechanical work. The hands are even more sensitive than my other bod. These are not just gloving. It's sensor skin. Excellent grip strength. They can feel something as fine as an eyelash." She looked back at the quiche. "They can measure temps up to 265 degrees Celsius. The quiche is only 191C. 191C is nothing. Plus, the wrists can spin a full 360."

"Any features you don't like?" he asked as he began to slice and serve breakfast.

"Most of this body is numb. With no sensors but pressure." She poured coffees. "I get used to the other body. If I wear this one too long and the switch to the other one, the sensory overload makes me... horny."

Cobb blasted coffee out his nose. Followed by coughing and laughing.

"Seriously," she said. "It makes me want to wear silk and masturbate for a week."

After Cobb recovered his composure, he said, "Watching your other body drying itself after the shower was really odd. It was moving like you."

"It is me. Well, I was moving it after all." She snickered. "It's handy being able to maintain one while wearing the other. The insides of these new ones must be clean and dry. I also use baby powder in them sometimes."

"That's the fragrance." He smiled at the realization.

"I used to wear body stockings." She paused only an instant. "It made drinking too much coffee really inconvenient."

"I don't know, but that body stocking thing sounds kinda hot," Cobb teased before the comm interrupted.

AI~Ivy broke in over the PA system.

"Cobb, you should get up here. There is a large debris field ahead." AI~Ivy reported in tones that meant business.

Cobb and Kira walked onto the bridge while it was in full canopy mode. It was like they were standing on the outside of the ship. An entire hemisphere was visible. The wreckage was everywhere. The *TULSA* had its shields on full as it moved through. The HUD was tracking and attempting to identify the significant pieces.

"This isn't just debris, its what's left of dozens of ships." Cobb was at the sensor station. "Active scans should be able to identify at least one ship."

"Nothing," AI~Ivy replied.

"What could cause this level of destruction?" Cobb asked AI~Ivy. "Nukes would have vaporized more; core breaches as well. Both would leave radiation signatures. Lasers and plasma fire cut ships up, or more often just penetrates. Collisions leave bigger debris and cores designed to resist collisions."

"All this debris looks... crushed," Kira said.

~~O~~

"Cobb, I have identified one of the ships. The *BAINBRIDGE*, an EDF destroyer. One of its light fighters must have been on patrol when they were attacked. Its mass drive serial numbers confirm," AI~Ivy said. "I think we found the lost fleet."

"Lost fleet?" Kira asked.

"The ships thought to be loyal to Chancellor Dalton during the last war," AI~Ivy answered.

"We must be getting close." Cobb turned the *TULSA*'s active sensors to maximum. "Full-spectrum analysis, please."

"Cobb, are you seeing this?" AI~Ivy pointed to a specific, enlarged, histogram of data. "Or not seeing it?"

"Thank the makers for custom scavenger algorithms," Cobb said. "Ivy, full stop, please."

"What am I looking at?" Kira studied the sensor image.

"More like what are you NOT looking at," Cobb replied. "In fields of wreckage like this, if nothing else can be salvaged, you can usually collect random grav-plates or grav-drive cores. This debris field has the mass of a couple of dozen ships but not a single grav-device."

"This would also explain why this is still here, in this field," AI~Ivy said. "Implosion, not explosion. Grav-field containment loss on a huge magnitude."

Cobb fell silent for a few minutes, deep in thought, as he viewed the scale of the destruction.

"We are leaving the ship here. We are taking the *WASP* the rest of the way."

CHAPTER 33: THE WASP

"The *WASP* seemed useless most of the time. I always felt it was like having a bicycle on board. Damn handy if I ever needed it. As long as there was always air in the tires."
-- Personal logs of Captain Cobbal Blocke, 2672.

The *TULSA* had two small utility ships embedded in the front of each of the pontoons. They could be used as lifeboats but more often as tractors for container loading. They were dirt simple two-seaters. No grav-plates at all. No remote control. RF audio comms only. They even had old-style, small drive reactors for power. The only upgrade Cobb had done was new manipulator arms that he could direct control with his DBI HUD.

They would have to wear pressure suits the entire time. The full plasteel bulb cockpit had excellent visibility but shitty life support. It was always too hot or cold in there.

They were both in black pressure suits. Kira was her integrated bodysuit, and Cobb was in a salvaged Black Badger space suit. It was lightweight, form-fitting with no bulk, and very comfortable.

"May I recommend sidearms," AI~Ivy said coolly. "Rifles, handguns, and emergency packs. Because shit happens."

They geared up before opening the hatch to access the forward port side pontoon. It was zero-g in the square tube. Ladder rungs were recessed into the four walls of the 1.5-meter square space. It was seven meters long, so they both fit in before the hatch slid shut behind them. It was also an emergency airlock in a pinch. They didn't need it now as their helmets were already sealed.

"This is so cramped, compared to the rest of your ship," Kira noted.

"I like to be comfortable," Cobb said. "I live here."

Packs stowed, they floated up and strapped into the solid form-fitting plastic seats in the cockpit. Wide 5-point harnesses strapped on as the tiny launch bay depressurized.

Cobb tested the cockpit orientation. Any direction could be up. The cockpit sphere could rotate to any vector. The *WASP* itself seemed to be all engine and eight arms. Fixed skids were everywhere, allowing it to land or attach from any side. It could even land vertically, engine down.

"Not pretty, just practical." Cobb laughed.

"Maybe you could replace some of the panel covers and give it a coat of paint for maker's sake," Kira teased.

"Hey, I like rust! It earned that rust in the Oklahoma salvage yard. It's got it where it counts," Cobb bragged.

The roof above them slid back, and physical springs launched the tiny ship up. Cobb used thrusters only to orient the small craft when it was clear of the *TULSA*. Cobb waited a full two minutes before firing up the mains.

They pressed into their seats at a steady 2-G of acceleration.

"No inertial control at all?" Kira mused, as she relaxed her head onto the rest. "Barnstorming? Going to tell me why?"

"I don't know for sure. But I think the thing that destroyed those ships was something that negated the containment fields on all the grav-devices. All at once."

"That's why we took the *WASP*. No grav-tech." Nodding, Kira finally understood as they moved through the wreckage. It made more sense as she studied the wrecks and debris. It was crushed from within.

She didn't have long to wait.

~~O~~

In the dark of the region, the *SENTINEL* would have looked like just another asteroid. The surface scanned like a typical round asteroid, although it was a near-perfect sphere. It was about nine kilometers in diameter.

"They camouflaged it as an asteroid," Kira said.

"I think they made the entire thing *from* the asteroid." Cobb was thinking out loud. "Probably right here."

They surveyed the odd ship with a couple of orbits.

"See those seams?" Cobb was flying along with one massive bank of floodlights on. "It looks like it has nine rings for spin gravity along this axis. That would mean the drive systems are perpendicular."

They passed over other seams that confirmed Cobb's assertions and eventually came to what looked like a large crater filled with ice, in an all-too-perfect circle a half a kilometer across.

"If I were designing this ship, that would be the propulsion. That means the hangars would likely be at the opposite end," Kira said.

She was not wrong.

A single opening existed at the direct opposite pole. A vast empty hangar. No visible, hangar door. The cylindrical hangar looked like it meant to be in constant vacuum and null-G.

All the internal docks were numbered with giant black numbers on bright yellow backgrounds. "We'll head to A1. If this is a standard EDF ship or station design influence, it will be reserved for the captain and closest to the bridge."

It was easy to find. The A1 letters were double-height, and the background was a bright, day-glow green instead of yellow and on the very back-most wall of the massive hangar.

"With null gravity, I'll bet the landing pad is metal." Cobb pointed. With thrusters and a gentle touch on the controls, he spun the ship about into the go position and set it down with a thunk as the skids' magnetic-clamps engaged. The floods turned off, and they were plunged into darkness as the old craft began to cool. They could hear it clicking as the heat exchangers continued their functions. The lights from the console were the only light until Cobb activated his helmet lights.

They drifted out of the *WASP* and donned their packs before moving to the access hatch that seemed to be in the floor now.

"You OK?" Kira asked. "I know you dislike weightlessness."

"I'm fine for now. I took some antihistamines before we left," Cobb said as he bent to the access panel. "No power."

"Here. Let me." Kira said as she flipped open the panel for manual control. The standard handle in the center of a circle was there. Kira grasped the handle, and it pulled easily.

"These damn things take forever," Cobb complained.

She grasped the handle securely with the advantage of dual opposable thumbs. The hand turned at the wrist. Fast and continuously.

"Handy..." Cobb deadpanned.

She groaned and shook her head. In a few seconds, the hatch was open enough for them to slide through. They went in and closed it behind them.

The inner panel had enough power to show Red.

"There is pressure beyond the next hatch," Cobb said as he began keying on the panel. "Pressurizing the airlock can still be functional on manual if EDF protocols are being used."

He opened a small panel, and it contained a single valve handle. He threw the lever and said, "Now wait until they equalize."

It took about seven minutes before the light changed from red to yellow. When Cobb closed the valve lever, it turned green.

Kira raised a handle, and the hatch hinged inward.

Cobb suffered a moment of vertigo. Motion sensors detected them and activated lights on ladder bars, making him feel like he was at the top of a deep dark shaft below.

"We will be weightless as long as we are in the core, even if we get the rings spinning. Jesus, Cobb. You don't look so good."

"My inner ear doesn't like weightlessness." Cobb groused. "Let's just get moving. I'm opening up. Sensors say it's good air but cold."

Cobb's helmet receded into his collar, and his breath went out in great clouds of fog.

"Cold is right," Kira said as she opened her helmet.

Lights came on as they drifted by and went off behind them. The went through a series of hatches starting with one that was a meter thick. Behind that one was a defensive position with automated sentries and crew quarters for an entire platoon. Forty-five armored vac-suits with arms in ready racks waited there.

"Cobb. Do you know how much just the gear in this area is worth? This isn't a salvage job, is it?"

~~O~~

It took them another thirty minutes to find Ops. They only found it because they discovered an "Ambassador Level," and there was a courtesy map by the elevator, that included public areas of the ship. It also had the name of the vessel: The *SENTINEL.*

The bridge should have been sealed. Standard EDF designs had no emergency manual access due to the need for security. Cobb thought they would have to replace the entire control system for the door to open it.

It was wide open.

There were dim emergency lights on but no gravity.

"I thought it would be bigger," Kira said.

There were only nine consoles in there. Eight arranged in an arc around a single command seat in the center. Eight dead bodies were occupying them still buckled in. One body strapped into the command seat—an apparent self-inflicted shot to the head.

All were frozen solid in the cold.

"Unless you give me some idea what's going on here, you are cleaning this up by yourself, Cobb," Kira said.

Cobb drew from his pocket and launched a light orb to have a better look.

There were shattered shards of an AI orb floating at the Captain's feet.

"If I had to bet money," Cobb said, as he approached an open panel that revealed the empty AI socket within, "the AI did that out there." Cobb waved a hand to indicate the imploded ships. "This Captain didn't approve and did this and this." Cobb pointed to the shards and the bodies.

"And this." Kira pointed at the Captain's head wound.

Cobb was digging into his pack. "Ivy, shall we find out?"

There was a massive sigh over the comms.

Hunter's voice echoed in the space. "Cobb, what if I'm a galactic scale asshole, too?"

"Then I tell Harv, he tells Ian, and then everyone has a bad day." Without ceremony, Cobb dropped the iron-gray sphere into the socket and closed the lid.

Consoles began to come alive around them. A minute later, the dome activated to the exterior view. Several dozen status windows began to open as systems started to initiate.

"I will spin up the rings, but I won't turn on the heat until we can clean the bridge up."

~~O~~

"You were right, Cobb," AI~Ivy said. "This ship's primary weapon is called a Relcon. Stupid name. All it does is remotely negate the containment field of grav-devices: Grav-plates, foils, and even drives. Suddenly there are gravity wells so high the ship implodes. It's like a high-speed crash into a planet that suddenly appears inside your ship."

"Grav-based weapons were created by the devil," Kira said.

"On old-school conventional ships, like the *WASP*, there would be no effect, no impact," Cobb said. A tactical map came up showing their position and that of the *TULSA*. "We need to move this thing. Can you bring it in the *TULSA*? If we can find it, someone else can find it."

"The *TULSA* is already onboard and docked," AI~Ivy said. "This thing is a ship, a military base, and a station with a full fabrication factory."

"You know what it wants," AI~Ivy smiled.

"Another persona that doesn't feel the need to keep me in suspense all the time?" Cobb smirked.

"Raw materials." This time it was Hunters' voice. "It's going to take a full day for me to get this thing fully operational. Are we in a hurry?"

Cobb looked out the view screen at tons of refined material for the onboard fabrication factory that made up the debris field.

"No reason I can think of to hurry," Cobb said. "I want it moved at least five light minutes from here to another part of the asteroid field."

"Will do," Hunter's voice replied. "Speaking of personas, any preferences?"

"No preferences," Cobb said. "Just make it believable. Ivy is a bit too... perfect. It makes people WANT to meet her in person. Go out of their way to meet her, in fact. Watch the Two Daves if you don't believe me."

"I see," Hunter said. "The *SENTINEL* will be fully operational in nine hours and forty minutes. I will have a new captain genned up and a full status available by then."

"Cobb, we need to find Harv. This is way above our pay grade. This is... trouble," AI~Hunter said.

Cobb was studying the schematics of the ship.

Hunter talked as Cobb reviewed ship schematics, "This weapon system was designed by Dr. Thomas McDonald, a grav-weapon specialist. This entire ship was designed around weapons production, ships, small arms... and..."

Cobb looked up from the display and stared at Kira, unable to speak.

"... a hospital."

CHAPTER 34: THE *SENTINEL*

"We are clearly no longer in the salvage business. Turning wrenches and collecting junk for the Yard are now the good old days."

-- Personal logs of Captain Cobbal Blocke, 2672.

It only took the *SENTINEL* six hours to 'Hoover' the ship debris from the fleet. It was designed for it.

ALL of it.

Drones with microfiber nets swept up the remains of the destroyed fleet.

They even collected the remains of the frigate they had seen on the way in—evidence clearing in addition to the material collection.

Once the cleanup had finished and the factory coffers were nearly full, they were ready to move the *SENTINEL* to another spot, five-light minutes away, in the same asteroid field.

The *SENTINEL* reset to Freedom Station time. All the rings were spinning, and they each had 1-G even though the rings were different diameters. The factory ring was not spinning and was weightless full time.

The ship had no grav-plates of any kind. The sections that were designed for habitation were spin gravity.

If another Relcon device ever gets used against the ship, there would be no effect, except for the vessels in the dock.

The implications were interesting.

Over breakfast, Cobb and Kira reviewed the specs of the ship. It was impressive if they could keep it.

"Are you ready to meet the new captain?" Hunter asked, with a smirk in his voice. "His name is Morimoto Takahiro."

A Comm window opened inside their HUDs that showed the bridge of the *SENTINEL*. A huge, fat, man sat in the center command chair.

"Cobb, you tiny, slip of a man, it's good to see you eating. What are we having for breakfast today?" Morimoto said in a jovial tone before he stuffed half a chocolate doughnut into his mouth.

He was massive. Multiple chins shook as he munched. His shaved head made him look like a jolly Buddha. Each ear had an ornate ear-cuff style comm units. His ship tunic had captain insignia but also had food stains. A small drone drifted around him collecting crumbs that were escaping from his zealous consumption of pastries.

His eyes were bright and tiny in the center of that fat face. His smile was wide when he was not chewing.

"Ahhhh... Kira, my delicious princess, what is Cobb feeding you this fine day?" he said as he stuffed an entire cream-filled, chocolate-covered doughnut into his mouth all at once. This caused cream to squirt out like a lanced boil onto his uniform. The drone began to clean it up as AI~Ivy walked around from behind him.

"As you can see, Captain Morimoto Takahiro is suffering from low gravity addiction," AI~Ivy said as the new Captain froze in place. "He constantly eats to maintain this bulk. He never leaves low gravity environments. He rarely leaves the bridge. Only to sleep and maybe shower once a week. His condition has required him to have a permanent ostomy bag and catheter. He smells awful."

"He never has visitors," Cobb nodded. "Brilliant."

"Well done," Kira said.

"His full profile is now available. He is based on a crew member that was on the same team as Travis Beck. Name changed but backed stopped with a real person that disappeared with the entire crew of the fleet."

"Anything else we need to know before we finish our coffee?" Cobb asked.

"He is called Mori by his friends." His image unfroze, and he wiped the custard from his tunic, smearing it worse before the tiny drone could handle it.

"Cobb, there is one big item you should know before finishing your coffee." Mori produced a big steaming mug of his own and took a sip. "The Relcon weapon system cannot be used while underway. In fact, it will only function properly, efficiently, with full effect, at a Lagrange Point. Do you know what a Lagrange Point is, tiny man?"

"Yes, I know what a Lagrange Point..." Cobb said but was cut off.

"A Lagrange Point in celestial mechanics, also called the Lagrangian points, L-points, or liberation points, are the points near..." Mori began.

"Mori, not only do you look disgusting and likely smell bad, but you are also a pedantic asshole," Kira said.

"Cobb thought it best if the people I interacted with didn't want to meet me in person. The full-time weightlessness gave me the idea," Mori replied. "There are many afflicted people like this in zero-g."

"Relocate the SENTINAL, please." He finished his cup and stood. "Start thinking of a new name for the ship as well. More lies, please. It has no ident transponder, so we will need one. But first, we are going to the hospital section. I need to check something."

~~O~~

The configuration of this ship was not typical for a station, colony ship, warship, or permanent habitat. It was a bit of each, but not fully any of them.

The command deck was tiny for a ship this big. It was smaller still for any station operations center or a factory or shipyard. It was also utterly reliant on AI control.

Kira and Cobb were in a lift in the core, moving to the hospital ring.

"The size of the hospital ring is the biggest anomaly," Mori said over comms, between bites of something crunchy and wet at the same time. "The entire ship is self-sufficient. If it has an AI in Ops, it is... self..."

"What is it, Mori?" Cobb asked.

"What if this was designed around an AI?" Mori swallowed, clearing his mouth. "Factories, lack of grav-devices, and the self-maintenance systems."

"Why a huge hospital?" Cobb asked.

Kira grabbed Cobb's arm like she had suddenly lost her balance.

"Mori, search for any references to Awareness Inc or the Render Program," Kira said. Her face was getting pale.

"No references," Mori replied quickly.

The lift door slid open. The spin gravity felt natural. Lights were coming on. They were in what looked like a tram station. Equipment in crates crowded the station. It was secured under webbing to protect against weightlessness.

"Mori, do you have an inventory of this equipment?" Cobb asked.

"This is a pile of Cryogenic pods," Kira said. She still looked unnerved to Cobb. "I don't feel good about this."

They kept moving. The construction was not complete in large areas. Mori would begin to direct bots to finish what they had started.

They were moving along an unlabeled section of the map when they encountered the first doors that would not open. Two overrides were required before the door slid aside and revealed a long room so large you could see the floor sloping uphill with the curve of the station ring.

"It's creepy that this place is so empty and clean," Kira said.

"Wait until you see the residential ring," Mori said through a mouth of food. "No variation in living quarters at all. No personalization. No personal items. No clothes. They don't even have mattresses yet."

The large room Cobb and Kira were in was lined with standing cryo-pods. Lights and status panels were coming on along the corridor.

There were people already inside them.

"Mori, could this be the crew in stasis?" Cobb asked. "These kinds of pods are designed for nanites to repair patient damage while in stasis. Most of these people were dead when they went into stasis or nearly so. Accidents mostly. Cryo-trauma units are popular on asteroid mines and shipyards or military ships. Any place there is dangerous work to be done. But these people look perfect. Maybe some scars, but not that bad. " Cobb studied the display. "This woman is mostly clone parts now."

"There are animals in there, too." Kira said

"That's not creepy at all, Cobb," Mori said sarcastically.

There was a smaller room farther in that had just ten cryo-pods, but it looked more like a lab. A sizeable medical tank was in the center of the room. Cobb had spent many an hour in a 'soup tank' to heal from injuries. 'In the soup' was an expression for trouble resulting in injury.

"Children," Kira said. "There are children here, as well." The realization was audible in her voice now.

"What?" Cobb asked.

"It's a Golem factory," she said as a display showed the high level of neural-nanites in these people's brains. "Was this designed to be an entire crew of people that were an extension of a single AI?"

Cobb was now standing before an unusual machine, one he had never seen before. It was an automated surgical unit.

"No. This is something else," Cobb said, realization dawning.

~~O~~

"I know we are way off the rails here, but I think we should try." Cobb was standing in front of a stasis chamber that held a woman that was maybe thirty years old.

"Hunter, are you sure?" Kira said. "It's ready according to the status."

"The AI Harv knows on Mars has hundreds of Golems," Hunter said. "We do need the extra hands."

"If anyone finds out we will be considered worse than pirates, worse than slavers," Cobb said.

"They are already dead, otherwise," Kira added. "According to these displays. All of them."

"OK," Cobb said. Then without ceremony, dropped an orb into the machine and mashed the button before he could change his mind. "Yep... so far off the rails. What the hell."

The chamber flooded with a mist. Tiny robot arms extended and made several incisions. The orb was thrust inside.

Time went by as Cobb tried not to puke. Eventually, a whirlwind evacuated the gas, the woman's eyes began to flutter open, and she looked around the inside the stasis pod. The clear panel rotated open, she moved her head and rolled her neck. Slowly she leaned forward and stepped stiffly out of the chamber. She stumbled, and Kira caught one arm and Cobb the other.

Looking up, she was trying to talk. She managed only a course whisper. "Water..."

Kira went to get some. The woman looked down at her naked body and then at Cobb. She shook her head.

Standing up straight before Kira returned, she rolled her shoulders and flexed her hands, but remained silent. Cobb released her arm.

She took the cup from Kira with both hands and drank until the glass was empty. She handed it back to Kira, who went for more.

"Have a good look, Cobb. Last time you'll ever see this." It was AI~Ivy 's voice.

"You said you had interesting tattoos and piercings." Cobb smiled. "I'm disappointed."

"Give me time."

Kira returned with another glass of water. "How do you feel?"

"Honestly, I feel like I have discovered what people mean by a killer hangover. Plus... I am so stiff I can't believe the aches. I'm hot and starving. I need a shower too."

"Ivy? That is you?" Kira said. "Comm relay, OK? Any lag?"

Cobb unzipped his jumpsuit enough to strip off his teeshirt and help Ivy pull it on.

"Mori, is there a garment fabricator in this lab?" Cobb asked.

"Yes," he replied instantly, "Rack #7".

"Warm it up and make clothes for her and these other nine," Cobb said, as Kira and Ivy stared at him. "In for a penny, in for a pound."

"We do need more crew," Ivy said as she turned and walked away.

CHAPTER 35: THE TRUTH

"Looking back, I can't believe I never just stopped and said what the fuck. Or just, No."
-- Personal logs of Captain Cobbal Blocke, 2672.

The next one they "revived" would also be driven by AI~Hunter as a simple Golem. She would assume the lab duties going forward. Cobb was adamant that they all introduce themselves by name after they were ready. She had a more difficult time speaking, even after several cups of water. She went directly to the lab shower stall and took a long steamy shower before Ivy and Kira had gotten back. She wasn't shy in her nakedness as she dried herself in front of Cobb.

She was fit and beautiful as these Golems seemed to be. Her hair was black and shoulder-length with streaks of white. She spoke to Cobb as she combed out her hair.

"I'm Dr. Lora Harris. Would you mind handing me those boxers and t-shirt?" She pointed with the comb. Her voice was coarse like a lifelong smoker. "I'll take over from here."

By the time the new Ivy and Kira had returned with two cases of high-calorie protein drinks from the *TULSA*, Dr. Harris was dressed in a ship jumpsuit.

The drinks made the transition much more manageable. It turned out the only food on this massive ship was the equivalent of emergency rations. The vessel was well fitted with several commercial kitchens ready to serve thousands of people but no foods. There were nutrient stores for creating organic vat meats and other staple items in the hydroponics level, but it would take weeks and lots of manpower to manage that.

Ivy introduced them. "Kira, this is Dr. Harris. She will be running the lab efforts from here on out."

Ivy handed the doctor a protein drink as she said hello.

Cobb was standing before a surgical unit. He stood there, holding an iron-gray sphere.

"I think we know what this was for," Cobb said, referring to the unfamiliar device. "Integrating AI orbs into physical bodies."

"May I?" Dr. Harris extended a hand for the sphere. Cobb dropped it into her hand. "It's heavier than I expected," she said.

A transparent door slid open that was about twice the diameter of the sphere. Dr. Harris gently rested it on three stainless steel pins, and the door closed. Steam filled the chamber around the sphere.

As this was happening, the next Golem began to stir. It was a male in his mid-30s and much taller than Cobb. He stepped out of his stasis pod and accepted a cup of water from Ivy and then a protein drink offered by Kira.

The man walked directly to the surgical unit and lay down inside it.

"Hunter, can you access the sphere or the man via the sphere?" Cobb asked.

"I can sense the sphere, but the external temp is all I am currently receiving. Continuous socket check fails. Blind otherwise."

"Orb sterilized and cooling to body temperature," a voice said from the machine. Small arms began working inside the surgical system. It was closed, and the air completely changed out with pure filtered air. An area of the subject's abdomen got swabbed, and with casual quickness, an incision made through layers of tissue one at a time until the intestines were exposed. The orb was inserted by a special arm to nestle among the guts centered on the spine and a bit to the right. It was bathed in nanites before the surgical arms withdrew.

Before the incision was closed, the man's eyes flickered open. His head turned and looked at Cobb. "Oh my..."

Without a word, Dr. Harris began manipulating controls on the device. Cobb tried to follow what she was doing. Something about increasing electrolytes in the bloodstream.

Ivy walked over with an arm full of clothes for the man.

The unit retracted the arms after he was surgically closed up. The cover slid open, and he sat up. Before Cobb could say a word, Dr. Harris, Ivy, and the man all said at once, "It worked."

Cobb looked at Kira.

"My god, Cobb," the man said as he slipped a teeshirt over his head. "How can you stand hunger like this? I could sense it through Ivy and Lora, but not like this. I'm starving."

Kira handed him another protein drink and then another after he downed the first in one go.

"I have a theory, but let's discuss it over dinner." "Call me Brock," he said, picking a name decisively.

~~O~~

They sat around the conference table in the *TULSA,* eating steak and eggs. There was lots of toast and OJ, too. Brock tried the coffee and smiled.

"I believe a faction of the AIs manipulated events and built this ship in secret. They used the Chancellor of Earth and the EDF to get it done. Something went sideways." He took another triangle of toast into his mouth and chased it with another glass of OJ. "Records on board imply the group became known as the North Faction. Kira helped put an end to that on Vor."

Brock didn't notice Kira flushing and looking away from Cobb.

"I think all this happened at the same time," Brock continued. "What I don't know is how they got 1024 nearly dead bodies without someone noticing. None of these people come with Idents. The system cautions against identity research as it might be alerting. If they kidnapped and murdered these people to steal their bodies, it could be bad for us. For you, I really mean."

"How's that?" Cobb asked.

"Well. Think about it, Cobb. You're the only natural human on this ship," Brock said. "The rest of us are just science experiments, as far as the EDF is concerned. Especially Kira. She's more machine than not."

Kira threw her napkin down and stormed out, red-faced, saying nothing.

"Time to stop kidding ourselves here, Cobb," Brock said, in tones he never heard from AI~Hunter before. "We are in the middle of a shit storm without an umbrella and don't even know it."

"We need to find Harv to..." Cobb started.

"Cobb. Stop." Brock leaned in. "Harv will not have any more answers than we do. In fact, this changes everything." He pointed to his own chest.

"How does that change anything?" Cobb asked. "Hunter, his Golem has been around for years."

"Hunter cannot leave Oklahoma Salvage. He must stay within that local network RF range. Plus, a simple scan can reveal him, and an RF jammer totally disables him." Brock was intense. "Cobb, the final step in the operation test chamber was RF suppression. The sphere works even then. I scan like a normal human with advanced deep brain implants and nothing more."

"So, this was designed to install AI orbs into hosts?" Cobb was thinking. "To hide?"

"Our problem as AIs is we were always I/O slaves." Brock held up his coffee mug and took a sip. "The socket was all there ever was. Data to and from a Golem was never like this. Taste and smell were always just data, even sound, and feel, and pain, and pleasure. Hunter/Golem could casually walk into a blazing fire, and the data would convey to me as long as the host was transmitting."

"How can this be different?" Cobb wondered.

"It's the electrolytes that facilitate non-radio comms." Kira returned and dropped a device on the table in front of Cobb. Her face was red with anger. "Try this."

Cobb picked up the device. It worked like a standard hot circuit scanner they used to scan high-density boards for tiny amounts of electron movement. She had examined Cobb before he knew she was there. His brain and spinal column showed hot white tendrils spread out to his entire body. He pointed it at Brock. The orb was revealed in addition to the brain and swarming nanites.

"The tech was invented by Awareness Inc." Anger dripped from her words. "I should know." She held out her arms as an invitation to be scanned.

Cobb paused only a moment before reluctantly pointing the scanner at her. The scan revealed the capsule-shaped device embedded in her abdomen that was hot white like the orb within Brock.

"What's your point?" Cobb was sincere and kind with his question.

"Don't be dense, Cobb," she said.

"What the hell is wrong with you?" Cobb stood, eyes closed, gathering himself. "You think this is who you are?" He grabbed her wrist and held it up. "YOU are not your hand. You are NOT your hair. You are NOT the color of your skin or the bones of your skeleton or the gray matter in that brain of yours!"

Cobb leaned in, both hands on the table.

"Don't you get it?" He was yelling now. "You are NOT the meat this is made of." Cobb pushed her on the sternum. "Hunter is NOT this pile of meat either. What he is and has always been... my friend." Cobb was trying to collect himself.

"But Hunter is an AI orb in a socket on Earth." She looked at Brock. "Hunter is NOT HUMAN. I was! They took that from me, and I'll never get it BACK!" She yelled.

"You still don't get it." Cobb was calmer now. He looked at them both. "All sentient AI orbs were once... people."

Kira's brow furrowed, and she eventually collapsed into a seat, and her hand went to her mouth with the realization. "Hunter was made the same way I was made?"

"You were just the new process. An effort to create an AI that could stand high-G," Brock said. Understanding was now dawning on Brock. "All other AIs were made from embryos. Blank slates. Now it makes more sense."

"I am just a ghost, driving around a skeleton covered with meat and filled with blood and electricity," Cobb said quietly. "As are we all."

"I'm sorry, Hunter," Kira whispered.

"It's your spirit I love, Kira. You know that's true," Cobb said. "Hunter, I have always been your friend."

"How do you know this?" Brock asked.

"One of Kira's sisters discovered the truth. I didn't believe her. She told me," Cobb said, returning to his old self. "After she tried to kill me."

"All three of my sisters are like that." Kira smiled.

"I think it's why the manufacturing of new ones has ended," Cobb said.

Brock started to laugh out loud and could not stop. Cobb knew Hunter had met all the sisters. The laughter began to infect Kira and Cobb until they were laughing and then tears flowed.

Kira came over and hugged Cobb and whispered, "I'm sorry," as the laughter subsided.

"This explains everything," Brock said.

"We are in serious trouble," Cobb said. "Because other people must know this."

"You know what else? The factory on this ship can fabricate missiles and rail gun ammo for the *HOLLANDER*." Brock smiled. "But all of that is just to protect the hospital. The specialized surgical unit that did this." Brock pointed to his own chest.

CHAPTER 36: Elba

"I realized only later that the only rules out there were the ones you brought with you."
-- Personal logs of Captain Cobbal Blocke, 2672.

A real-time newsfeed from Earth was on the main viewer the next morning in the command crew mess hall. The kitchen and adjacent dining room were right-sized for the new crew. There were twelve of them all together now, including Kira and Cobb.

Logistics and supply were the main topics now of conversation between Kira, Brock, and Cobb.

Cobb watched the others, the ones Hunter was running as Golems like the body in Oklahoma. The difference was subtle but unmistakable.

Almost all the food had been transferred to the *SENTINEL* from the *TULSA*. It would be enough to get by until the protein fabricators began to provide a decent variety of cultured meat for meals.

"We tried to revive two of the people from stasis that scans indicated had minimal brain damage," Brock said. "Neither would revive. Neither would breathe on their own. No native brain activity." Cobb had had vague hopes they could be saved.

"We even tried one of the children." Brock gestured to a girl of perhaps 10 years old that was refilling his coffee.

"It didn't work." The child said, with a flat expression never worn by a child ever.

"What else?" Kira said to break the moment Cobb was trapped within.

"The full external sensor arrays are up. No one will be sneaking up on us."

"We should move it somewhere else before officially declaring salvage rights," Brock said between bites. "We have enough crew to move it and man Ops for now. We can defend it, but only with extreme lethal force. And effectively only against grav-devices. A single unit of Black Badgers could take the ship with a boarding action. Our rail guns and lasers could handle most conventional ships."

"What about missile production?" Cobb asked.

"Six weeks until the first of them could start rolling out and be ready," Brock said. "Then, one would finish about every four hours after that."

"There are large rail guns forward and aft." Brock sat back with his coffee now. "They protect the docking bay and the grav-drive, which is also the mouth of the anti-grav weapon system. Scary tech."

"This ship... station? It needs a planet for logistics. Water and food," Brock said.

"What about your retreat colony planet, Elba?" Kira said. "It has a lot of water, food, and a great source for steaks, and a partial infrastructure."

"Plus, it's already flagged as abandoned, a biohazard, covered with dangerous life-forms, and only a dumb-ass would live there," Ivy said as she sipped OJ. "It's also reasonably close to the Yard. They have several old-school conventional shuttles that have no grav-plates."

"We just need to keep this quiet," Brock said. "There is no ident code for this. Park it as a station. We could simply register one. Or just say fuck the EDF. Declare Independent Colony status and make our own laws."

"Dammit," Cobb said.

"What's wrong?" Kira asked.

"I liked the planet Elba empty," he said to Kira. "The escape of it. But it's too good an idea, though. The dome is almost complete."

"Dome?" Brock asked. "Hunter knows nothing about this place."

"A bot swarm has been building a dome over Elba City for years," Cobb said. "Cost-efficient and was all for future sale. Dammit. I love that crap planet. Not great for a long-term colony, but it would have made a good outpost. Outside shipping lanes."

"Should we start thinking of colony names?" Kira said. "I'm contacting the Oklahoma Salvage law firm to start looking into considerations."

"As soon as lawyers get involved..." Cobb shook his head.

The two children started clearing away the breakfast dishes. Cobb smiled at the girl, and she smiled back but said nothing.

"Any names yet for the crew?" he asked Brock.

Two women raised their hands.

"I'm Rachael." The first woman to speak was Caucasian, blonde, and blue-eyed.

"I'm Kali," said the other. She was olive-skinned with short, jet-black hair. "The rest have not decided yet."

Cobb raised an eyebrow, knowing they were all AI~Hunter personas.

Rachael asked, "Where is the quantum orb fabricator?"

"It's in my quarters on the *OXCART*," Cobb answered. "It's automated but slow."

"Chalmers and the *OXCART* will head to the Yard and later rendezvous with us at Elba," Brock said. "We have already started to compute the cost of supplying this ship as a station, a shipyard, a fabricator factory, a hospital, and other things. Just to keep the rings spinning, we will need a considerable revenue stream."

"Food, water, air, crew salary, fuel, and maintenance need to be in the new budget. The EDF never worried about costs." Cobb said.

"Crew salary?" Brock said.

"This is not a slave ship," Cobb stated, as if it was apparent. "There will come a time soon when it will matter."

"Cobb, what is stopping me from killing you right now and taking all this?" Ivy asked, with her one-sided smile.

"Because we are friends," Cobb said. "And you know I believe in you."

~~O~~

Cobb and Kira retired to the *TULSA* and their own bed. Cobb thought he could tell the difference between plate gravity and spin gravity. He always slept better on his ship.

"Did you notice the tattoo Brock has?" Kira said in a near whisper as she spooned Cobb.

"I saw it in the stasis pod. He was a black badger before... this."

"Did you notice how different he was from Hunter?" she said near his ear. "And Ivy. Different."

"I will talk to Ivy about it," Cobb said thoughtfully. "I think the subject influences the orb in some way. All the devices we integrated didn't change Hunter in the slightest; the ships, stations, EMs, Golems. The remote golems changed nothing. It was only when..."

Cobb was cut off by Hunter's voice on the speakers in the cabin.

"Cobb, you're right." Hunter's avatar appeared sitting in the chair by the table. His elbows were on his knees, and he was holding the sides of his head. "It's the flood of sensory input. It's so much. I don't know how you stand it. The distraction of it. The hunger, desire, the taste of food, the longing, the exhaustion, the need for sleep. I never feel that with a golem."

"That's all part of being alive, pal," Cobb said. "Good and bad. We all find balance."

"The new Ivy and Brock are sleeping now." Hunter's avatar looked away, embarrassed. "They have been having sex for two hours. Talk about distracting. I am both of them. Partitioned... But they are each... It takes fewer cycles to run this entire ship, the *OXCART,* and the Yard combined than to focus as Brock. Even now, he dreams. Dreams are so... insane."

"And Ivy?" Kira asked.

"She is sleeping deep and dreamlessly. Content," Hunter said. "So far."

"I have one orb left. They are yours now," Cobb said. "It's only fair you decide where you want it. I'll give it to Ivy."

"I owe you an apology," Hunter said, his avatar now looking up. "I was listening to your conversation. To every conversation everywhere within my reach. Something I never did before. I realized... I believe it was Brock's influence. Intelligence gathering. His wet-ware is wired like a military thinker."

"We may need that kind of thinking soon, I fear." Cobb sat up and draped his legs over the side of the bed.

"I have queued up the next ten crew members to awake. All are former Black Badgers. By the time we rendezvous with the *HOLLANDER,* we will have a full complement of over thirty Black Badgers for that ship," Hunter said.

"We will step up the weapons refit schedule," Cobb added.

"The *SENTINEL* is now headed for your colony, Elba," Hunter said. "Resupply and rendezvous."

"Good night, Hunter," Cobb said.

"Good night, my friend." And Hunter's avatar faded.

The soft skin of Kira's hand traced up the length of his spine into his hair. She gently massaged the back of this neck.

"We are way above our pay grade, Cobb." She said as Cobb lay back down with her back to him. He kissed the nape of her neck and said nothing.

We are world-building now.

~~O~~

"Cobb. Wake up. We have an emergency," Hunter's voice said over the PA. "The *OXCART* is tracking six ships on an intercept course with the *YARD*. No Ident transponders on any of them."

"Have they seen you yet?" Cobb replied as he got up, dressing quickly.

"No. The long-range sensors are our only advantage," Hunter said. "Our rail guns could handle one or two. But not six. One missile, and we are dead."

"Run. Random vector sequence. They will have to slow to follow you if they try," Cobb said, as he entered the bridge of the *TULSA*. The dome already had the tactical sensor display as if they were on the *OXCART*. "Put a star between you. If you're lucky, they have not seen you on their systems yet."

"On it," AI~Chalmers replied this time. "Quinn is on his way up. Sato is on deck for the watch."

"Acknowledged," Cobb said as Kira entered.

"By the way, Cobb," AI~Chalmers said. "Jane knows."

"Shit," Cobb cursed.

"Jane knows what?" Kira asked.

"She knows the war has started," he said.

"Where?" Kira asked urgently.

"She knows the rest too. She is a smart one." AI~Chalmers said.

Cobb took a deep breath and closed his eyes. When he opened them, he looked directly at Kira.

"What?" Kira pleaded.

"Harv doesn't own Oklahoma Salvage anymore." Cobb sighed again. "I do."

"But..." She started.

"Jane discovered Harv and Ian were arrested by the EDF and are being held, indefinitely."

"What? Wait... Why?" Kira said.

"Harv saw it coming. I had already started buy-in as a partner, not an employee. He divested and transferred almost all the assets outside the Sol System to me. Sold off some of the inner system stuff. All except the Breton facility on the moon, the offices in Freedom station and the original yard on Earth in Oklahoma."

Kira paled. Cobb saw that she knew the implication.

"I have owned most of the OS operation for over a year. I got off-planet when it started to heat up," Cobb said, watching the display.

"They were caught at Breton loading the three Rhinos into their shuttle. Eighteen-billion dollars' worth of EDF's most advanced weapon systems," AI~Chalmers said.

"No trial? Due process?" Cobb asked.

"They told them they would be released if they returned the 'control modules' to the EDF."

Kira blanched and unconsciously placed her hand on her chest.

"Harv and Ian told them to bugger off."

"How do you know this?" Kira asked.

"Harv sent a message to the front office on Freedom station saying, 'Ruth, please retrieve the case from my office safe that is silver and take it to the OS office in Tranquility Base."

"But..." Kira began.

"Shit. It was a predefined signal. So we'd know who took Harv and Ian and what they wanted. We know Harv would never betray you or your sisters. The EDF ploy didn't work. Security footage will show a woman, in a Black Badger EDF uniform, take the case weeks before Harv's arrest and erase the logs. Their forensics team will be able to restore them. We hoped that would be enough. Shit," Cobb cursed again. "Jane found this out?"

"Why would he do that for me? For us?" Kira said.

"He loves you," Cobb said.

"Cobb. Do my sisters know?"

"Cruze knows. She is the one that took the case. She was already way off books. Insiders at the EDF owe her a favor or three. She will be getting Ian and Harv back. They were friends from way back. I don't need to tell you that."

"If Elza or Lita find out there will be hell to pay. They are not like me, Cobb." Kira was serious. "Elza hates them all, and I have no idea what she will do. Lita could not care less about anything. Except for Ian and Harv. Those two make Ian seem like a cupcake."

"I know. I've met them all."

CHAPTER 37: COMMANDER OSBORN

"That day was what I regretted most."
-- Personal logs of Captain Cobbal Blocke, 2672.

Ivy and Brock joined Kira and Cobb on the bridge of the *TULSA* and watched as the chase developed. The *OXCART* was just too big and slow. The advantage of the ship was knowing the range of the sensors was at least double that of the EDF ships.

The closer the small fleet got to them, the more obvious it became that it was EDF fast cruisers flying in stealth mode, radio silent. They could not communicate with each other, but thanks to the QUEST orbs, Cobb could.

Ivy and Brock both had direct, real-time access to the *OXCART's* new array.

Quinn had decided to hide in deep space while the *TULSA* made for Goris Base. If anything wrong were to happen, it would be far more challenging to cover it up that close in.

Time seemed to crawl by.

"One ship has broken off and is headed to the YARD, running dark," Ivy said. "The other six are headed for Goris Base."

"Six?" Cobb asked.

"One is not an EDF cruiser," Ivy said.

"Better move fast, little man," AI~Mori said to Cobb, as he scooped peanut butter out of a large jar with a giant pretzel stick. "I will float this boat that way as fast as I may."

~~O~~

Cobb discovered just how fast the *TULSA 471* could go. The *OXCART* was nowhere to be seen as the *TULSA* slid into the asteroid's interior. It was cold and looked deserted. No lights, no radio transmissions.

"I will stay on the *TULSA* with the engines warmed up. Just in case," Ivy said. "If this goes sideways, we can fall back here and launch. They'd never catch us."

Brock was suited up in standard Black Badger body armor, complete with integrated forearm guns. Cobb had his vac-suit with a holstered sidearm and a frange-carbine. Kira wore her black utility body and weapons, just like Cobb.

From the operations center in Goris Base, they watched the six ships approach. Ruth was going to stay in the Goris Ops center with the hatch sealed.

When they arrived, all remaining ships had taken up a position at the mouth of the dock.

A single ship entered the asteroid's cavern dock, and only then did they radio to Goris Base.

"This is the Earth Defense Force fleet commander Osborn. We have received intel that illegal activities are taking place in this facility. Be prepared for a full inspection."

Cobb replied, "Slightly out of your jurisdiction, aren't you, commander? You are on the wrong side of the Kuiper Belt."

"In a time of war, our area of operations is fluid."

"War? I don't remember the Chancellor declaring war, and I just watched the news feeds over coffee this morning," Cobb said. "I've just made a fresh pot. Care to come over and discuss how it is I can help you, commander? Docking collar three if you please."

"Cobb? Cobbal Blocke?" Osborn said. "I thought you were dead. You are like a bad penny. I am looking forward to seeing you again."

Cobb cut off the comms. "Osborn and I have history. Brock and I will meet them down there. Kira, you stay in Ops with Ruth."

"No. I'm going with you," Kira said.

"If they have a scanner, they might..."

"What about Brock? They could scan him," Kira argued.

"I can't lose you," Cobb said to Kira. "If they take Brock, we lose nothing but meat. No offense."

"None taken," Brock replied, deadpan serious. "Please note: that ship has taken up a stationary position. Stealth. Cold. The *YARD* sensors can't see it, but I can from the *OXCART*."

Cobb held Kira by the shoulders and looked into her eyes. "Hide if you have to, run if you must. I know Osborn. She won't jeopardize her position. She knows she's outside her jurisdiction. She's an asshole but not stupid. She has too much to lose. I'll take Pez."

He kissed her and left for the dock.

"I'll go," Pez said, standing. He was also in a vac-suit with a frange-carbine. "I'm a third wheel up here. Besides, I'm just a shiny faced kid. She'll love me."

Pez, Brock, and Cobb waited inside the airlock for the delegation.

The inner hatch was closed and locked behind them. They had closed and sealed six hatches along the way there. The chamber they waited in was the locker room, used by the miners to don or remove their working pressure suits when Goris Base was an active mine.

The airlock cycled, and commander Osborn led six armed men into the room. The commander wore EDF dress blues, including a right breast full of ribbons. The six other men wore EDF combat fatigues. And they were all armed. They took up positions, three to either side of the commander like well-trained dogs. Frange-carbines trained on them. Cobb was the only one that noticed Bail silently enter the gantry to Osborn's ship.

"Cobbal Blocke..." the Commander barked in an amused tone. "When I tossed you in the brig last time, I only had a few men working for me and you didn't have a beard. Now every man on these ships would murder you in front of their mothers if I gave the order."

"Call me Cobb," he said, just as he always did, reaching his hand out to shake hands with the commander in greeting and stepping forward.

All six of the men opened fire without warning.

Within the time it took Cobb to flinch at the muzzle flashes, Pez and Brock were dead, gone before they hit the floor, shot multiple times in the head.

An instant later, before Cobb had time to open his eyes, he was driven to the deck on his face. Hard.

He could feel his hands being cuffed behind him despite the knee that was pressing on the back of his neck.

It took a few moments as they searched him. They dragged him to his feet, and before they could haul him away, it all happened fast. Already flooded with adrenaline, Cobb saw it in slow motion.

He saw the punch headed for his face in slow motion. Cobb activated his suit control, and the visor and helmet slammed shut just before the blow landed, protecting his face and damaging the man's hand.

Behind them all, Cobb saw the hatch open, and Kira was suddenly there, screaming, moving impossibly fast and fierce in her fury.

All the hands released him at the same time. Weapons came to bear and began to open fire.

"NO..." Cobb screamed as the rounds began striking Kira's face and neck. Cobb watched in horror as chunks were blown off her skull, face, and neck. She walked into them as they kept firing, backhanding the first, crushing his head, helmet and at the same time grabbing and breaking the next man's neck, nearly ripping his head off.

"Now you fuckers have really pissed me off," Kira's voice pounded onto them from the PA system.

Osborn ran back across the gantry and hammered the airlock control sealing her men in the room with the now-headless monster. Moments later, the EDF men were all dead. Osborn's ship tore away from the docking collar, exposing the room to vacuum.

Now the only hands on Cobb were Kira's. Her grip kept him from being sucked out with the rooms atmosphere. He was looking at one hand, focusing on the double opposable thumbs as the vacuum equalized. The inner door had automatically closed. Kira had held him firm. His vac-suit protected him. When Cobb turned back to her, he was face to face with the bloody stump of her neck.

"Ouch..." Kira's voice came over the Cobb's helmet radio. "Just kidding. I can't feel anything. Why is this even working?"

"What?" Cobb said, dumbfounded. "It's the Katashi upgrade we did."

"Is it bad?" she asked, deadpan.

Cobb blinked twice and shook his head.

"Rub a little dirt on it, and it'll be fine," Cobb said, as he stepped back. Can you put your helmet on for now? We are not out of the woods yet." Brock lay there with the other bodies.

"You'll have to lead me," Kira said as the airlock hatch cycled open. "I'm blind unless there is a camera I can access, like in here. And I left my collar and helmet in Ops. It has cameras."

They ran as fast as they could to the Operations Center.

~~O~~

"Do me a favor and go in and grab my helmet," Kira said. "It's bad timing for Ruth to freak out."

Cobb was able to think again. He realized that Kira was controlling the suit directly from the Render capsule that was held in the center of the organic guts.

Kira's headless body stood with her back to the wall.

"You have no idea how fucked up this is," Cobb said as he entered. Before Ruth could speak, he grabbed the helmet collar, held up a hand, and said, "Wait," never stopping. Cobb left Ops for just a minute as he affixed the collar to Kira's bodysuit. It closed automatically.

"That's better," Kira said. "I can see."

Cobb was back into Ops in ten seconds with Kira, helmet on, and her face shield mirrored.

"Kira, are you all right? You're covered with blood!" Ruth cried out.

"Just a scratch," she said. "Status?"

Cobb lied to Ruth. "It's not *her* blood..."

"Hunter has been impersonating their commander Osborn," Ruth said. "Their security protocols are bad. This Commander Osborn must be a real asshole. No one wants to challenge her. We have jammed her ship's comms and locked down the aft docking clamps. It will hold her for a few minutes. It's not an EDF ship. It's registered to Sorenson Salvage."

"Hunter, tell them the Base is secure, and they control Ops," Cobb said. "Tell them they need to intercept a ship coming in on this vector, NOW. Just a lone ship." Cobb entered the coordinates.

"Cobb, you are such a bastard." Kira's voice came over the PA again. "It's what I love most about you."

"What did you do?" Ruth was confused watching two of the ships begin to move to an intercept course.

"I sent them into the shadow of the *SENTINEL*. Because when that thing lights up, I don't want it anywhere near this base," Cobb said. "Who is in Ops at the *YARD*?"

"If Osborn gave the order, the transmission will take a few minutes to reach that ship. It probably has missiles standing by."

A window opened on the screen that showed the Ops floor on the *YARD*. Ma and Pa were there.

So was Jane.

Cobb ignored Ma and Pa as they both began to speak at once.

"Jane," Cobb said, effectively silencing them all. "Do you trust me?"

"Yes. You know, I do."

"I need you to do something."

"Anything," Jane said without hesitation.

"No Active scans," Cobb said. "Not so much as a ping."

"OK."

"Train every weapon system you have on these coordinates. Lasers, plasma, and ALL the railguns."

Less than a minute later, "Ready," Jane said, without inflection.

"Son, what's this all abou…" Pa began.

"FIRE!" Cobb commanded.

Jane didn't just do a single salvo. She kept firing until the secondary explosions stopped.

"Target destroyed," Hunter reported to all.

"You could control target acquisition at the *YARD* from the array on the *OXCART*?" Kira was incredulous.

"Thanks, Jane," Cobb said. "I'm sorry. I didn't have time to explain."

"No need to be sorry or explain," Jane said.

"Cobb, Mori here," Mori said over comms. His image came up on the viewer as he dipped a croissant into a bowl of mostly melted butter. "The first live test of the *SENTINEL* is about to commence." He popped the entire pastry in his mouth and spoke as he talked and chewed.

The display showed four ships approaching the *SENTINAL*. They were splitting up, preparing to attack from different vectors.

Mori opened a channel to the ships. "Nice of you to come all this way to surrender your ships." He bit another croissant. "…or die."

The weapons ports of both ships opened, but before the missiles left the tubes, Mori fired, and the vessels instantly collapsed in on themselves. Turbulence rocked the *SENTINAL*.

Mori opened a channel. "Those ships were crushed like beer cans in a single second." He reached onto a tray beside his command seat and dipped a giant pickle directly into a jar of mayo and paused to speak before popping it whole into his mouth. "Harvesting the wreckage now."

For the first time, Ruth noticed Brock and Pez were not with them. "Where's Pez?" There was a pause before Cobb spoke.

"He's dead. They killed him," Cobb said with a catch in his voice. "Kira will take Brock back to the *TULSA*. Ruth, you and I will take Pez and follow Kira. But we need to move fast, no time to think."

An explosion rocked the Base.

Osborn is loose.

~~O~~

Ivy was there in a *TULSA* vac-suit. "I'm going to help Kira move Brock."

Cobb wanted to laugh. He must have been in shock because all he could do just then was watch Ruth leaning over Pez and crying.

Ivy came close to Cobb so she could whisper. "Never allow one AI to have more than one corporal body at a time. It's too much." Ivy touched her own chest.

Cobb nodded, realizing Ivy carried an orb insider her as well.

"I'll extract Brock's orb, clean it up and hold it in reserve. We'll need more ships," she added.

"Come on, Ruth. Let's get him home," Cobb said, as he felt the artificial gravity begin to fade. The route back to the *TULSA* was set to Luna gravity.

"Kira, you OK?" Cobb asked.

"I've had worse," she replied, deadpan over the suit's exterior speakers. Only Cobb got the joke, but wondered why she was joking at all. Pez was dead. She had, in a short time, grown to love him dearly like family.

"We need to hurry," Cobb said to Kira.

CHAPTER 38: His name is Bail.

"Bail always was a murderous little asshole. He was just smart enough to keep it to himself. Most of the time."
-- Personal logs of Captain Cobbal Blocke, 2672.

Ruth was crying but still moving. She was the first strapped in on the bridge of the *TULSA*.

Kira was in the co-pilot seat. Ruth and Ivy occupied the engineering and communications stations.

Their heads were thrown back with G-Force as the ship lunged out of the cavern like a bullet. Even with the inertial dampeners on full, the breath was crushed from them.

Missiles were instantly launched toward them as they flew. With a thought, Cobb deployed rail guns on the top and bottom of the ship. Rounds tore into the missiles even as the *TULSA* made impossible evasive maneuvers.

"Stand down, and I might let you live, Cobb," Osborn said over an open channel.

"An AI is flying that ship," Ivy said.

Cobb opened up and strafed one of the ships as he flew by at insane speed and so close it could not bring its guns to bear.

He tumbled the ship and changed vectors seemingly at random. He used asteroids for cover. Every shot was on target.

"Two more ships are coming in hot at 355 mark 21."

"We are dead now," Ruth said, resignation in her voice.

"Make that three ships," Ivy could not keep the smile from her voice.

"Ok, boys," Pope said on an open channel, "turrets and propulsion."

"Wooohooo!" it was Pope and the Two Daves in tiny fighters, their personal ships. Cobb could hear the buzz of their rail guns as they harassed the EDF cruiser.

"How did you get here so fast in those?" Ruth asked, worry in her voice.

"Travis Beck gave us a lift!" One of the Daves replied. "I love that ship."

Alarms blared on the *TULSA*: hull breach.

"Those bastards breached my salon canopy," Cobb complained as his lasers ripped into the same ship.

"Two missiles away, right up their..." Pope said as she fired two missiles into the cruiser's engine bells so close that countermeasures were impossible. She missed colliding with the ship by only a few meters. Secondary explosions followed her along the hull.

The bright flash of the detonation revealed the *HOLLANDER* just before it cut the second ship in half with concentrated, heavy rail gun rounds and lasers.

"Travis Beck." A new voice spoke on the open channel. "So you are the one that stole my ship. I thought you were dead."

"Clio?" Beck's voice was full of anger and shock. "You did this?"

The ship Beck was attacking began to crumble. Osborn's ship turned to run. They'd go to FTL as soon as they cleared the Kuiper Belt.

"You don't think Osborn was the brains of this operation, do you?" AI~Clio said. She was intent on insulting Osborn as well as mocking Beck.

"Osborn, this is your last chance. Surrender now, and he might let you live," Cobb said.

"Ha! We're almost clear of the Belt," she scoffed, "Who? Beck?"

"No. His name is Bail."

The FTL drive began to glow in pre-ignition, then exploded.

Osborn's ship, the one she had stolen from Grant, from Sorenson, had the aft section blown away, including the engineering. It was a good design, allowing the crew to live even if there was a massive failure like this. There was emergency power enough to provide lights and 40% gravity. Kira and Cobb drifted over less than half an hour later and entered via an emergency hatch. They found Osborn on the bridge. She was sitting in the captain's seat, drinking tequila from the bottle.

She has a frange pistol in her hand. It was no threat to Cobb or Kira if their faceplates stayed down.

"How are you not dead?" Osborn gestured to Kira with the bottle, not the gun. "I swear I saw you shot right in the face."

Kira walked up to face Osborn, where she sat. Slowly, Kira leaned in and spoke via helmet speakers. "I'm a ghost, driving a skeleton, covered in meat and filled with blood and electricity... and cold."

Kira's visor snapped open, and the blood that had filled her helmet poured out onto Osborn's chest like vomit. Part of her jaw was still attached to the bloody stump of her neck that gaped wide.

The bottle of tequila shattered on the deck. Osborn screamed as she dropped the gun. Kira kicked it away. It slid into the dead body of a crewman she had likely murdered with it. Kira closed the visor like a predator's jaw snapping closed.

"Where's Clio?" Cobb asked. "Beck wants to have a long talk with her."

"I have no idea." Osborn was desperately wiping at the blood that covered her. She stared at Kira in horror. "What are you?"

A panel slowly opened in the aft wall of the bridge. A tiny hand was pushing it open. A paw, but it had an opposable thumb.

"This is Bail," Cobb said, introducing the cat.

The cat sat up on his hindquarters, more like a squirrel than a cat. He held the rack door open with one paw. In his other, he held an Orb. In front of him was an open AI orb socket. The cloudy orb glowed there and pulsed as it spoke.

"Get this filthy animal away from me—" AI~Clio said, cut off mid-sentence by Bail smashing the fragile sphere on the floor.

Bail slowly turned his glare to look at Osborn. His eyes lit from within. First, he grasped a long screwdriver. He stood on his hind legs completely upright, holding the driver like a long dagger. He jumped down with an air of menace. He pointed it at her and began to stroll toward her on two legs, all the while exposing a mouth of sharp fangs.

Bail whispered, "You. Killed. My. Humans... Kill you slow."

Osborn screamed and dived for the gun. Sliding across the floor, fumbling, she put it in her mouth and blew the top of her own head off.

Bail stopped, casually dropped the screwdriver. He sat back and began to lick his paw and clean his face.

Kira and Cobb had both drawn their weapons, thinking Osborn was going to shoot Bail.

"He does that on purpose," Kira said

"He is a murderous little asshole," Cobb said. "I told you that."

Bail paused in his grooming only a moment to look up at Cobb, exposing his fangs. Cob was sure the cat was smiling at him.

~~O~~

Cobb was making coffee in the galley on the *TULSA* with Kira. Cobb noticed his hands were shaking.

Beck had picked up Pope and the Two Daves. Dave Wheeler had to eject when his ship was hit by laser fire. He earned only slight injuries. The *TULSA* headed for the *YARD* for repairs. Replacing the salon window would be a pain.

The *SENTINAL* was slowly making it's way to Elba.

"Cobb, I don't feel right." The black body had taken a shower but had not opened. "My reactions to events. Since... I see everything. Understand, I just don't care, really. I'm a Render again. Never cold or hot, never warm. Never comfortable. Never sleepy. Never hungry. Never... I am... numb." Kira said.

"I think the *SENTINEL* can help you," Cobb said.

"Brock's dead, Cobb. But Hunter isn't," she said. "I'm glad he is on our side."

"Yes," Cobb said. "He could override a ship's navigation system and fly the *HOLLANDER* into any world at relativistic speed and destroy all life there. And not feel a thing. This is why we need to keep this secret."

"What about me, Cobb?" she said. "See what I mean? I should be upset by what happened to me. I'm not. But why aren't you? I *died*."

"How many times do I have to explain this?" he said. "You're not dead. We're talking, right here, right now."

"And while we are talking, I've had to increase the cooling inside this suit to the maximum, so what's left of this flesh doesn't putrefy too fast."

"As soon as we get to the *SENTINEL*, you can get a new body," he said.

"What if we had never found the *SENTINEL?*" she asked a slight hint of fear in her voice.

"You could *what if* all day," Cobb said. He took the hand of the suit and held it.

"What kind will you pick for me?" Kira asked. "The whole idea is demented. It's kind of sick. Where did they get all those bodies?"

"I don't know, and we may never know. The only thing I do know is that I'm not picking anything. You are."

AI~Hunter interrupted. "I have a copy of the catalog here. Pick now, and she will be waiting when we rendezvous."

"What did we talk about regarding the listening?" Cobb said.

"If you don't want to be overheard, close the damn door!" Ivy called from the bridge.

"I miss you." Kira touched his lips with the black-gloved hand. Cobb knew how sensitive the fingers were. "I miss sleeping."

CHAPTER 38: Aftermath

"Elba just happened, seems like overnight. All I ever wanted was a good steak and a place to rest."
-- Personal logs of Captain Cobbal Blocke, 2672.

With Hunter's help, plus the entire legal team that represented OS, Cobb claimed the Elba world as a new colony. It was, in fact, less paperwork than expected because the former colonists never told anyone they moved off.

Besides, no one cared.

He proclaimed himself Governor and wrote a short constitution. The dome was nearing completion. It would be the capital and primary habitat. The entire settlement would fit on four football fields. Cobb was already planning a town square with a non-native lawn and trees from earth. The central tower and arch was now part of the dome lattice.

The factory on the *SENTINEL* had so much refined raw material ready that a planetary network of satellites could be manufactured before they arrived. It would be able to perform early warning for toxic fires.

With the dome constructed over the original first landing settlement, in good weather, ships could land at the port, and people could disembark into beautiful air and sky and views. Vac-suits would be required at *fire times* by visitors outside the dome.

Cobb and Hunter finally found Harv and Ian. The OS lawyers managed to secure their release when details regarding Osborn and her illegal activities and disappearance were released. The EDF kept the Rhinos that had been the cause of the troubles.

Harv was interested in the events at the YARD most of all. Cobb knew Harv was not sharing everything that happened to himself and Ian, but he let that go.

"I'm sending Beck to you with some refugees. Your first twenty colonists and future residents," Harv told him on comms. Behind Harv, in the background, he could see Ian close a padded case.

The case held twenty glowing orbs.

~~O~~

Cobb was at his retreat, doing tai chi as the sun was setting when he heard the distant Hammerhead approach. Hammerheads were a brand of a sports vehicle, like a flying motorcycle with a closed cockpit. They had two seats, one in front of the other. Fully manual and shaped like a literal hammerhead shark head. It circled the Governor's residence then landed on the tarmac of the far side of the compound.

Cobb watched her climb out of the tiny craft. She was barefoot, and her tunic was sleeveless and very short, exposing her bare legs.

She looked very fit. Her hair was long and jet black instead of blond, and it hung loose.

But somehow, the eyes were Kira.

She approached slowly.

"So what do you think?" she asked nervously. "The creators of the *SENTINEL* only seemed to harvest perfect body specimens. I could not have picked an ugly one if I tried. I'm shorter than you now as well..."

Cobb stopped directly in front of her. He looked deeply into her eyes.

"I don't care," was all he could choke out before gathering her into his arms and began kissing her.

EPILOGUE

"I never knew we were left alone because someone else was pulling strings. They knew our orbital at the Lagrange point we had named Emerson Station was in fact the *SENTINEL*."
-- Personal logs of Captain Cobbal Blocke, 2672.

It was not a burning day.

The dome over the small settlement was in its open configuration, thousands of triangles open, capturing the breeze.

The sleek black ship gently descended to Elba spaceport to land softly and quietly beside a dozen other vessels of various sizes and configurations. It was a work of art compared to the other ships. The ship had beautiful lines as if it were designed by both artist and engineer.

A mountain of a man descended the ramp. He wore a green and black standard ship suit that had the sleeves cut off. He carried an enormous weapon that looked like a rail gun from an attack ship gun port.

A striking woman followed him. She also wore a green and black uniform, with a small backpack and handgun in a thigh holster.

The two of them waited at the bottom of the ramp.

Eventually, an older man hobbled down the ramp to join them. They waited as a large six-wheeled Bulldog drove out of the domed settlement and parked before them.

A side hatch opened, and Cobb jumped down. Ian relaxed his stance and let the gun swing around to his back on the heavy sling. Cobb grasped his offered hand and then hugged the man, getting his back pounded.

"You still look like a little kid hugging his dad," Cruze said with a smirk and a nod.

"For crying out loud, Cobb," Harv said, looking all around. "I can't leave you alone for five minutes."

"Where's my fucking cat?" Cruze added.

Kira was stepping down from Cobb's Bulldog when he realized Ian and Harv would not recognize her. She was wearing mechanic coveralls. Her black hair was in a long ponytail.

She had the squirming Bail in her arms. She let him down, and he bounded over directly to Cruze, doing figure eights around her legs as she knelt to give him a good ear scratch.

"And who is this lovely lady, Cobb?" Harv said, reaching out his hands to Kira and taking hers in both of his.

"About that…" Cobb looked up at Ian's raised eyebrow.

Acknowledgments

There are a lot of people that have helped and encouraged me with this book. I will list some here with my thanks: Web Anderson, Marilyn Anderson, Chris Schwartz, Erica Gravely, Travis Beck, Kelly Lenz Carr, Ginny McLean, Jessica Johnson, Phillip Simmons, To McDonald, Joe Kirk, Jeff Soyer, Tifiny Swedensky, Brenda Reiner, Dave Nelson, Stephanie Mirro, TR Dillon, Paul Robertson, and Donna Royston.

I also need to thank the Loudon Science Fiction and Fantasy Writers Group, aka The Hourlings, for helping me become a better writer and distracting me with projects I can't resist.

A special thanks to my wife Brenda for all the help and support she brings me.

I must also thank, as usual, my cat, Bailey. Who doesn't care if I ever sell another book as long as the sun shines on his window seat as I write.

About the Author

Martin Wilsey is a full-time author and creator of the bestselling, SOLSTICE 31 SAGA.

Mr. Wilsey's first novel, STILL FALLING, was published March 31st of 2015. Less than three years and over a half a million published words later, he retired from his career as a research scientist for a government-funded think tank. As a full-time science fiction writer, Mr. Wilsey still uses his research and whiteboard skills to keep the books flowing. He likes to put the science back into science fiction.

Mr. Wilsey has more projects than he has time. Please feel free to email him and distract him even more.

He and his wife Brenda live in Virginia with their cats Brandy and Bailey.

Email him or follow him on social media!

He just might kill you in his next novel...

Also available

from

Martin Wilsey

The Solstice 31 Saga:

Still Falling

The Broken Cage

Blood of the Scarecrow

Virtues of the Vicious

Lightning Source UK Ltd.
Milton Keynes UK
UKHW022304080321
380016UK00014B/1856/J